When Next We Meet

J B Millhollin

Grey Place Books, Nashville, Tn
ISBN: 978-1-7358745-1-7
Library of Congress Control Number: 2021921518
Title: *When Next We Meet*
Author: J B Millhollin
Digital distribution | 2021
Paperback | 2021

This is a work of fiction. The characters, names, incidents, places, and dialogue are products of the author's imagination, and are not to be construed as real.

Previous novels by JB Millhollin:

Brakus
   Brakus, Book 1
   Everything he Touched, Book 2
   With Nothing to Lose, Book 3
An Absence of Ethics
Forever Bound
Out of Reach
Redirect
Whisper of Hope
To Hide from a Northern Wind: Spencer Creek, Book 1
To Hide from a Northern Wind: Wilson County, Book 2
To Hide from a Northern Wind: Nashville Divided, Book 3
To Hide from a Northern Wind: River of Tears, Book 4

Coming soon:

Plausible Deception
The Reporter
An Unacceptable Conclusion
The Prosecutor
I Guess I'll Never Know
Compassion!
Life Altered Book 1
Life on Hold Book 2
One More Time
My Turn

Prologue

Nashville, Tennessee
6:50 p.m.

She sat on the edge of her bed watching as her mother continued putting on her makeup.

"Now, I don't want to have to tell you again, honey. You remember our conversation, don't you? I'm really sorry, but I just *can't* take you with me tonight. Mommy likes this guy, but I'm really not sure what he would think if he knew I had a five-year-old in the house. So, we can't take that chance. You understand what I'm saying?"

She said nothing.

Laura Johnson continued to fix her lashes and work with her hair. "You've done this before. This isn't the first time. You know the routine. Just keep still when he comes to pick me up and when he brings me home. They'll be plenty of time for you to meet him when he and I are a little closer."

Annie was way too involved with her dolls to respond. As she continued to line them up exactly as she knew they wanted to be, her mother looked at her and said, "You just stay in the bedroom, right here, when he comes to get me, okay? And when he brings me home, again, you make sure you're in here and the door is closed. Do you understand? Just like we've done before."

Annie never looked up as she said, "I understand. Can I open the door a crack like I've done before and take a quick look at whoever it is you're going with? Would that be okay, Mommy?"

"No, no, that *wouldn't* be okay. You just stay in here, *with that door closed,* and go to bed in a while, like you always do. I'll wake you up when I get home and he leaves. Keep your little light by your bed on, but that's it. This isn't any different than the three or four other times we've done this. You've always done it just right. Make sure you follow the rules this time."

She returned to her makeup application as she said, "He's tall and good looking. He would make a great father for you. I just don't want to scare him away before we even get started."

Rags, her small poodle, jumped up in bed with Annie.

"Rags get down, *right now*. You know you're not supposed to be up on this bed, *ever*."

He never moved. Laura reached down and shoved him off the bed. Slowly, he walked into the living room and jumped up on the couch, nestling down in one corner, apparently content to sulk on his own.

"Don't you let him up on this bed, Annie. Leave him out in the other room if you have to, but I don't want him up on our bed, do you understand?"

She continued to play with her dolls, until her mother looked at her and once again said, *"Do you understand?"*

Annie looked up, smiled and said, "I'll keep him in the other room and just keep my dolls in bed with me, just like you tell me to."

Laura had finished preparing for her date. As she started to leave the room, she said, "Time to shut things down for tonight, Annie. He'll be here shortly. Now why don't you get under the covers and play with your dolls, but be very quiet until we leave."

Annie looked up and said, "Why isn't Carol coming tonight? Why isn't she staying with me?"

Laura sat down on the edge of the bed and said, "We've talked about this before. I don't have the money to pay her right now. She'll be here with you next week anyway—when I go see that lawyer about having your last name changed to my last name. Besides that, you've stayed alone for short periods of time before anyway. Are you afraid tonight? Is there something you and I need to talk about?"

"You won't be too long, right?"

Laura smiled. "No, not tonight.".

She stood and turned on the small nightstand light, then leaned down and kissed Annie on the cheek. "I'll crawl in bed with you as soon as I get home. Love you."

Annie never looked up, continuing to focus on her dolls as she said, "I love you, Mommy."

Laura walked through the door and into the only other room of their small, one bedroom apartment. As she did, she turned off the overhead bedroom light and shut the door behind her.

Annie, a short time later, heard their apartment door open, some muffled conversation, and the sound of the door closing. Before long, she was too tired to keep her eyes open any longer.

She sat up in bed. She could hear loud voices—a man and maybe her mom. Why were they so loud? They seemed so mad. She needed to see. Rags was barking as loud as she had ever heard him bark.

She quietly left her bed, walked to the bedroom door, then opened it only a crack. Her mother and this man were arguing. She didn't understand what they were arguing about. She kept telling him to leave. He kept saying not until he "got something." She couldn't understand what he meant. What would he want from her mother?

He told her to stop the dog from barking. Her mother quickly turned to Rags and said, "Rags keep still. You keep still." That didn't seem to have an effect on Rags, as his barking continued. Finally, the man looked down one more time and kicked him. She watched in horror as Rag's rapid journey through the living room came to a sudden stop against the wall. Once Rags dropped to the floor, he never made another sound.

Annie watched as her mother screamed, then she grabbed the man's sleeve, pulling him toward the door. As he turned toward her, he swung, hitting her in the face. She fell backwards, her head striking the wooden floor with a resounding thud. She never moved.

The man leaned down. He moved his hand over her nose. When he looked up, he looked around the room, then looked directly at the bedroom door. Annie didn't know what to do. She quickly ran into the closet, quietly closing the sliding door behind her. She left a small opening between the door and its frame, hoping that would be enough to watch him and still not be seen.

She heard him as he slowly opened the door to the bedroom and watched as he turned on the bedroom light. He walked around the room, stopping only by the nightstand on the other side of the bed.

He reached down and picked up a picture frame containing a picture of her mother and herself, looking first at the picture then quickly looking around the room, his investigation coming to a halt as he looked directly at the closet doors. He put the frame down and started to walk around the end of the bed, toward the closet. Annie heard a siren. They were close. It sounded as if they were right outside.

The man heard it too. Once those sirens stopped outside the window, he stood motionless. He never finished his walk toward the closet door, altering his path as he ran through the apartment door, then closing it with a resounding slam after he walked out.

Annie looked through the crack in the closet door until a policeman in a blue shirt found her. She looked down at her mother on the floor of the living room, now covered with a sheet, as the officer handed her off to some other woman in the hallway of their apartment complex.

A few weeks later, she was taken to a home. There she was told that her mother was gone and wasn't coming back. Annie cried for days, not only for the loss of her mother, but for the loss of her dog. The police brought her a small box which contained some of her personal possessions. She never took the lid off the box. The new people she lived with finally bought her a new dog—she named him Rags.

Chapter 1

Twenty years later

Starbucks
West End Avenue,
Nashville

Ann sat quietly waiting for her cousin, Sally Hart, to join her. She had asked Sally to meet her today at 9:00 a.m. sharp. This was her first day on the job. She had worked hard to find a position since graduating from law school—she sure as hell didn't want to lose it as a result of being late the first day she walked in the door.

Ann waved as she watched Sally walk toward her. She was always anxious to see her. Sally, always upbeat, always confident, always positive about life, was one of the reasons Ann had remained relatively sane and a functioning member of society.

One of these days, however, they would need to have a discussion concerning the extra weight Sally carried around. She wasn't fat, and it wasn't, as of yet, enough of a problem that it could possibly affect her health. But it was enough that Ann knew she had to be uncomfortable. She had decided long ago she wouldn't raise the issue unless Sally raised it first. That, as of yet, hadn't happened.

"Hi, Sally. Glad you could make it."

"I can always make it when you call, you know that." She sat down with her coffee cup in hand, and said, "So, today's the first day, is it?"

"This is it. The start of something new and the end of a two-month nightmare. Hopefully it will all work out. I'm just glad I found the job here, in Nashville, and I didn't have to travel to

Memphis or Knoxville to find something. I didn't want to leave here."

"So, what's this old guy like?"

"Well, first of all he's not that old—he's only fifty-five. He seems like a great guy. He practices alone. His wife helps with the office work. They have one full-time secretary. He just has more to do than he can handle. He wants out of the criminal justice field and, of course, that's the field in which I want to practice. So, I think all and all, this is going to be a pretty good fit."

"I guess I didn't know you were interested in that field. Why criminal justice? You really don't seem the type to want to specialize in that particular area."

"You mean, because I'm so laid back?"

"Well, yes, I guess. You're just not really very assertive. I mean, please understand, I don't know you very well as a lawyer, I know you as my cousin. Because of that, I've seen you around your friends, and you just never appeared to be the type of person that would have an interest in crimes, criminals, jail...you know...all that kind of stuff. No offense, but you just don't. You're a wonderful person and...I mean not that lawyers aren't, but...Oh hell, I don't know what I mean. Forget I said anything."

Ann laughed and said, "I understand. I may not be suited to this type of practice, but I've wanted to work in this area of law since I was—well, for a long time. I'm not going to walk away now until I know I have no ability. Then, I'll start looking for work with an insurance company, the government, or in some other field. But not yet. Not until I've convinced myself I'm no good in this field of law. I want to represent people that aren't guilty, or that can't help themselves, whether they are guilty or not."

"Does that somehow stem from your mom—her situation—maybe?"

"Oh, I guess. Hell, I don't know. Do you mean just helping people that need help, like she did? Probably. It's just what I've wanted to do for a long time, and I've come too far to turn back now."

"Speaking of your mom, has there ever been anything turn up concerning her murder? I know it's been a long time, but have the cops just quit calling—quit touching base with you?'

"Pretty much. I don't hear from them and don't talk to them at all unless I go to the station and find someone that will discuss it. They avoid me on the phone. They've never had a lead of any kind. Breaks my heart. I lost her, then on top of all that, the person that killed her can't be found—losing situation on both counts."

"I'm so sorry, Ann. I know how traumatic it's all been for you, but you've done amazingly well. Graduated college, graduated law school, and now this great job. I'm really proud of you. Oh, and a great boyfriend—pretty good looking too."

Ann said, "Let me grab a refill. Be right back."

She walked to the counter, got a hot cup of coffee, and as she was ready to sit, she said, "He's a hoot. He's trying some case now—a criminal case here in Davidson County. He wants me to come sit in and watch when I have time. He thinks I might learn a thing or two. I told him I'd try to today, but the new job comes first."

"So, is your new boss going to start you out right away in criminal cases? Has he mentioned what he wants you to work on, like on your first day there?"

"That was one of the things I asked for—to hit the road running, and he told me those were his thoughts too. So yes, I expect to go to work on criminal cases as soon as I walk through the front door."

"Would you let me know when you're in court? I'd like to watch you in action."

"Sure, when I'm ready. For now, you're just going to have to take my word for it that I was actually there, actually representing some guy that should have never been charged. When I'm ready and have a little confidence in myself, I'll give you a call."

"On a personal basis, I want to hear a little more about that lawyer buddy of yours?"

She smiled, as she said, "Now, just to make sure—are you talking about *my* man—the man I love? You talking about *Jack*?"

"You know who I'm talking about. Certainly, Jack. What's going on with him? I have no excitement in the world of romance whatsoever, so I have to follow your life. You'll find out what it's like when you're married for well over ten years to the same man and you have three young kids. Your idea of romance changes completely. A romantic situation for the two of us is each with a Big Mac in hand, in the front seat of the car, with all the window rolled up, the radio on, and the kids locked in their bedrooms. Now *that* cousin, *that's* a big evening for *us*. Tell me about 'your man'. You've only briefly discussed him in prior conversations and, of course I've never met him."

She smiled. "He's great. He's five years older than I am, and been married once, so he knows a little more about life, about relationships, than I do. But he's been easy to live with, although we've only just celebrated our six-month anniversary. As I said, he's trying some criminal case in Davidson County this week, and he's preparing to try one in Wilson County before long. He does a lot of business in that county. In that case, they're trying some guy for theft, so it's not a high-profile case, but if they all pay a retainer, it really doesn't matter how big the issues are, as long as you're getting paid for what you do—at least that's his theory."

Sally hesitated. She took a sip of coffee and finally said, "You still miss her? You still miss your mom?"

"Every day. Every fricken day of the week, I miss her."

"Would it help you to find out who did it or does it really matter anymore?"

"I think it would help—I guess. She's gone and nothing's going to change that part of the situation whether they find the guy or not. However, in my own mind, fair is fair. He did something wrong—now he's supposed to pay the price. It's simple. That's how it's supposed to work. But in this case, it's not working at all."

Ann thought for a moment, as Sally remained quiet. "You know, that's the part of all this that *really* bothers me. The whole process, the final piece of the puzzle in situations like this, I believe happens when that last piece *fits* and the perpetrator is punished. This puzzle isn't complete. It's missing a piece. I'll do what I can to continue to push law enforcement until someone uncovers the piece that's missing and fits it into the puzzle, or I'm dead. That's how I feel about it and probably always will."

"Well, that's an interesting way of looking at it, I guess. Never thought of it quite that way."

"I better go. I need to be there by nine-thirty."

"The office isn't far away. You sure you can't hang just a few more minutes? I love talking to you."

"Thanks, but you know this traffic. It could take ten minutes and it could take an hour. I do *not* want to be late."

She stood, as did Sally, and they embraced.

"I'll see you soon. I'll give you a call when I know what my schedule is. If there's something I feel you would enjoy watching in the courtroom I'll let you know."

Fifteen minutes later, Ann walked in the front door of the Harold Dale Law Firm. Harold took her through all four separate rooms, finally ending up in her new office. She took a seat as Harold walked out the door. She smiled as she looked around the four walls of her *own office* and opened the next chapter of a life which had already been full of more surprises than most people encounter in a lifetime.

Chapter 2

Ann sat at her desk and once again checked the time. It was only a few minutes before ten—not even midmorning. But regardless of what time it was, she could barely keep her eyes open.

It wasn't the work that tired her, it was those damn dreams. Since her mother's death, almost every other week she would dream about some aspect of what she observed that night so many years ago.

There was little consistency in the content of the dream. Sometimes he would notice her watching through the small opening between the door and the doorframe. Sometimes he would stop her on the street and ask her if she was the little girl that saw him kill her mother. But she could never make out his face—it was always a blur.

The only consistency in the dreams, was that she could plan on it happening at least once every other week. The content varied. Most of the time some of what she dreamed wasn't even part of what she actually observed. She always woke up, normally sweating through her nightshirt and normally succeeding in also waking Jack.

Once in a while, the dream would point out a new tidbit of information she had forgotten. That would again bring up the whole episode and she would wonder what that new sliver of information might mean as concerned the totality of what occurred that night.

Again, last night was no exception. She awoke at two-thirty and it took her at least an hour to fall asleep. The aftermath was always the same—when it was time to rise and get ready for work, she felt as though she had just finished a marathon, rather than a night's sleep.

"Morning, Ann. How was your evening?"

"Fine, fine Mr. Dale. I'm a little tired this morning, but I'm fine."

Harold Dale sat down across the desk from her. He was clearly overweight to the extent he had trouble fitting in the chair, which had arms. In addition, he was tall. All in all, he was a large man in every respect.

His horn-rimmed glasses made him look studious, and once she had a chance to visit at length with him, it helped solidify her first impression of him. He was truly a geek in every sense of the word—a wonderful man, but a geek.

"Hang in there—it's only seven more hours and you'll be able to go home and take a nap."

His laugh resonated off the walls of her office, and she couldn't help but laugh too—even though there was nothing to laugh about.

"Okay, we need to calm down now. I have some serious business for you. After you left last night, I had a family come in whose son has been charged with sexual abuse. The boy wasn't with them, but they tell me he had nothing to do with it. I told them to send him in tomorrow morning. In fact,..." He looked at his watch, "About right now. I want you to visit with him, get his story, and tell him we'll discuss whether we want to take his case. We'll let his family know when we decide what we want to do."

All thoughts of a lack of sleep quickly faded away. She opened her desk drawer and took out a legal pad.

"Well, okay, I...can...do that...Mr. Dale...I..."

"Hold on, Ann. Look at me. *Ann, look at me.*"

She stopped making notes on the pad, looked up and said, "Okay... Mr. Dale."

"Take a deep breath."

She said and did nothing.

"No, I mean it—literally. Take a deep breath."

She did as he asked.

"I know how overwhelming all this can be. But it's just one step at a time with these cases. First, get the facts, which shouldn't be a big deal for you. Then, you and I will assess the case, and we'll decide what we want to do, okay?"

She continued to look at him, but failed to respond.

"Ann, do you understand?"

She took another deep breath, then said, "Yes, I understand. I'll get the facts, then discuss them with you. Sorry, Mr. Dale, it's just all so new to me. I'll be fine—I think."

"Just take your time with him, find out what happened, take good notes. We'll go from there."

He stood and walked away, but came to a stop in the doorway. He turned around as he said, "By the way, call me Harold, everyone else does."

He let out an enormous burst of laughter and laughed all the way to his office.

She started jotting down questions she would ask the young man, right up until the secretary buzzed her and said Randall Kingston was waiting to see her. Ann told her to walk him back to her office. He arrived a few moments later.

There was little to him. He was short, cute and very young.

She extended her hand and he shook it as she said, "Have a seat, Randall. Do you go by Randy or Randall?"

As he sat down, he said, "I didn't do this. I didn't do what they say I did."

She smiled as she said, "I understand. But what do you want me to call you, Randall or Randy? Let's just start there first."

"Randall, just call me that for now—Randall."

She smiled. "Okay… Randall. You can call me Ann. Tell me a little about yourself."

"Well, I'm a freshman at Belmont. I've lived here all my life, and I didn't do it."

"Okay, well I guess that's at least part of the basic of 'basic information,' that I need, and since you're so anxious to tell me what it was you 'didn't do,' tell me what they've charged you with and why."

"This girl I was dating, this girl from Kentucky, said I…she said I…raped her." He looked away for a moment, and when he reengaged in conversation, he stared at her, and said, "But I didn't. I didn't do anything. She's lying and I know why."

"Where did this supposedly happen?"

"In my car."

"First of all, I assume you were with her the night it happened?"

"Yes, but we never did nothin' like that. I kissed her. We made out. But I never touched her…down there…if you understand."

Ann continued to write.

"You say you know why she's saying this?"

"Yes."

"Why?"

"She wants paid off."

"Has she contacted you in that respect?"

"No, but why else would she say that? It just didn't happen."

"Did she report this to law enforcement the night it supposedly happened?"

"Yes."

"Apparently she went to a hospital and was checked out?"

"Yes. There wouldn't have been any of that…you know…"

"Semen?"

"Yup, that's it, because she told them I wore a condom when I raped her."

"So, do you know if there was any evidence that she had just had recent sexual contact?"

"They never told me that. I swear on all that's holy I never raped her. I would never do that to a woman."

"When and where did you meet her?"

"I met her through a guy that I met. He knew her from high school. He was in one of my classes, and he lined me up with her."

"I assume there were no witnesses to what she claims happened?"

"No, other than they told me one of her classmates, some girl friend of hers, said she came home that night crying and told her I had raped her. She took her to the hospital. But as to the actual event, no there were no witnesses. Couldn't have been. I didn't do it."

"When were you told to appear next?"

"The cop said something like they would present everything to a grand jury. After that I would be told when to appear."

"You're out on bail?"

"Yes."

"Have you heard from her since it happened?"

"Yes. She tried to contact me, but I never took the call."

"At this point, I wouldn't talk to her at all. Ever been charged with anything before?"

"Oh, some small stuff, traffic violations, but nothing like this."

"Where did this supposedly take place?"

"In my car out west of town on some old country road she took me to. I should have been more careful. At the time, I thought it was kinda strange she knew right where the road was. I had never been there before and I've lived here all my life."

"Is there enough room in your car for this to happen?"

"No. I have a vet. Actually, I was driving my dad's car that night and yes, that thing's big enough to haul a building in the back."

"Did they search his car?"

"Yes. They found nothing, but they said that doesn't mean a thing."

"Okay, Randall, here's what I want you to do. I'll walk you down the hallway to our conference room. There, I want you to take a legal pad and pen, and write down everything that happened that night, from beginning to end. Once that's finished, you can go home. We'll file an appearance for you in the case. That way they will have to notify us when you're to appear. I'll appear for you from then on. We will, of course, plead not guilty and just take it from there. You say you haven't talked to her since, so she's never asked you for money?"

"No."

She stood and handed him a legal pad and pen. He followed her out the door and into the conference room, where he sat down and started to write. As she turned to leave the room, he looked up at her and said, "Believe me, ma'am, I swear to God, I didn't do this."

She smiled and said," Hang in there, Randall. I believe you. We'll do all we can for you."

As she walked down the hallway, she quickly concluded this case would indeed be an interesting way to start her practice in criminal court. Unless there was some type of separate independent evidence he either didn't know about, or he just didn't tell her about , the first case she would handle in her career would be a *he said, she said.* She had learned about those types of cases in school. Whether you represented him or her, they were considered difficult to win. She would start her *own* investigation as soon as she got the paperwork from the courthouse and had the opportunity to review all the facts with Mr. Dale.

Chapter 3

Ann finally arrived home near 7:00 p.m. She was barely able to exert enough enery to turn the key in the lock. As she opened the door, she heard Jack yell, "I'm in here."

She laid the files she brought home from the office, on the coffee table and walked in the kitchen. Jack was standing over the sink. He turned his head ever so slightly as she walked in the room "Hey, glad you're home. What's that new boss like? You think it's all going to work out, or did you make a mistake going to work for him? I thought about you all day. I wanted to call, but I didn't want to interrupt anything."

She walked up behind him and wrapped her arms around his waist.

As she continued to hug him, she said, "Everything went well, I think. I mean, it went as well as I hoped it would, I guess. Hell, I don't know how it went—I got nothing to compare it too. I'm just glad to be home. I'm tired, I'm hungry, and I've missed you all day. I have no idea how many times I thought of you and wished you were with me, guiding me, explaining things to me. It went fine, but it was a long, long day, for sure."

"I really wanted to call, but I didn't want to bother you, especially your first day on the job. I remember how that first day was for me—*not fun*. I made it through, but it was one of the longest days I've ever experienced. Now, tell me about it."

She turned and walked to the refrigerator. "We got any beer left? I just need one…or maybe two…three if I don't have to run somewhere to buy it."

"I think we've got some left. I haven't looked yet. I just got home a few minutes ago myself."

She found one in the far corner of the refrigerator. After sitting down at the kitchen table, she continued to watch as he fixed supper. She wondered how she was ever so lucky as to warrant someone like Jack. He was tall, handsome, and honest to a fault.

In addition, he had also been a great help while she had continued to search for that one job that would specifically suit her.

He winced as he turned to walk to the table to join her. "Damn back has been bothering me all day. You know, if we buy a house, we're going to have one with a jacuzzi in it or we're not buying it. I thought the pain would end the day I left the hospital—or at least it would somewhat back off. Little did I know it would stay with me this long after the accident."

"Turn just a little. Let me rub."

He swiveled in his chair, but even with that movement, he sucked in air, as he felt the pain not only from swiveling, but from her firm fingers digging into the painful area.

"Well, tell me how you got along today."

"Good. I think I got my first client. He's just a kid. I really want to represent him. I'm going to talk to Mr. Dale tomorrow and suggest we take the case."

"What kind of case?"

"Sexual abuse. They charged him with rape. The case, at least as far as we've discussed it, sounds pretty iffy to say the least. I think we got a fair chance of getting him off. Of course, what the hell do I know? I'm a flat-ass rookie."

"Your gut instinct concerning most things in life has always been pretty good, Ann. If you think it's a good case, it most likely is. He been indicted yet?"

"No. I'm waiting for that paperwork before I do much of anything. Once he's indicted, I'll take a few depositions and get it on the docket as quickly as possible. I really want to keep it moving—get it in front of a judge as soon as we can. This kid's life is totally on hold until the case is tried. *He* thinks it's a shakedown. But he hasn't been approached by her and, as of yet, there's no indication of that at all."

"What's this guy, Harold whatshisname, going to be like as a boss?"

"Today everything went well. Of course, I haven't been there long, but both he and his wife seem like wonderful people. I certainly have no complaints concerning either of them."

"Is he helping you with this case all the way through?"

"I don't know, but if he doesn't, I may need your help. I'm telling you right now, if I need help and Mr. Dale hasn't got the time, I'm calling on you to assist me. By the way, how'd your trial go today?"

"Not bad. This case is a close call. I'm just not sure what the jury will do. The identification of my client is really weak, but he has no alibi for the night it happened and that hurts us. Hopefully, we'll come out okay." He smiled through the pain. "Now isn't this fun just talking about our cases like this. One day, I hope we'll be in the same office, working together on cases."

"So do I. But as for tonight, right now, I'd really like to have a bite to eat, then lie down on the couch and watch some TV—just relax. Everything about ready to go?"

He stood, walked to the oven, opened the door, and said, "Everything's ready. Let's eat."

Later that evening, after she had reviewed the office files she brought home and as they watched TV, both of them nodded off for a moment. He woke up, nudged her and said, "Hey, wake up. You ready to go to bed?"

She sat up and said, "What time is it?"

"What's it matter? If you're that tired, which after the dream you had last night and the day you had today, I'm sure you are, then we should go to bed."

She stood, and walked toward the bedroom door. As he turned off the TV and followed her, he said, "By the way, if I find the right case for us, I'd like to try one with you. Will that work out okay since you're now employed by Harold?"

"Sure. Well, anyway I would think so. I'll talk to him about it. That would be great if we can work it out."

"Let me see what comes up. I'll let you know if I take on one that needs us both."

"I'd have to run it by Harold, but I'd certainly be interested. I would love to work and to learn, from you."

As they both started to undress, he said, "When are we going to start thinking about opening our own firm?"

"Oh, hell, I don't know. I suppose when we both start making enough money to pay the rent and all associated expenses with our own office. I'm really excited about doing that, but I'm just not sure when we'll be able to handle it financially."

He crawled into bed and grabbed a book he had started to read as she crawled in beside him. He looked at her, then laid the book down. She wore only a night shirt. She was lying on her back as he turned toward her. His hand made its way up her stomach until it came to a stop, nestled securely on her breast.

She opened her eyes, and said, "Are you serious? Now?"

"Well, kind off. It's been a few days and I just thought maybe…"

"Remember last night. Remember me waking up in the middle of the night and not being able to get back to sleep? Then there was a ten-hour day on top of it. Why don't you hold that thought until tomorrow? I'll be ready for you tomorrow. Okay?"

He smiled. "I'll hold on 'till then, but no longer." He picked up his book, and about ten minutes later, laid it down, turned toward her, and said, "By the way, let's get married."

She was breathing softly and showed no sign of responding.

Softly he said, "Hey, let's get…hello…yoo-hoo…I finally tell you I'm ready and you fall asleep."

She turned over on her side, away from him. Once again, he turned over on his back, grabbed his book, and started reading. A few moments later, he put the book down, turned out the light, and whispered, "Hey, you awake? Got a great idea. Let's get married."

She said not a word.

Chapter 4

Ann was all settled. She had her cup of coffee, she had reviewed the files of clients she expected later in the morning, and she was mentally refreshed after a dreamless night. She had now worked for Harold all of four weeks and was just starting to get into a routine which suited her.

She was still smiling as she remembered the events of a few weeks ago, when they had started the morning with sex and immediately thereafter, Jack had proposed. She told no one. There would be plenty of time for that.

It had been the first time he had approached the subject on his own and without some initial comments by her as she tried to ease the conversation in that direction. After his proposal, Ann told him she had been ready for a long time. She was just waiting for him to wrap his head around the concept. They agreed they would start making plans immediately. That's just what they had done, although very slowly, which was the way both wanted it.

As Ann started to, once again, review her notes and prepare for her appointment with Randall Kingston, Harold walked in her office.

"Good morning, good morning. You all ready to begin a most glorious day? I mean it's beautiful outside, isn't it? Just a perfect late summers day."

"It is at that Harold, it is at that."

"You got that Kingston kid coming in today?" He took a chair in front of her desk as she responded.

"Yes, I do. He'll be in around nine-thirty."

"Is everything pretty much ready to go concerning his trial?"

"Yes...I think so. We still have about five weeks before it's tried. I've done everything I felt was necessary to prepare. Depositions are over. I've done as much investigating beyond that as I could."

"I believe you're ready. I've suggested that you do everything I would have done, and you've done that. I'll try to find time to second chair you when and if you want me to, but I want you to handle this. By *'this'* I mean try the case and handle each and every aspect of it by yourself. I'll try to be there with you, but I want you to first chair it all the way through, okay?"

She hesitated. "Are you sure this is the way you want it? I'm just not certain…"

"Wait." He stopped her in midsentence. "You've been here a month now, and if there's one thing I notice about you, it's that you're consistent—you really underestimate your abilities. Whether it involves handling people, *or* it involves your approach to solving a problem, *or* it involves your analysis of legal issues, you continually underestimate yourself. You are way more capable than you, yourself, believe you are. Go with your instincts, Ann, just go with your instincts. If you do that, without a doubt, you're going to come out way ahead in this business."

She could feel herself blush as he finished his statements.

"That's kind of you, Harold. I know I'm a bit insecure, but I'm working on that. I think it'll all get better the more I learn, the longer I practice."

"You don't have to wait, Ann. You're there now. You have all the intelligence, all the ability you need, right now. Sure, you're going to make a mistake or two along the way. We all do—even those of us that have already practiced a hundred years. Don't let the mistakes bother you. Just learn from them and move on. In the scope of things, they won't amount to much when you review the whole body of work you've accomplished." He stood. "That's all I've got to say. I'm done for today, and I bet you're damn glad." Again, he let out his now infamous belly laugh.

"Thank you. I'll remember what you said."

He left once her secretary indicated Randall was waiting for her.

"Morning."

He sat down as he said, "Morning, Ms. Jackson."

"Just call me Ann, Randall. I would feel more comfortable if you would just call me Ann."

"Okay. Do we have a trial date yet?"

"Yes. Five weeks from Tuesday."

"Have you had a chance to talk to the prosecutor about resolving this? I think you said his name was Mr. Leonard."

"Yes, I have. He indicated he would resolve it by dropping it one level. You'd still have to plead guilty to a sexual abuse charge, but it wouldn't be as serious as the one you're charged with."

"Jail time?"

"Not as much, but yes."

"Sexual abuse registry?"

"Yes."

"Then no, I'm not doing any of that unless I no longer have a choice."

"I understand. That's what I figured you'd say."

"What did you want to see me about today?"

"I just want to go through the procedure you can expect once we get to trial. We'll go through it many times, but I just want to start introducing it to you now. I don't want you surprised by the procedure once we get to trial."

"I'm ready."

"Okay, first here is a list of jurors. I want you, with your family, to review the names. If there's anyone on there that presents an issue, I need to know so I can strike him. We'll end up with twelve people, but I want to make sure it's the *right* twelve people—not ten that are unbiased and two that have an axe to grind with you or your family, okay?"

He took the list, folded it up, and placed it in his pants pocket. "I'll have my parents go through these names with me, and I'll talk to you about it the next time I come in."

"Great. Okay, now as concerns the witnesses, what are your thoughts? They've all been subpoenaed. You've heard their position through the depositions we took. You told me you wanted to review their testimony and let me know where the mistakes were. What are you thinking?"

"Well, really other than the testimony of Charlene, I can't say there's much that I took issue with."

"Okay let's go through the major witnesses. First, there was Johnny Stark—he introduced the two of you and is from the same town in Kentucky she's from. No problem with what he testified to?"

"No, not really. He did introduce us, so he told the truth."

"What about Thelma Wells. She testified that Charlene came to her after you raped her and told her all about it."

"Obviously she's either lying or Charlene lied to her. But the most important fact she testified to couldn't have happened because I never raped Charlene in the first place. Beyond that, I guess she told the truth about everything else."

"Then there's Charlene, Charlene Cartwright. Obviously, she's lying, so I won't even ask you about her."

"Yes, she's lying." He looked away, as he said softly, "How in the hell did this happen? How did I get hooked up with someone like this? Am I that stupid? How did this happen?"

"Hey, don't beat yourself up over getting involved with this woman. How in the world could you have known? I'm sure she presented a pretty picture when it all started. There was no way in the world you could have known it would end like this."

"I know, but putting my parents through this—I just feel like such an idiot."

"Look, it is what it is. We're definitely going to have to try the case. So, rather than focusing on that aspect of the problem, let's focus on getting the jury to find you not guilty. Now, I've prepared a list of questions I'm going to ask you at the time of trial. I want you to review them carefully, Then, the next time we talk, I'll go through each of them with you."

He nodded, then took the questions also folding them up and shoving them down in his pants pocket.

"Make another appointment for about two weeks from today. At that time, we'll review the rest of the process."

After she answered a few more questions he asked which were of a general nature, he left, setting up an appointment two weeks from today.

Ann sat quietly in her office, waiting for the next appointment but thinking about her time with Randall. Either he was already a really, really good liar at his young age, or he was truly innocent. She was way more inclined to believe the latter than the former, but what the hell did she know—she was, after all, the epitome of the word *rookie*.

Chapter 5

It had been a demanding five days—a difficult work week, to say the least. The past few days had made law school look like kindergarten.

Even though she would come to the office at least a portion of the day tomorrow, she would spend the rest of her time over the extended Labor Day weekend, with Jack, doing as little as possible. They hadn't talked about it yet, but she could see some hiking, a movie or two, and a cookout in their immediate future.

As for this moment, she kicked off her shoes, put her feet up on her desk and enjoyed her last cup of coffee for the day.

Everyone else in the office had left for the day. She had remained to work on a couple of items that were on her mind, and now that they were cleaned up, before she went home to her *other* environment, she wanted to take a deep breath…breathe deep for just a few minutes before she left.

Her phone rang. She checked to see who the caller might be before she answered. It was Sally. They hadn't "caught up" for a while and she wanted to know all about her new life as a lawyer. Rather than visit over the phone, Ann just told her to come to the office. They *did* have some catching up to do, and coffee in the office was free.

A few minutes later, she heard Sally walk in the front door. She walked out to greet her, locking the door before they walked back to her office.

"Wow, this is nice."

As she poured her a cup of coffee, Ann said, "It's not the best of the best, but I love it—it suits me perfectly."

Sally took a chair, as she said, "How's it all going? Is this something you're going to enjoy, or is it too much?"

"It's perfect. I love it here. I guess we haven't talked in a while. I got my first jury trial coming up in a few weeks."

"Wow. Are you nervous? Can I come?"

Ann hesitated as the smile left her face. "Sure. While you're at it, why don't you bring all your friends too? It starts a week from Monday, here in Nashville. It's a criminal case, and no I'm not nervous at all."

"You're not? Good for you. I'll be there. I'll take some time off work and come watch you in action."

Ann leaned forward. She smiled and whispered, "Sorry, Sally, but you don't get it. I'm scared to *fucking death*. But just keep that between you and me, okay? Don't tell any of your… *friends* you're bringing to court with you."

Sally's eyes opened wide, as she said, "You're scared to death? You were just *kidding* me about not being scared?"

"Now come on. It's my first trial *ever*. Sure, I'm scared. I think about it, I almost throw up. Yes, I'm scared to death. I've been trying to practice *not* showing how scared I am, but every time I think about it, I sweat through my blouse. Now tell me, how's that going to work out? I'm going to have to wear a fucking blouse made out of leather or something to cover that up. No, I'm petrified. It'll be fine though, it'll be fine…I'll be fine…it'll be fine…it will all turn out okay."

"I'm sorry, Ann, I wish there was something I could do."

Ann sat back in her chair and released the grip she had on the edge of her desk. She smiled and said, "Change the subject."

Obviously flustered by Ann's outburst, Sally looked around the room for a moment, before she took a long drink of coffee, then said, "Okay, sure, I'll be glad to do that. Let's see, what about the rest of your work here? Is it all going okay?"

"Yes, it's going great. I love the people I work with, and all in all, I couldn't be happier. You?"

"Oh, me…I'm happy, I'm really, really happy. Could we go back to that trial thing again? Would it help if I didn't show up and didn't bring any of my friends? I hate seeing you like this. You're never like this. I don't think I like this side of you."

"Okay…I'm sorry. I may have gone a little overboard there, but yes, I'm really nervous about it. You can come. Your presence won't alter anything. Bring your friends if you wish— won't help or hinder me. I'll still have to try the case."

"Thank you. Now, this is the side of you I like. This is much better. I'll be there rooting you on. Let's talk about something else. What about Jack? How's he?"

Ann smiled. "Oh Jack, he's fine. He's so even-keeled; he stays about the same day after day. Great guy. Love him to pieces."

"You're right about that. He's…"

"I told you we're getting married, didn't I? I can't remember if I told you that or not."

Sally sat quietly for a moment, then started to smile. She jumped up, grabbed the front of Annie's desk, and screamed, "You're what? *No,* you never told me. What the hell…I thought I was your best friend as *well* as a cousin, but you never said anything to *me* about it. Oh my god, that's huge, that's huge. Come over here…right now!"

Ann stood and walked around her desk, where Sally grabbed her. Together they jumped up and down, until Ann said, "Okay, that's good. Sally, that's good. Stop Sally, we're good here."

Sally finally let loose, and as Ann again took her seat behind her desk, she said, "When, where, what time?"

"I'm not sure about all those details yet, but you'll be the first to know. I want you to be my maid of honor."

Sally jumped to her feet again, and said, "Yes, yes, yes, I'll do that, now come on over here, right now."

"No, no, no. Here, just shake my hand."

She extended her hand, which Sally shook as she sat back down.

"I'm so excited for you. Do all your other friends know? Does everyone know, but me?"

"No, you're the first I've told. We're just keeping it to ourselves until we get some of the arrangements figured out. Now what about the family—how are the kids doing?"

"Good, we're all doing just fine, just fine." She was quiet for a moment, before she said, "Ann, I wish I could help you with this trial coming up. I know how important it is to you. I just wish there was something I could do to help."

"I know you do, but there isn't. It's all up to me. I really feel this kid is innocent, but it'll all be up to the jury. Not knowing exactly what to expect is so disconcerting to me. I don't know the prosecutor, although I do know he's good and of course, I don't know the judge. I'm just so much in the dark about all this. But my boss said we have all been there at one time or another—there was a first time for all of us." She smiled, and said, "I know he's right. So, I'll hunker down, do my homework and hope it ends the way I want it to."

"You're all prepared, I assume?"

"I've gone through everything so many times, I can recite it all in my sleep. Yes, I'm as prepared as I'll ever be."

"You'll do fine, Ann, and I'll be right behind you all the way."

Later that night, as she repeated Sally's comments to Jack, she felt lucky to have so many people in her corner—standing behind her. But unfortunately, that wasn't the issue.

At this point, she wished there was someone in *front* of her, someone to actually lead the way, lead her through it, perhaps handle part of the trial, and not leave all this responsibility completely on her shoulders.

But she knew that wasn't going to happen. No matter how the trial turned out, when that verdict was finally rendered, she was either going to end up with all the glory...*or all the blame.*

Chapter 6

Ann sat in the stillness of early morning, alone, in her office. No one but her had yet arrived to start up the daily madness and the march of potential clients that always seemed to happen as soon as the front door was unlocked. But this morning, instead of unlocking it and leaving it unlocked as she normally did, she left it locked. She needed time to sit and think about the event which would literally start her career on a positive note or a negative note, one way or the other.

Randall's trial was scheduled to begin tomorrow morning. She had worked on her opening and closing statements most of the weekend. Jack had helped her, which was certainly beneficial. But the bottom line was that when the gavel fell for the first time tomorrow morning it was her, and nobody else, that would need to take hold of the reins and handle the buggy.

As she sat reviewing all she had accomplished during the weekend, she heard the door open and knew it had to be either Harold or their secretary. She looked up as Harold appeared in her doorframe.

"Here pretty early, Ann. Were you here all weekend too?"

"Not really. I went home for a while both days."

He smiled, but said nothing.

"Okay, I was here the majority of the weekend."

He remained quiet and never moved.

She hesitated, then started thumbing through some of the paperwork in Randall's file as she said quietly, "Okay, to be honest I guess I was here almost all of the weekend."

Harold smiled. "You all ready to go?"

She hesitated, then looked at him as she said, "I…I'm not…"

He walked in and sat down in front of her desk. "Again, are you ready—are you prepared for this trial?"

"She leaned back in her chair, took a deep breath, and said, "Hell, I don't know, Mr. Dale. I guess so. I hope so. I think I am."

"You got everything written down?"

"Yes."

"Give me all your notes. Let me take a look and make changes I feel are appropriate while you drink your coffee and look at something else for a while. By the way, I'll be sticking my head in and out of the courtroom door, but, as I told you, I can't be there all the time. I just have too much going on."

As she assembled all her paperwork for him to review, she stopped as he dropped that tidbit of news on her. "You're kidding. I thought you would be second chairing me at least part of the time. Are you sure it wouldn't be better if you tried this? I just don't know if..."

"No. This is your case, and besides that, there's no better way for you to get your feet wet, than to...get your feet wet." He laughed, which tended, at least for the moment, to break the tension in the air.

She smiled, and said, "Okay, I hope you know—I hope we *both* know what we're doing come tomorrow."

The rest of her morning was spent getting ready for Randall's appointment right after the noon hour and cleaning up a few additional matters that demanded her attention prior to commencement of the trial. She had no idea how long it might take to try the case, and there were other issues that needed to be resolved before tomorrow.

When Randall arrived for his appointment, she first reviewed procedural issues with him, which really didn't involve his actual participation.

When she had completed discussing those issues, he said, "So, what do I need to do when it's time for these things to take place—your opening statement, picking of the jury, and then the final closing statements? Do I just sit there, or do I leave the room?"

"No, you'll sit by me. That's especially important while I pick the jury. As we've already discussed, we'll quietly evaluate each prospective member of the jury as they are being questioned, and we can dismiss those individuals you feel uncomfortable with.

Now, as concerns the reading of the instructions by the judge to the jury at the end of the trial, and my opening and closing statements, you'll just sit and listen."

"When those witnesses all testify, do I just sit there too?"

"Yes. Make notes if need be. If there's something that doesn't sound right to you, or isn't the truth, other than the fact you didn't rape her, you need to let me know. Write it down and we'll discuss it when we get a chance."

"Have you discussed my case with the prosecutor again?"

"Yes. There's no chance to resolve it. He's made his final offer. It's no different than it was from the beginning, so all discussions with him about that are over. We are just going to need to try the case."

"By the way, I heard from Charlene. Did I tell you that?"

Ann leaned forward in her chair, as she said, "Why didn't you call me?"

"Nothing happened. I didn't think it was important."

"What'd she say?"

"She wanted to meet with me—see if we could work this out some way."

"What'd you tell her?"

"I told her to go to hell and hung up."

"Did she happen to say what she met by 'work this out?'"

"No. I told you what she said. That wasn't the first time. I've heard from her before. The calls never started until I met with you. I've hung up on her every time, because I really had nothing to say to her. We discussed nothing, so I didn't think it was important to tell you."

"You may have been right from the very beginning. This whole thing may have originally been just a shakedown. You still have the number she called you from?"

"Yes."

"Let's try to call her right now. Don't respond to anything she might say. Just call her and ask her what she wanted to talk about. If she wants to meet tell her okay and ask her when and where. I'll hook you up with a recording device and we'll go from there."

He pulled out his phone and hit redial. It rang a number of times, until he finally just terminated the call. "What now?"

"It's probably just gone too far. She's gone too far down the road to try that now. She could also have concluded we may be trying to catch her, now that you've had time to discuss all this with an attorney. If she calls again, don't talk to her until we have a chance to record the call. I imagine she's done, but from here on, no conversation with her until we can record it."

"Okay." He looked down, as he said, "Sorry, I didn't think the call was important. So I never told you about it. I haven't been through this before—I just didn't know what I was supposed to do."

"I understand, but you *do* know now. She's the enemy here, Randall. She's trying to put you away for a long time. We just need to be careful, that's all."

"I understand." He looked up at her, as he said, "So what about my testimony. I've reviewed all the questions again, and you and I have reviewed the answers—anything else I need to do?"

"Let's just review your general demeanor when you testify."

"You mean when I'm actually up there on the stand and you and Mr. whatshisname are asking me questions?"

"Yes. Now, first of all, you understand you never try to answer a question you don't understand, right?"

"Right."

"When you're up on the witness stand, don't fidget around. Sit still and talk loud enough so everyone can here. Look at the person asking the question. You don't need to maintain eye contact with the jury. Look at the person that asked you the question."

"Will the judge ever ask me anything?"

"No. Only the attorneys will ask the questions. Now, when you answer the question about whether you actually committed this act, be firm when you respond. Don't let there be any doubt in anyone's mind you didn't do this."

"Okay. I'm kind of afraid of what the prosecutor might ask me. Will he ask me questions I can't answer?"

"Probably not. I don't know what he's going to ask you, but if you don't understand the question, or you just plain can't answer it, tell him so. Do not try to answer a question you just don't know the answer to or don't understand. And don't argue with him. You can't win an argument with him—don't even try."

Ann kept referring to her notes—notes concerning direct and cross-examination she had pulled from books she had reviewed on the subject. Obviously, she had no firsthand experience concerning these issues she was discussing with him. But the information she had gleaned from the books made sense, and she would follow the rules until for some reason or other, they didn't fit the problem.

"Will the jury take long to decide?"

"They'll take as long as they need, or until the judge declares a mistrial if they can't come to a conclusion. It's all up to him."

"Can I take a quick break if I need to ask you the answer to a question I'm not sure about?"

"Nope. When you get up there, you're on your own. If you don't know how to answer, or don't know the answer, just explain that to the one that asked the question."

"What are our chances here, Ann? We going to win or are they going to believe her?"

"The state has the burden of proving beyond a reasonable doubt that you did this. I personally don't think they can meet that burden, but I guess we'll know the answer to that sometime after Wednesday."

"How long's this going to last?"

"However long it takes. There's no rule about how long a trial is or isn't supposed to take. You just try the case, and it ends when it ends."

"What if we lose? What happens then?"

"Let's worry about that if it happens. For now, let's just have faith in the system—hope it all works out."

She didn't want to think about losing. She had studied the procedure that would take place if they lost, but she was afraid if she discussed it with him, it might scare him enough he would run. They would take this a step at a time—in the manner Harold had suggested. Hopefully, when the trial was over, they wouldn't have to consider the next step—they would only savor the victory. *Hopefully, that wasn't just wishful thinking.*

Chapter 7

Ann heard the door open, then watched as Jack Connors slowly eased his way through the door and into their townhouse.

As he turned and saw her, he smiled and said, "Hi, hon."

She gave him a kiss and said, "You having trouble with your back?"

"That damn wooden chair in the courthouse is hard as hell. The longer I sat in it, the harder it got. You know, I just keep paying for not wearing my seat belt the day that kid hit me. I guess I'm just going to keep on being punished the rest of my life for not having it on."

"You want me to rub it? I'll be glad to."

"No, no. I know you would, but I'm fine."

"What's in the sack?"

"I stopped at the liquor store for a moment on the way home. I thought we might try a new Merlot tonight. It was a little pricey, but I just figured we might try something new for a change."

"Great. By the way, where you been? That trial last until now? You're later than usual."

"Oh, the judge in Wilson County decided to let the jury keep deliberating after the foreman told him they were near a verdict. So, how was your day?"

Ann hugged him, and said, "Good. Today was good, but tomorrow…well tomorrow scares the shit out of me."

She walked in the kitchen as she continued to prepare supper.

He walked up behind her and put both arms around her waist.

"It'll all turn out fine. You've got a good head on your shoulders, Ann. You'll figure it all out as you go."

She turned around, and said, "I'm just so worried…not only for myself, but for this kid. He's a good kid. I have no doubt he's innocent. But I'm so uncertain, so concerned about how it's going to turn out. Today, Harold again reconfirmed he wouldn't be around to help, so I'm on my own."

"Do you want me to sit in? You know, maybe just sit in one of the back rows of seats and give you my thoughts at the break? I'll be glad to do that if it would help."

"No, no I'll handle it one way or the other. Besides, you got your own trial going on."

Jack walked to the kitchen table. He took the bottle of wine out of the paper sack, held it up and said, "Actually, I don't. It's over. We won—they found him not guilty."

She turned around as she said, "Are you kidding me. Why didn't you tell me? I'm so proud of you. What happened? You never seemed that sure you were going to win. So, this is your second win in a row. Wow. I'm really, really proud of you."

He pulled the cork screw out of the drawer and started to remove the cork.

"Would you please get one of those new-fangled openers for wine bottles? We've talked about it a thousand times. They're so much easier than dickin' around with this old dinosaur. In answer to your question, I never really felt they had that much on him in the first place. In fact, I was really surprised when the district attorney's office said they were pursuing it. He had a believable, although somewhat weak, alibi, but identification on behalf of the state was also weak. I just think in the end, the jury felt *all* the evidence was weak and the state failed to establish his guilt. I haven't had a chance to talk to any of the jurors yet, but that's my take."

"Bet your client was out-of-his-mind happy."

Jack smiled. "That's the best part of it all—experiencing the joy, the relief of getting someone off like that, someone you really felt was innocent all along. That makes it all worthwhile. Believe me that makes all the hard work and all the preparation worth every minute." He poured both of them a half glass of wine, smiled, and said, "Of course, getting paid is a nice perk, but the joy of getting an innocent man off is worth it all, in and of itself."

She sat down at the kitchen table, and after tasting the wine said, "Wow, this is really good. Tastes expensive."

"It was more than we normally pay, but it was a good day for me, for us. Unfortunately, the problem now is that I've got an incredible amount of shit to clean up at the office. I've disregarded everything else while trying this case. I should have stayed late at the office this evening, but I just wanted to get away from it all for a while—just have a little wine, a good meal and be with you,"

"That's sweet of you." She leaned over and kissed him. "With all you have to do, I wouldn't even consider you helping me. I'll just give it the best I have and go from there." She hesitated. "You know, I just hope I get to experience the type of gratification with my case, as you did today with yours. I got a healthy retainer, so getting paid won't be an issue. But actually, it never was. I want to win. I don't care about the money. I really like this kid, I truly believe he's not guilty, and I would probably represent him for nothing, just to get him off."

Jack frowned at her and said, "Unfortunately, you don't have a choice when it comes to getting paid. You know as well as I do, you got to get the money, win, lose or draw. We all still have to pay the bills. All you can do is the best you can do under the circumstances. I know how badly you want to win, and you will—maybe not this case, but you are, and always will be successful at whatever you do. You work hard at it, you're smart, and you're not a quitter. Just because you don't prevail with this kid, doesn't mean you won't win many, many other trials after you get some experience under your belt. Are you ready to cross-examine the complaining witness?"

"Yes, I think so, but this case is clearly a he-said she-said kind of case, and I'm afraid it's just going to come down to who has the most witnesses and who's the most believable. I'm afraid if it's a tie, they'll tend to believe her, not him."

"Let me come tomorrow and at least sit in the back of the room. I can listen to what's going on and give you my thoughts at the break."

"Nope. Harold will be in and out, at least for part of it. He can do that. You've been out of the office for a long time trying your case. I'm sure your desk is a mess. I'll handle this, Jack. I'll get through it come hell or high water—if I don't have a heart attack first."

"Okay, it's your case. We can discuss it when you get home. Maybe I can offer some advice then. Oh, by the way, it appears our office is going to take a case out of Wilson County concerning a man that killed his wife. I don't know if you've heard anything about it or not."

"Really? What are the facts?"

"It's all a little sketchy to me at this point. I just haven't had time to look into it because of all I have going on. But apparently, he and his wife were having some issues and he stabbed her—killed her. No one's talked to him yet, and it looks like I'm the one they are going to have him talk to. I haven't discussed it at all because of the trial I've had going on, but when I talked to my secretary briefly between witnesses this morning, she said someone was asking about my schedule, trying to find a time for him to see me. Apparently, the guy has a little money too, or someone would have already been appointed by the court to represent him."

"Sounds like an interesting case. Of course, with your experience, you're starting to get some high-profile cases. Hopefully I'll be in your position in a few years."

"Tell you what. Why don't you try this one with me? I'll recommend you and suggest both of us try it together. You up for it?"

"Oh, I don't think it's me you want helping you. I can't bring much to the table, Jack."

"Bullshit. If I didn't think you could do the job, I wouldn't be asking you, believe me. Now, why don't you talk to Harold and if he's okay with it, let's give it a shot."

She looked away for a moment, then she started to smile as she turned toward him and said, "All right. I'll ask Harold in the morning. If he says it's okay, I'm in. But just remember, this was your idea, not mine."

"Great. It should be a good learning experience for you, and I'll enjoy working with a partner."

She stood. "Here's to our newly formed partnership."

He stood, and they touched glasses. He then leaned over and kissed her, as he whispered, "Is this the type of thing what warrants a short trip to the bedroom to really, really seal the deal."

She turned and walked into the kitchen as she said, "Hell no. The pasta's almost overcooked now. There will be time for that later… *partner*. Let's eat."

Chapter 8

She sat quietly, as the judge made his way through the door leading from chambers, then up the steps to the bench. They had already selected a jury, but it had taken all morning. The judge had to help Ann through the process, advising her in front of the jury panel when she made a mistake. She figured it had to be obvious to the panel, that she was a novice but she couldn't stop long enough to think about it. She needed to keep up—to continue with jury selection, as well as anticipate the next step in the overall process.

Once it was time for their noon break, they had succeeded in selecting 12 people to listen to the evidence in the case and determine her client's guilt or innocence. Ann continued to learn as she completed the process, jotting down notes for reference the next time she selected a jury.

Immediately after the break, the judge explained the rules the jury would need to follow while the case was being tried—rules that explained what they could and couldn't do while they were serving as jurors.

Once completed, both the state and the defense presented opening statements. She muddled her way through, with the most obvious problem being her inability to remember her own client's name about halfway through her opening. Once she proceeded past that initial blunder, she finished up strong.

The judge then took a mid-afternoon break, and they were now ready for the state to start presenting evidence.

Prosecuting attorney Arnold Leonard presented testimony from the doctor that initially saw the victim and from a couple of cops that had initially interviewed Charlene. They were now ready for the testimony of Johnny Stark.

As Ann reviewed her notes, she quickly concluded the testimony of the examining doctor was interesting and beneficial to the defense. He testified Charlene wasn't a virgin and that he observed no sign of semen. But he did testify as to some bruising on other areas of her body which appeared to be recent. He also testified that they did find the defendant's DNA on her clothing. However, the fact that at the time of the incident he couldn't testify she had been sexually active within the recent past, was definitely a plus for the defense.

Johnny Stark was the first witness called by the prosecution. He testified that he met Randall at a party. He also testified he knew the complaining witness. He felt both Randall and Charlene might be a good match, so he introduced the two of them. His testimony was nothing that created an issue for the defense. It really presented little value for the prosecution either. Ann was unable to determine how cross-examination would assist in any respect so she never even questioned him.

They were nearing the end of the day, but the state asked the court permission to introduce one last witness before they adjourned.

Thelma Wells did not present a pretty picture. She looked barely a teenager, was extremely thin, and was poorly dressed. After the basic foundational questions had been asked and answered—those basic questions asking the witness who she was, and what her overall status was at the time of the incident—he then started to question her concerning the issues which were the subject matter of this case.

"How do you know the complaining witness?"

"We've known each other a long time. We're from the same town in Kentucky—Louisville—and we grew up together."

"You both move down here at the same time?"

"Yes."

"You both apparently continued to remain close, to remain good friends even after leaving your home town and moving here, is that correct??"

"Yes."

"Can you tell us what happened involving you and your friend, Charlene Cartwright the night of July 15?"

"Well, I really don't know what happened earlier that evening because I wasn't there, but later that evening Charlene told me she was raped by that guy sitting next to his attorney."

Ann stood up. "Wait, wait, Your Honor, that's hearsay...I think. I'm pretty sure it is. I am going to object to it on that basis."

"You know, I think you may be right. Mr. Leonard just have the witness testify as to what she observed herself, at this point in her testimony, and let's keep the statements of the complaining witness out of it for now unless you can show there's an exception to the rule in play here."

Ann had to smile as she sat down. First time for an objection, and it was sustained—one for one.

"Can you just tell us, Ms. Cartwright what her physical appearance was when you first saw her late that evening?"

"Sure. She was crying, she was bruised, her sleeve on her blouse was torn."

"Would you describe her physical appearance as very distraught?"

Ann jumped up, as she yelled, "Objection. Isn't that leading?"

"You don't have to yell, Ms. Jackson, I'm right here. I'm going to overrule that—he's just summing up what she just testified to. Please proceed."

Ann sat down. It was leading. There was no doubt about it. The judge was dead wrong. He should know better. Not much she could do about it, but he was wrong, that son-of-a-bitch.

"Yes, she was clearly distraught."

"Did she tell you what had just happened to her?"

"Yes."

"Did she indicate to you it had *just* happened?"

"Yes."

"Tell us what she said."

"Objection, Your Honor. It's hearsay."

"Well, now, it may be, but the state has established, in my opinion, one of the exceptions to the rule. The event had clearly just occurred, and the complaining witness was explaining what had happened. I'll allow it. Proceed."

Thema said, "Charlene told me she had been raped by that guy sitting next to his attorney."

"What did you do or say to her?"

"I told her we needed to get her to the emergency room and have her looked at by a doctor."

"Did you take her?"

"Yes."

"Did you take her back to the apartment after they examined her?"

"She stayed with me the rest of that night and for a few nights after that. She was afraid to stay in her apartment alone."

"Did she tell you where this occurred?"

"Yes. She mentioned it happened on a country road out west of Nashville."

"How would you describe her mental state after the rape?"

"Objection. He's assuming a rape happened. That hasn't been proven yet."

"I'll rephrase, Your Honor. How would you describe her state of mind after that night?"

"It definitely changed her. She was afraid to go out alone. She wanted nothing to do with him, the defendant. She wasn't as cheerful, as quick to make friends. It changed her. She hasn't been the same since it happened."

"Did you ever discuss this issue with the defendant?"

"Yes. I told him what I thought of him."

"Did he respond?"

"He called me every name in the book, as he did Charlene. He yelled at me. I was so embarrassed. I finally just waked away. He surprised me. I thought I knew him. I never figured he would do to anyone what he did to Charlene or say what he yelled at me."

Randall leaned toward her and whispered, "That never happened. No way in hell. She's lying about all that."

"Okay, we'll discuss it when we recess for the day."

"That's all I have, Your Honor."

"Cross?"

"Yes, Your Honor. Ma'am you weren't with them that night, were you?"

"No."

"So, you just can't be certain what actually did happen can you?"

"I know Charlene. She's not a liar, if that's what you're implying."

"Please just answer the questions I ask you. You cannot be certain what happened that night, can you? You weren't with them."

Thelma looked down for a moment. She looked at Ann, and said, "No, I wasn't there, but I have no doubt it happened as Charlene said it did."

Ann stood and said, "May I approach the witness?"

"Yes."

She walked toward Thelma, stopping only a few feet from the witness stand.

"Where did this conversation with the defendant take place?"

"On campus."

"Who heard it? Who do you know that actually overheard that conversation?"

"Well, really no one I know of, I guess."

"So, there's no one to confirm the conversation ever took place, is there—I mean, if you say it did happen, and he says it didn't? "

"Lady, it happened. Maybe no one overheard it, but it happened, believe me."

Ann, having taken all of her overbearing, arrogant attitude she could handle, grabbed the front of the witness box with both hands, stared at the witness and said, "Well, Ms. Wells, that's what *you* say. My client knows it's not true, and so do I. Judge, I'm done with her."

The prosecutor stood, and said, "Your Honor, I object to the insertion of council's personal opinion into the record. It obviously doesn't matter what she thinks. It's the jury that matters. The jury determines who's telling the truth and who isn't, not her."

"You're right. After this Ms. Jackson, keep your opinion to yourself. The only opinion that matters in this case is that of the jury."

Ann stood and said, "I understand, Your Honor. But it's tough to sit still when you know the witness is lying through her teeth and..."

"Stop, councilor, or I'll find you in contempt. Do you understand?"

Ann looked down, as she said, "I do, yes I do, Your Honor."

Shortly after the colloquy between Ann and the judge, they terminated proceedings for the day. Just before they did, the judge said, "Ms. Jackson, I want to see you in chambers before you leave."

Once the courtroom had cleared and Randall had left, Ann walked in chambers talking a chair in front of the judge's desk. He was reviewing a file concerning another case, but put it down as she walked in.

He looked at her for a moment before he started to speak. "Ann, I know this is your first case, but I can't have any more of that kind of bullshit I heard today. You can't browbeat a witness like that using your own opinion to do it. You know better. You understand?"

"Yes, I do Judge, but it's hard sitting there and..."

"Just stop. Do you know what you did wrong today?"

"Yes."

"No excuses next time. You know what you did, it can't happen again, end of story."

Later that night she explained the situation to Jack.

"You can't let your emotions rule the day. You know better than to do what you did. Learn from it and move on."

Jack was right—and the judge was right. She knew it—she knew she was wrong at the time. The first day, other than her one misstep, went fine, although perhaps the most positive result of the day grew out of a negative situation—*she hadn't been thrown in jail for contempt*. Ann would remember her mistake and try not to get carried away like that again. After all, it might indeed prove to be impossible to keep Randall out of jail if *she* ended up behind bars before the trial even concluded.

Chapter 9

There was only one left—only one remaining prosecution witness for the jury to hear. But the state had saved the best for last. They wanted to make sure the last witness that testified on behalf of the state, was this young lady who was innocent, pure as the driven snow, and treated so inappropriately by the defendant.

Once she had been sworn in and her basic information had been provided to the jury, Arnold said, "Can you tell us about your relationship with the defendant prior to July 15 of this year?"

She presented an extremely calm demeanor and was dressed to testify. She was attractive. In fact, attractive beyond the type of woman that would most likely pursue a relationship with the defendant. She apparently had people present that were supporting her. At least there were a couple of older individuals in the courtroom toward whom she glanced from time to time.

"Yes. We were good friends. I thought maybe it would turn into more than that. I really cared for Randall. He was kind and considerate. Obviously, that all changed."

"How long had you known the defendant?"

We dated most of the spring. We were excited about spending the summer together."

"So maybe about three to four months give or take?"

"Maybe, yes."

"Prior to the incident you had not been sexually involved with him?'

"No. Neither of us pushed the relationship in that direction. I thought it might happen, but the time was just never right, and I really wasn't that sure where the relationship was going. So, I, or rather we, just waited to see where it was all headed before we committed to each other in that fashion."

"You had apparently, at least according to the doctor's testimony, been sexually active prior to your relationship with Randall, is that correct?"

She looked down. "Yes, that's why I knew this time, because of that prior relationship, I was going to be darn sure where this was going before I gave myself to him, if you know what I mean."

Ann had already concluded this woman was either sickening sugar-sweet by nature, or she had been well-coached. Her demeanor, her appearance, was over the top squeaky clean. She could tell the jurors were eating it up as quickly as she could dish it out.

"Tell us what happened the night in question."

"Well, we went to a movie that night and after that, he asked me if I wanted to drive to a quiet place he knew about, and just listen to music—spend some time alone. I said sure, but I told him I wanted to be back in my apartment by midnight."

Randall leaned toward Ann and whispered, "She's the one that knew about the road. Hell, I had no idea it was even there."

"Then what happened?"

"We drove to the road, he turned the lights out and the music on. We started to kiss, and he said 'Let's take a walk.' The moon was shining really bright, and I said 'okay.' We got out of the car and walked down the road a ways and when we walked back to the car, he said, 'Let's get in the back—it should be more comfortable.' I said, 'Okay, but nothing more than kissing.' He said 'Okay.' Now, as I look back, I guess I was really naïve, but I didn't have any idea what he was going to do. I really didn't. I trusted him."

"Go on."

"When we got in the back of the car which had those seats that fold down, I should have known when they were already down, something was going on. We started to kiss. He got more forceful, and he told me to pull my jeans down. When I said no, he said, 'I don't want to hurt you. Now pull them down.' I did and he raped me."

By then she was crying. The jurors were all looking at the defendant as if they expected him to respond at that very moment.

The judge pushed a box of tissues toward her as the prosecutor asked, "What happened next?"

"When he was done, he said, 'If you know what's good for you, you won't tell anyone this happened.' Once I told my friend Thelma what happened, she told me I had no choice. I had to go to the doctor, which I did."

"And the man that raped you, is he in this courtroom today?"

"Yes."

"Where is he seated?"

"Next to his attorney, right there." She pointed at Randall.

"I have nothing further, Your Honor."

"Cross-examine?"

"Yes, Your Honor. Now, Ms. Cartwright, apparently, you've had sex with at least one other man, or boy, is that right?"

"Just one. And I thought I was going to marry him."

"Have you ever accused anyone else of raping you?"

"No, absolutely not." Once again, she started to cry. Ann had anticipated the crying would start up again—that it was only a matter of when, not if. She didn't trust this girl any further than she could throw her.

"No one saw any of this did they—no one else was present when this happened?"

"No."

"Isn't it correct you were the one that knew about that road, not Randall?"

"No. I don't live around here. How would I know about it?"

"Just answer my questions, please, Ms. Cartwright. So, you're saying he overpowered you in the back of the car? Look at him. He's not a very big guy. Do you really expect the jury to believe he's tough enough to overpower you and take advantage of you?"

Charlene looked at the jury and said, "Yes I do, because it's the truth."

"You been trying to contact my client, since this happened?"

"Yes."

"Why?"

She looked away. "I guess I just wanted to tell him I was sorry. I never expected this to go this far. But now I don't care. I've had time to think about it, and what I'm doing is the right thing to do. I would never want this to happen to someone else."

"You've never been involved in anything like this before anywhere else?"

"No."

"You weren't harmed or injured, were you?"

"No. And as I said, this doesn't have so much to do with me, as it does just not wanting it to happen to someone else. I figured I wasn't the first, and I didn't want it happening to another victim like it did to me."

"That's admirable of you."

For the next hour, Ann repeated questions and tried to dig into other areas of Charlene's life, but either an objection concerning relevance, or 'the question had been asked and answered,' stopped most of her questions before she ever got an answer.

She finally ended her cross-examination as the trial moved into late afternoon. The prosecutor had no additional questions, and the state rested its case.

Ann met with Randall in one of the conference rooms just prior to both leaving for home.

"This doesn't sound very good to me, Ann."

"No, but that's always the case after only one side of the story has been presented. It will be up to you to tell *the rest of the story* tomorrow. Are you ready to do that? You have any issues we should discuss before you get up on that stand tomorrow morning?"

He looked away, as he thought. "No, I don't think so. I'll think about it tonight and let you know in the morning, if that's okay with you."

"That's fine. Get a good night's sleep, Randall. Tomorrow's a big day."

As she slid into her car seat and started her car, she just hoped he understood how big a day it really was. The verdict, if he was found guilty, could be a tragic ending to a life which, it appeared to her, held *so* much promise.

Chapter 10

Ann left the courthouse and drove immediately to her office. Even though it was near 6:00 p.m., she needed to check on other cases, phone messages and new appointments before she did anything else.

There were well over 20 phone messages. In addition to reading each of them, she noticed appointments with five new clients. Some of them wanted to see her and some of them were people Harold wanted her to see. She concluded it didn't make much difference why they were coming to see her—whether it was because of what they hoped *she* could do for them, or whether it was because Harold sent them to her. She needed to continue to build her business, her clientele, until she simply had no more hours in the day and had all the business she could handle.

Hopefully that would happen in a fairly steady manner. Hopefully she would reach the maximum of what she was capable of achieving about the time Jack concluded he was ready to form their partnership. She could then push business over to him that she just simply didn't have time to handle.

Once she finished reviewing all the messages, and making notes for her secretary, she drove home, where she found Jack reviewing office work he had brought home for the evening.

"You're late. Something going on I don't know about?" He smiled. "You're not seeing some other guy are ya?"

She laid Randall's files down on the coffee table and kissed him. As she walked into the kitchen she said, "We got anything to eat?"

Jack stood, and said, "Okay, you didn't respond to my question, but I'm assuming your answer was 'no'. There's some of that mac and cheese I had to fix for myself that's still in the frig if you want it."

"I'll take it. Sorry I'm so late, but I went to the office after I left the courthouse. It looked like it was a madhouse there today."

As he sat down at the kitchen table, he said, "Sooo…since you haven't yet brought it up and since I've been crazy out of my mind worrying about you today, how did things go? I've thought about you every minute of the day. I know you were especially worried about the testimony of the complaining witness. What happened?"

She sat down with a plate of warmed up mac and cheese, and a beer, as she said, "Went exactly as planned. I'm not sure my cross did any good at all. It's like I said from the very beginning, it's going to come down to which one of them the jury believes, no more no less."

"Your client testifying tomorrow?"

"Yes. I'm going to have his mother testify too. I'm hoping she can lend some credibility to Randall and the family in general. She can testify she remembers the night this supposedly happened and remembers Randall coming home without issues. I'm also going to have a couple of girls he has dated testify he was a perfect gentleman with them. I hope I don't have trouble getting that into evidence. Arnold said he wouldn't object, but we'll see."

"You really don't have many witnesses, do you?"

"Hell, no, Jack. There were no eyewitnesses. There's no alibi…he admits he was with her. It's really frustrating." She hesitated, took a drink, and said, "You know, I don't understand how you do it. How do you handle… how does *any* lawyer handle all the things they do in a general practice on a daily basis without completely losing their minds? In addition to trying this case, I have so many things on my mind right now, I'm about to scream. How do you do it?"

Jack smiled, and said, "It can be difficult, but I think it's organization and compartmentalizing that takes care of the problem. You know, just learning how to pull all the pieces together, and organize your practice, so there's a time and place for everything you do. You'll figure it out or you'll quit the practice. Or maybe you'll quit trying to handle three or four areas of law and concentrate on one or two. You've only been at this a few months, Ann. Be patient. It'll all work itself out."

She frowned at him, then once again began eating, without responding.

"Oh, by the way, I hate to throw this in the mix on top of everything else, but I got that new case—that one in Wilson County."

As she finished her single course dinner, she said, "So what happened?"

"He's been accused of killing his wife. I guess it's a good family, but there had been some tension between the two of them. She ended up dead and he's been charged. I don't know the specifics, but I do know he can't make bail. The grand jury is going to review it all next week."

"When do you meet with him?"

"I told him I'd try to see him in a few days, before the grand jury convened. I have no doubt they'll indict. You still want me to work with you on it?"

She thought for a moment, then looked away as she said, "Why not? I don't have anything else to do. Just add more to the stack."

"Now look, you don't have to do this if you don't want to. I'd love to work with you, but it's pretty clear after tonight's conversation, you already have a lot on your mind. It's no problem for me one way or the other."

"No, no, no I want to do it. I need the experience, and I want to work with you whenever it's possible. I think this trial will be over in the next couple of days. I'll plan on going with you when you talk with him."

She met with the judge and prosecutor before court reconvened the next morning. The judge wanted to be sure they were all on the same page as concerned the remainder of the proceedings. It was clear after a short conference, that they were. The meeting ended, and Ann went to meet with her client before court convened for the day.

Randall, along with both of his parents, were waiting for her when she arrived.

As she sat, she looked at him and said, "Are you ready to do this, Randall?"

"If I have a choice, no, I'm not. Do I have a choice?"

Ann laughed and said, "No choice."

"Then I'm ready."

"Ms. Kingston, are you ready to do your part?"

"Yes. I'm nervous but I'm ready."

"I just peaked in the courtroom. Both of the girls I talked to about testifying for us, are there. I had them subpoenaed even though I figured they'd show up. Now, the order of business this morning will be you Ms. Kingston, then both girls and finally, Randall, you'll finish up our case. I was somewhat concerned about the district attorney's position concerning testimony from both you Ms. Kingston and both girls. But he wants the jury to hear all the evidence available as I do, so he's going to allow all three to testify without objection. Of course, none of you know anything about the facts concerning what actually happened that night, but I'm glad he's allowing what you *do* have to offer, into evidence. Now, any questions from anyone?"

"When we all finish with our testimony, what happens then?'

"The judge will read the instructions, and each side will give a closing statement."

Might it just be dismissed?"

"No. There's plenty of evidence to convict if the jury wants to. I didn't file a motion for acquittal at the end of the state's testimony because I felt it was really a waste of my time and your money. It's all going to come down to who they believe. Before long, it will simply be a question of whether they believe her or him—nothing more, nothing less."

"So, what do you think?"

"I don't know. I know everything both sides have to offer will be before them. It'll just be up to who they believe. I would guess, and this is strictly a guess, we are about 50/50."

"That's not very good."

"No, it's not, but that's what you get into with this type of case."

She spoke as if she had a basis for her comments—she didn't—she had nothing whatoever to base her conclusions or her comments on. She was as much in the dark as everyone else in the room.

The continuing issue of the uncertainty that pertained to all juries, when added to the inability of an attorney with zero experience, created a match made in hell as concerned predictability. But there was nothing she could do now except finish as strong as she could, and hope, somehow, someway, the jury would find this young man not guilty. She would continue to do all she could do. Hopefully, it would be enough.

Chapter 11

The testimony of both girls was allowed into the record without objection, as was the testimony of Randall's mother It had achieved its intended result. All three witnesses had established the picture of a calm, mild-mannered young man, who might be somewhat backward when it came to socializing, but had never been mean to anyone, nor spoken an angry word in his short life. Ann wasn't sure how much weight the jury would place on their testimony while deliberating, but it had served *her* purpose well—they were better off with it, then they were without it.

Now it was time to hear from Randall. As he took the stand, he looked like the proverbial deer caught in headlights. The one thing she had continually advised him not to do—squirm around in the witness chair—he was doing. There was nothing Ann could do for him now. He was on his own. The case would most likely rise or fall based upon his appearance and his testimony.

After all his basic foundational information had been entered into the record, she said, "Tell us when you first met Charlotte, Randall."

"Well, Johnny, a guy I met early in the school year introduced us. He had previously told me she was lonely. This was her first year here in Nashville, and she really only knew one or two people. So, he introduced us, and we hit it off right away."

"Did you start dating as soon as you met?"

"Yes."

"What did you do—where did you go on these dates?"

"We would go to the movies, or just go downtown and listen to some of the bands. Sometimes we would go to my folks house and just watch TV."

"Never sexually active?"

"No."

"Ever been sexually active with any girl?"

"No, ma'am."

"Were you interested in becoming sexually involved with her?"

"Maybe. We discussed it a time or two, but we finally both concluded we would just wait a while and see where the relationship was heading. I was fine with that."

"So, what changed?"

"Nothing. We agreed to that right up until this all started."

"Tell us what happened that night."

"Well, we were having a really good time and had just left one of the bars downtown. She told me she didn't want to go back to her room yet. She asked me if I wanted to go to this quiet place—a road out west of Nashville—and look at the stars. I said fine."

"Is that what you did?"

"Yes, that's what we did."

"What happened once you got there?"

"I parked and turned up the radio. We kissed a bit, but that was it. The next thing I knew they were haulin' my ass to jail. Nothing else happened out there."

"Okay, now Randall, watch the language here. Remember where you are. As I recall, she said you were the one that knew about the road. Is that true?"

"Hell no...I'm sorry...heck no. I had never been down that road before."

"Did you touch her or do anything other than kiss her that night?"

"No."

"Why did you have your father's car?"

"His was parked in front of mine in our driveway. He wanted to leave. He was going to work. I said just take mine—I'll take yours. At first, I was just joking, but he said, 'fine' so that's what we did."

"You never crawled in the back of the car with her that night?"

"No ma'am."

"What reason might she have for making this all up?"

"I have no idea. All I know is that nothing like that happened."

"Nothing further, Your Honor."

"You may proceed, Mr. Leonard."

Arnold Leonard stood, and said, "May I approach, Your Honor?"

"Certainly."

As he approached the witness stand, he said, "So, let me just make sure I understand. You were dating her—that part's correct, right?"

"Yes."

"You did go out with her that night. That part's correct, right?"

"Yes."

"You took your dad's car that had plenty of room in the back portion to have sex or do whatever you wanted to do in that respect, right?"

He lowered his head. Ann thought he looked guilty. *At this moment in time, she thought he looked like he had literally raped the hell out of her.*

Randall looked up and said, "Yes."

"You've lived here all your life, correct?"

"Yes."

"And at the time you started dating, she had been here but a few weeks, or at the most, a month, correct?"

"Yes, that's correct."

"But *she* was the one that knew where this quiet place, this road was and you didn't, is that what you're telling us?"

"Yes, because that's how it was."

"Doesn't make a lot of sense though, does it? I mean, that she would know where this road was. It would just stand to reason that normally someone that had been living in the area all their life, would be more likely to know about such a place, than one that hadn't only lived here maybe a month, wouldn't you say?"

He said nothing.

"Go ahead and answer the question I asked."

He whispered, "I guess."

"So, other than a small difference of opinion concerning who knew about the road, the only portion of all the testimony you disagree with is whether the two of you had sex that night in the back of the car. Everything else she testified to yesterday was absolutely accurate, correct?"

"Yes, I guess."

"What about the testimony of Johnny Evans? Was it accurate?"

"Yes."

"And to the best of your knowledge, was the testimony as concerns what Thelma testified to, concerning, and only concerning Charlene and what happened that night involving only the two of them, accurate?"

"I guess so. But that story she told about me and her having that conversation..."

"I didn't ask you about that, Mr. Kingston. That was only between the two of you. I want to know about Thelma's testimony and what she testified to involving her observations and her comments involving Charlene. As far as you know, what she testified Charlene said to her, and Charlene's appearance that night was accurate, is that correct?"

"Yes, I guess so. I wasn't there so I don't know."

"So, out of all the testimony introduced in the last few days, really the only portion of it you dispute is the part where you raped her...everything else was the truth to the best of your knowledge?"

"Yes, but the only part that really matters *is* the part where I raped her. That didn't happen."

"You sir, conveniently disagree with the only sliver of testimony that convicts you. How convenient that out of the whole body of testimony presented by these witnesses in the last few days, you completely affirm everything except the part that gets you in trouble."

"I didn't do this—I swear I didn't do this."

Ann was watching the jury. They were hard to read. Some started to look away beginning about halfway through Randall's testimony. Some remained engaged in the colloquy between the prosecutor and the witness, others appeared not to be interested from his first word, apparently already having made their minds up.

As he faced the jury he asked, "You've never been involved sexually with another woman?"

"No."

He turned around to face Randall, raised his voice and said, "So this pretty little thing comes down from Kentucky, and you figured this was the one—this was your time and you took advantage of her, didn't you?"

"No, I swear…"

"You know what, Mr. Kingston, I've heard enough. And it's my belief, the jury's heard all *they* need to hear, too."

He turned around, walked back to his chair, and as he did, he said, "No more questions, Your Honor."

"Redirect, Ms. Jackson?"

Ann knew redirect questioning had to address new information that had come out during cross. But there had been nothing new presented. Mr. Leonard's entire cross was directed at testimony that had already been introduced into evidence during Johnny's direct testimony. She had nothing new she could properly ask him.

"I have nothing else, Your Honor."

It was late Friday afternoon. The judge was ready to adjourn for the day. The only order of business left to finish was for the jury instructions to be read to the jury and the attorney's closing statements. They would handle both those issues first thing Monday morning, then submit the case to the jury for deliberation.

Ann walked out the courtroom door knowing the only subject of any consequence that would occupy her mind all weekend would be those remaining issues that she needed to tighten up for court when they reconvened Monday morning.

She would spend Saturday morning reviewing office messages, along with checking for appointments set for next week. But Saturday afternoon, along with all-day Sunday, would be spent reviewing and tweaking her closing statement along with making sure the judge's instructions to the jury were correct.

It was nearly finished. One more day in court and everything would be submitted to the jury. Hopefully before the week ended, they would have the result they wanted—Randall Kingston's complete vindication.

Chapter 12

Ann sat on the edge of her bed trying to remember. She looked around the room. It was light, so it had to be morning. She turned to look at Jack. He was already up. He was never an early riser. She was always up before he was, so she knew her day had already started off in an unusual manner.

She dreamed last night—about him. Ann glanced at the clock. She still had plenty of time to reach the courthouse before court convened.

Once she had dressed and put her makeup on, she walked into the kitchen where Jack was having a cup of coffee as he looked over some notes he had not had the opportunity to review during the weekend.

"You had a tough night."

Ann poured herself a cup and slowly walked to the table. "I know. I lived it. I remember."

As she sat, he said, "Should you start going back to that shrink? He helped you for a while."

"No, no I'm fine." She thought for a moment, while fixing herself something to eat. "You know, I can never see his face. I can make out most of him, most of the time, but I just can't make out his face. That's what's so frustrating. During the full extent of the time I dream, I am continually trying to make out his face."

"I waited, hoping you would stop on your own, but when you didn't, about three, I just figured with all you have going on today, I better wake you."

"I'm glad you did. It least I was able to get a little sleep."

He hesitated before he said, "You going to be okay? You got a lot going on. You going to be able to handle all this today?"

"Yes, I'm fine." She pulled some notes out of her briefcase as she once again prepared for her closing argument.

As Ann sat in the courtroom, she concluded this was not the way she had envisioned her morning. She was tired, depressed and nervous. She had, once again, dreamed the dream, but this time it reappeared at a very inopportune time. As usual, it had frightened her along with being terribly depressing, as she relived her mother's murder all over once again. And to top it all off, here she was just a few hours after it ended, trying to focus on her first closing argument before a jury.

The judge was reading through the instructions to the jury one at a time. There were many. The jurors listened intently as he slowly proceeded through each one, explaining what they were allowed to do and what they couldn't do while determining whether to find the defendant innocent or guilty.

Once he was finished, first the prosecutor, then Ann would be allowed, in their own way, the opportunity to sum up all the evidence the jurors had heard during the past few days. That would effectively bring the trial to an end and they would all sit on pins and needles while the jury arrived at a verdict.

Once the judge had finished, Arnold stood and addressed the jury. He started off with basic remarks, then summed up the case as he viewed it. Once completed, he told the jury what the state's position was and why he felt the defendant should be found guilty.

Ann found him convincing—in fact, to convincing. She worried that she wouldn't be nearly as convincing. She worried that even if she *was convincing*, they would conclude that since the cops and the prosecutor had charged him, they must be right, regardless of the evidence.

After about an hour of summery, Arnold took his seat. She was intently reviewing what she felt she should now emphasize, when she heard the judge say, "Ms. Jackson...Ms. Jackson please proceed."

She stood. "Thank you, Your Honor." She walked to the jury box, and started off with a brief summary of the facts, as she viewed them. She then reviewed the facts as they applied to each individual violation Randal had been charged with.

Finally, she said, "I want you, as jurors, to pay particular attention to the 19th instruction, because that, to us, is the most important one of all."

She pointed to the defendant and said, "You are obligated under the law, to find him guilty *if* the facts have established his guilt *beyond a reasonable doubt.* Now that instruction doesn't say, *'If you feel he did it, find him guilty.'* It doesn't say *'If he's charged by the officers and is being prosecuted, he's guilty.'* What it *does* say is after you've listened to all the evidence and considered it all, you must find him guilty if the state has, *during this trial,* established his guilt *beyond a reasonable doubt.* That's not a small burden the state has to overcome. Especially in this case."

"This case presents an unusual amount of difficulty for the defendant because it really does come down to Charlene Cartwright saying one thing and Randall saying another. There were no witnesses. There is none of that DNA evidence you all hear about on TV, nor is there even much medical evidence available. That's because she wasn't a virgin when this happened, and she says Randall used a condom. These are both really convenient facts for her, either of which could have conclusively established that at least they had actually had sex. Again, conveniently for her, neither of those issues are available to be considered by you."

She walked toward the other end of the jury box as she said, "So, who do you believe? Well, you don't actually have to figure that out. If it's a tie, you must find him not guilty. The tie goes to the defendant. It you are *fairly certain* he did this, you must find him not guilty. The standard you must follow is not, 'Well, maybe he did it, so we'll convict him.' It's, *'I am convinced beyond a reasonable doubt he did it.'* You can't just *think* he *might have* done it, or he *could* have done it, to convict. *You must be convinced beyond a reasonable doubt, he did it."*

"The testimony of Johnny had no impact on the case. The testimony of Thelma was important only if you conclude Charlene told her the truth in the first place. Charlene could have presented herself before Thelma anyway she wanted to—she had the time to get herself ready before she saw her."

"So, you ask, what's her motive? Why did she go to all this trouble?" She started her last walk to the other end of the jury box, as she said, "Who knows. I don't have any idea and neither does Randall. But really, does it matter? There is either evidence to convict beyond a reasonable doubt or there isn't. Regardless of the reason she acted in this manner, you either have proof beyond a reasonable doubt or you don't, and it's our position the evidence just isn't there."

"This young man, as you know, has no history concerning criminal activity. He's from a good family and he's a good student, as you heard during the testimony. This charge is completely beyond anything he has ever done or been accused of doing throughout his entire life. The evidence is incomplete. It just simply doesn't go far enough to establish his guilt beyond a reasonable doubt. And when that happens, when there just isn't enough evidence, you must do what juries have been doing in this country forever—you must find the defendant not guilty. Thank you."

Ann took her seat and listened while the prosecutor was given one last chance, during rebuttal, to respond to Ann's comments. He took little time, and once finished, Ann sat quietly, listening while the judge handed the bailiff a copy of the jury instructions telling him to take the jury, with their copy of the instructions, to the jury room so that they might deliberate.

Once the judge left the bench she walked, with Randall and his family, to the conference room they had used for the last week.

As they sat down, Randall said, "You did good in there Ann, you really did."

"Thank you. The only issue I can't tie down is her motivation. I just can't explain something to the jury I don't know or understand. I still feel this might have been a shakedown gone bad, but there's nothing I can do to prove it, or establish it— there's just no proof or facts."

No one said anything, until Ann said, "Look, I need to go back to the office and finish up some of my office work I've let go because I was here. They'll call me when the jury comes in. Just wait here patiently until they do. You folks alright with that?"

Randall's father said, "Yes Ann, go ahead. We'll let you know if we hear anything."

Ann stood as did Randall. She gave him a hug. "Hang in there. Keep your fingers crossed, and I'll see you when the jury's ready."

He nodded and sat back down.

She walked to her office and as she did, she prayed that the next time she walked into the courthouse, it was to hug him because he had been found *not guilty,* rather than to console him for being found *guilty.*

Chapter 13

There were a number of appointments already scheduled for later in the week. She started writing them down on her calendar and then just quit. She started reviewing phone messages from her clients and then again, just quit.

Ann walked into the back room, poured herself a cup of coffee, and stood there—wondering how long this would really take. Would she still be wondering what the jury would do a week from today, two weeks from today? How long would this jury be out?

She walked back to her office, and, as she sat down, Harold walked in.

"So, how do you think your first one went?"

"Oh fine, I guess. I really don't know. I do know I'm worried about the verdict. It's most likely a pretty close call. I just wish I would have had more evidence to present to them from the defense side." She looked away. "I just don't think I did enough, but..."

He sat down as he said, "Hey, it's over. I have no doubt you did all you could do. You know what they say, 'You can only do what only you can do', or something like that."

Once again, his boisterous laugh echoed thoughout the office. But she couldn't bring herself to smile. Not this time.

Harold said, "Hey."

She continued to stare at the wall.

"Hey, look at me."

She turned toward him, and said, "Sorry, sorry, I'm just a little discouraged, just a little lost today, I guess. Sorry, Harold."

"Look, I know you have a lot on your mind. I know that. And I remember how it was for me when I was your age. But, you know, I did a lot of research on you that you never knew about before I hired you."

He had captured her attention. She started to listen to what he had to say.

"I know how difficult life has been for you. I know all about your mother and what you saw when she died."

Ann said, "How did you find out about that? I never told you."

"Just listen. I know all about that, as I know how difficult it was for you to finish college, to get into law school and to finish law school. You've been a fighter from day one. That's one of the reasons I hired you. You never gave up. In spite of all that's happened in your life you never, ever gave up."

She looked away, as she felt her emotions become a factor.

"I knew if the past meant anything, that 'fighter' is exactly what I would get out of you if you worked here. You would never give up. People don't change as concerns the basics. They are what they are and you aren't, nor have you ever been, a quitter."

She looked at Harold and with tears in her eyes, said, "Haven't been so far. I'm not real sure who I am right now, Harold."

He sat back in his chair. "I do. You're the same person that persevered through all the problems you've had in your short life, to get to the point where you just finished your first jury trial. Win or lose you gave it your all, and you'll have that experience to fall back on the next time."

"I guess. I just don't want to lose. I like this kid. I think he's innocent and..."

"Hey, no one likes to lose. Even when you walk into the courtroom knowing you will most likely lose, no one, absolutely no one, likes to lose. I can tell you one thing. The client wants the best you have to offer. Nothing less. And if you give that to them, no matter how it comes out, 90% of the time the client will be good with that. They may or may not like the result, but they will be good with what you did for them. I know I don't need to tell you this, but you can never quit until there's nothing else you can do. If you lose the first round, you fight your ass off until there are no more rounds to fight, or until you finally wear the other side down and settle it advantageously for your client. But you never, ever quit."

"I agree with you, Harold, but it's so tough when you feel like you're on the right side and you get beat. I've been there before. I know you just got to get up and jump right back into the fray, but it's hard. I'll do it—I'm just a little discouraged right now—I'll do it, but it would be so much easier if they would just find him not guilty."

Harold laughed. "Yes, it would and maybe they will. If they do, that's great, but if they don't, I know you'll do what you've always done—you'll get up off your butt, and give 'em hell. You just needed to be reminded that's exactly what you've done all your life. We all need a little nudge now and again—today's the day you needed yours."

She looked down at all the messages, and leaned back in her chair, as she said, "Let me ask you something while we're discussing the practice. How in the world do you get everything done? I have this jury trial on my mind, and I look down and I have all these messages, these appointments, these people coming up with so many different questions about different aspects of law—how do you do it, how do you get it all done?"

"Organization, organization, organization. I organize absolutely everything and then have Beth help me set it all up. She's the best secretary I ever had. She can do wonders with a crazy schedule. One thing I've learned about *me* is—one thing at a time. I can't be thinking and won't let myself be thinking about the three or four appointments I have back at the office while I'm finishing off a trial. I work best when I schedule everything then just handle one thing at a time. If I have scheduled correctly, it will all work out just the way it's supposed to."

He stood. "I did *not* however schedule this time with you." He laughed as he said, "I got to go. Let me know when you hear from that jury."

Ann waited another hour to hear from the courthouse. When the call finally came, it was only to tell her the judge had sent the jury home for the night. She asked the clerk to send the Kingston's home and tell them she would meet them in the conference room tomorrow morning at 9:00 a.m., which the clerk said she would do.

She had just finished her first beer, when Jack walked through the door. "Hey, where you been?"

"Oh, I had a few things I wanted to review before I came home so I didn't have to bring them home with me. How'd today go?"

As he walked to the kitchen to find something to drink, she turned the evening news down and said, "Went as well as could be expected, I guess. The judge sent the jury home about five. They're to reconvene at nine in the morning."

As he sat down beside her, he said, "How'd you feel about it? Did it all go the way you felt it would? You concerned about the verdict?"

"Hell yes, I'm scared to death. I got everything into evidence I could, but I'm afraid it might not be enough."

"Ann, you gave it all you had. Sometimes it just isn't enough, but obviously if you got everything you had into evidence, you've done all you could do."

"Yeah, Harold gave me a similar pep talk today. I know you're both right, but right now, that doesn't seem to help. I don't know what I'll do if that kid goes to prison, I really don't."

"I do."

"What—tell me what you know I'll do? I want to hear this."

"You'll file a motion for new trial. If that doesn't work, you'll file a notice of appeal. If that doesn't work and you've exhausted all your remedies, you'll move on to the next case, knowing you did all you could do."

She stood, and walked toward the kitchen. "What do you want for supper? I'll fix it tonight."

"Didn't like what I had to say?"

She turned and said, "You know, tomorrow I'm sure I'll remember what you said, and what Harold told me, but tonight it's just like, blah, blah, blah, blah, blah. I can't compute. What do you want for supper?"

"Want me to order a pizza?"

She sat down near him, turned up the news, and leaned back against his shoulder as she pivoted to put her feet up on the couch. He put his arm around her as she said, "Yes. All I want to do tonight is eat pizza, drink beer, watch TV, and hope tomorrow never comes because, I got a feelin' it's going be a long fricken day."

Chapter 14

Ann had first met with the Kingston family, then left them waiting in the courthouse conference room. She returned to her office and was waiting for an appointment when Beth walked in her office door.

"You hear from the clerk's office?"

"Nope, I haven't. I just wanted to let you know your appointment is here. You know, you have them stacked up one right after the other. I figured today would most likely be the day the jury comes to a conclusion. If they do come in with a verdict, do you want me to have these people reschedule, or just have them wait as long as they can wait to see you today?"

Ann thought for a moment. "If the verdict comes in today, I'll have plenty to talk about with the Kingston's, which I would think will take most of what's left of the day, regardless of the time they come to a conclusion." She hesitated. "Tell you what, let's just handle one thing at a time. Let's handle each appointment until the verdict, and then call the rest of them and reschedule. How's that sound?"

Beth said, "To be perfectly honest, that sounds like what Mr. Dale might do."

Ann smiled, and said, "I've come to the conclusion he's probably not a bad guy to 'sound like.'"

She had completed four appointments when the call came. The jury had arrived at a verdict. She was needed at the courthouse.

When she arrived, the Kingston's were already seated at the counsel table in the courtroom. Once the clerk had informed the judge everyone was in place, he walked in from chambers and took his seat.

"The clerk informs me you have arrived at a verdict. Is that true, Mr. Foreman?"

An elderly gentleman seated at the very end of the jury box, stood and said, "We have, Your Honor. I have it here."

"Then I would ask the court attendant to take it from the foreman and bring it to me."

The court attendant walked forward, took the folded portion of paper and walked it to the judge.

He opened it, read it to himself, then without a trace of emotion, said, "We the jury in the above-entitled matter, do hereby find the defendant, Randall Kingston—guilty as charged."

She slowly closed her eyes, as she let it sink in. She didn't want to look at Randall—she figured everyone else in the courtroom was probably already looking at him.

"Please have a seat everyone. Ladies and gentlemen of the jury is this your verdict, one and all?"

A few said yes and the rest nodded affirmatively.

"Does either attorney want them polled, or is the written verdict sufficient?"

Both attorneys indicated the verdict was sufficient and they didn't need to be polled.

"Good enough. Ladies and gentleman of the jury I'm going to release you from further responsibility in this case. The clerk will inform you when you need to appear the next time. Thank you for your service."

She thought she was going to vomit. She still hadn't looked at Randall or his family. She wanted to walk out the courtroom door with the jurors, free as a bird, as they all were now.

"Please stand, Mr. Kingston."

Randall stood, as did Ann.

"Sir you have been convicted of..."

She only heard bits and pieces, while her mind tried to comprehend what was happening. The judge established his bond pending sentencing and subsequent appeal, in an amount which Ann knew would be way too high for this family to post, even in spite of the fact they lived very comfortably. The lower amount originally set had been somewhat difficult for them to come by— the amount posted today would be impossible. The judge set sentencing for three weeks from today pending the filing of any post-conviction motions. He then ordered that Randall be taken into custody. At that point she started to function again.

"Judge can I visit with him and his family for a few minutes in the conference room before he's processed and taken to jail."

"Yes, yes that's fine. Officer escort them to a conference room and give them a few minutes."

The officer escorted them to the room closing the door after they had all walked inside.

Randall's mother started to cry. His father, along with Randall, said nothing, waiting for Ann to begin the conversation.

"I'm so sorry, Randall. I am just..."

Randall's father, Bryce, held up his hand and said, "Hold on, Ann. We sat through it all. We heard every word that was said at that trial. We knew it would be a little tough to win. We felt you did absolutely everything you could possibly do to get him off. It didn't work. We need to move on to the next step. What are your thoughts?"

"Well, first of all, I assume it would be very difficult to come up with that amount of cash to keep him out of jail pending sentencing."

"Yes, I can't come up with that. I'll see about a bail bondsman"

"Okay. The first step is to file a motion for new trial. I'll do that right away. If that isn't ruled upon favorably, I'll file a notice of appeal."

Through her tears, Martha Kingston said, "But what happens to him while all this going on? Does he just sit in jail?"

"Yes, he does, unless you can put up the cash to keep him out."

"What are our chances for a new trial?"

"Probably not the best, but we need to go through the process. In the meantime, I'll continue to investigate, and we'll see what turns up."

Bryce said, "All in all, this doesn't look very good, does it? I mean, he was convicted. We don't have much more evidence than what we submitted if we *are* granted a new trial. It just looks to me like we're in real trouble here."

"You need to hang in there with me, Bryce. Let me check on a few things and get the motion ready. Do *not* give up hope. I promise you I'll see this through until we win, or until there's nothing else we can do."

Later that afternoon, as Ann was researching exactly what needed to be contained in her motion, Harold walked in her office. As he did, Ann said, "I thought you were gone for the rest of the day."

"Got back a little early. How'd the trial turn out?"

She leaned back in her chair, and said, "They found him guilty."

"The hell they did."

"Yes, they did."

"What are you going to do now?"

"I'm filing a motion for new trial. I doubt from what I read, we have much of chance of it being sustained, but I think I need to do it."

"Is that what all this is for?" He pointed at all the books and paperwork spread out over her desk.

"Yes."

"And if the judge doesn't sustain it?"

"I'll appeal it to the supreme court."

"You probably won't have much to appeal. It doesn't sound to me like there were many mistakes or errors made by the judge. It will most likely be a difficult appeal to win."

"You know, I don't give one shit how tough it might be. I'm not done with this case until I'm ready to be done with it, and I'm not ready. I'll take it as far as I can and that means, *first off,* a motion for new trial."

He smiled, stood, and walked out of her office.

Later that night, after the lights had been turned off, and as they lie cuddled up with each other, awake, both unable to fall asleep, Jack said, "I'm so proud of you."

"I think you misunderstood. I lost, Jack, I lost."

"You persevered through a tough case and got through it without a major problem or mistake. You had little to work with, and you're not done yet. The experience you gained, without help from anyone, was invaluable. I'm proud of you and I'm proud you're going to be my wife."

"Well, thanks for all that, but can we go to sleep—just stop the talk. I need to get what happened today off my mind. I'm not very proud of me. You might remember—my clients sitting *in jail.* He could be there a long time as a result of something I was materially involved in. Maybe tomorrow will be better, but right now, I'd just like to get some sleep."

The last words she heard, at the end of a long day, were, "I'm still proud of you. After today I love you more than ever."

Those were kind words for sure, but words that, at least for tonight, had little positive impact upon an otherwise extensively traumatized psyche.

Chapter 15

Sally was waiting for her when she arrived. They had recently agreed to meet at a small Starbucks not far from Ann's office, around 10:00 a.m. each Wednesday morning. Ann wrote in the time of their meetings on her calendar, and looked forward to the break from work each week to spend time with her friend.

"Morning. Get your kids off to school? Everything moving smoothly at your house this morning?" As she sat down, Ann studied Sally for a moment, then said, "Hey, have you lost some weight?"

Sally smiled. "Yes, I have. I'm taking a few pills, and I'm losing weight. It's going well."

Ann looked at the fingers Sally *didn't* have wrapped around her coffee cup handle. "You doing okay with the pills? Your hands…your fingers look a little shaky."

"Oh, they wire me up a little, but it's worth it. I only have to be on them until I reach my target weight. I've only got about 20 pounds to go. Hey, let's talk about you, not my fat. Is the trial over? I haven't seen you since the day I watched you in court."

"Yes, the trial's over—and no, I didn't win. He was found guilty. He hasn't been sentenced yet. I'm working on some post-conviction motions, but as of right now, he's guilty as charged."

"Oh no. Ann, I'm so sorry. I watched almost one full day of it, and you were doing so well. I was so proud of you. I know what I would have done if I'd been on that jury. I'm just so sorry."

"I wish you *had* been on that jury. It was difficult to accept, but that's what they did. I knew we had a lot to overcome, but I had always believed, always hoped, we would win. It's over—I lost—more importantly, my client lost. We're moving on from there—that's all I can do."

"Well, as to the part I listened to, I wouldn't have believed Charlene if my life depended on it. Of course, through you, I knew you already believed her to be a liar, but she wasn't convincing to me. What's the story on her?"

"Oh, she and those two friends that testified all came from Louisville. One of them set her up with Randall. The result was a rape charge. That's about all I know about her."

"Did you research them all? I mean, did you check into their backgrounds?"

"Yes. I searched the net, and I had Jack look into them too. Neither of us could find anything. None of them had ever been charged with anything, nor was there any other disparaging information about any one of the three that we could find."

"They had no police records? They had never been in court or anything?"

"No. We literally found nothing on any of them."

"So, what happens now?"

"I'm preparing a motion to ask the court for a retrial. I don't have much hope that it'll be sustained by the judge, but that's all I got. If it's overruled, I'll appeal the verdict, citing what I believe to be errors the judge made during the trial. I'll have Jack help me with it."

"What's he think about the Supreme Court doing anything about it?"

"He's not much more confident of it than I am. I'm sick about it. I can't sleep, I'm having trouble concentrating, I'm a mess about it all."

"Did you think you were going through your whole career and never lose? I mean you knew you were going to win a few and lose a few as they say. You're doing all you can, Ann. That's all anyone can ask of you."

"I realize that. I know that. I've heard all that from Jack and Harold, but for some reason it doesn't do me much good. I lost and that kid is going to prison if I don't come up with something."

Both were quiet, until Sally said, "Let's change subjects. That's enough about work. What about getting married? You set a date yet?"

"We're thinking about late next month, around Thanksgiving, but we haven't yet set the exact day yet. I'll let you know in plenty of time to make plans."

"I can't wait. I'm so excited."

"So am I. I'll let you know the date when I know."

Something Sally said earlier in the day concerning Randall's case caught her attention. She had trouble dismissing it. What if both she and Jack hadn't been looking where they should have been, concerning the background of all three of those kids?

As she sat at her desk, she wondered if maybe they had missed something. They said they were from Louisville, but what if they weren't. There were a number of public records that were unavailable to Jack and to herself while investigating their background. Could there have been something they missed or that they weren't, for some reason or another, able to access?

Later that night, Ann was waiting for Jack when he arrived home. Once he had had a chance to grab a beer and sit down with her, she said, "I hate to continue to discuss my losing cases with you...*but*...I'm wondering if we could have missed something in the background of those three kids in Randall's case."

"Why do you wonder that? We both looked on line and found absolutely nothing."

"Maybe I should have gone a step further. Maybe I was too laid back about the background of those three. I took it no further, because we initially found nothing and I concluded there *was* nothing. Maybe I made a mistake."

"I doubt it. But let's carry on with the discussion. What do you want to do now? I mean, what do you think *can* be done now?"

"I wonder about hiring a private investigator and having him look into all three of them. I mean, I don't really even know if they *came* from Louisville. I didn't think it would be necessary to know that. Maybe I made a mistake, Jack. Maybe I should have had someone look a little further into who they really were. What do you think?"

"I don't know, but I guess it wouldn't hurt. I have an investigator I use all the time and he's pretty good. Perhaps I could give him a call and discuss it with him. Wouldn't hurt, I guess. I could find out what the cost would be too. You want me to do that?"

"Yes. You find out what you can from him, and if he's available, get a price quote. I'll try to get it approved by Bryce."

"I'll contact him first thing in the morning."

Near noon of the following day, Ann received a call from Jack. He had discussed the case with Matt Armstrong, a good friend of his and a private investigator in the Nashville area. Matt was willing to handle the investigation and gave Jack a cost estimate, which he made sure to explain was *only* an estimate. Matt also informed Jack that he had a few friends in the Louisville area and acquaintances in the police department that he felt might be a big help in running down background material on Charlene, Thelma and Johnny.

She called Bryce, who agreed to pay the bill. The investigator, understanding this investigation was time sensitive, said he would start on it immediately.

Ann figured they had nothing to lose. She wasn't sure what she would do if they uncovered information that worked in their favor, but she figured they would cross that bridge if and when they came to it. Hopefully, he would find something that helped, because at this stage of the game, without it, she figured the kid was going to prison. Unfortunately, at this stage of the proceedings, even *with* additional information, she was concerned there was most likely nothing she could do about the conviction.

Chapter 16

Jack and Ann walked in the Wilson County Sheriff's Office and asked to see Thomas Cline. Jack had called first to make sure if they drove to Lebanon, the county seat of Wilson County, they would be able to meet with him around 10:00 a.m., and was told that was within their visiting hours.

He wanted Ann to come with him and she quickly agreed. But he had asked her to just listen—to let him handle the initial consultation with his client, explaining he had done this many, many times and she hadn't. She wholeheartedly agreed. In addition, at least for now, he was not Ann's client, and until they confirmed with Harold that she could work with him on the case, he would remain Jack's client and his client alone.

They watched as the officer brought his client to the meeting room table where he sat. Jack stood as Thomas Cline reached the table and held out his hand as he said, "Mr. Cline, my name is Jack Connors."

Thomas shook his hand, and said, "I'm Thomas Cline and I'm not guilty."

Thomas was short in stature and certainly not someone you would notice in a crowd. He was an uninteresting man to look at and his voice, soft and uncertain, would be nothing that would draw anyone's attention.

"Thomas, this is Ann Jackson. She may be working with us on your case."

Just as Jack started to ask his first question, another man entered the room and approached the table. He appeared similar to Thomas in both stature and movement. As he reached the table he said, "My name is Edward, Edward Cline." He sat down as he said, "I'm his brother and I want to be part of everything that goes on concerning this stupid, trumped-up charge."

Jack said, "That's okay with me as long as it's okay with you, Thomas."

"Yes, it's fine with me. My brother and I are close and if the tables were turned, I would be doing the same thing for him as he is for me."

"Thomas, let's start from the beginning. You're accused of murdering your wife. How long you been married? Do you have children?"

"We were married 23 years. No, we have no children."

"You always lived here, in Wilson County?"

Edward said, "They moved here about ten years ago after I encouraged them to. What's going to happen on all this? Can he plead to some lesser charge and get out of here?"

Jack said, "Let me figure out what's going on first, Mr. Cline. I need to know what happened before I can tell you what we can and can't do."

"Edward tends to get a little excited about things. He and I are somewhat different in that respect. But he's right. We moved here about ten years ago. Edward lived here and he told us it would be a good move for us, and it was, it really was."

"You employed? Was your wife employed?"

"Yes, I work in a factory between here and Murfreesboro. My wife wasn't employed, but I was making enough she didn't need to be. We had no children, we lived very frugally, and I didn't really want her to work."

"Okay, Thomas, why don't you tell me what happened.."

"Well, about six months ago, my wife and I started having a few problems. We never had any problems before that, but all of a sudden, it seemed like I couldn't do nothing right. We argued a lot. She didn't like much of anything I did, and she wasn't bashful about telling me about it neither."

"Mr. Connors, I saw this a lot. She would rip into Thomas for nothing, no reason at all. I mentioned it to him a couple of times—you know, asked him what the hell was wrong with her, but he didn't know."

"Did you ever confront her? Did you ever just flat out ask her what was wrong or did you just let it lie?"

"One day I asked her. She had been on me all day about little things, things that meant nothing. So, I just said let's sit down and discuss what's going on. She told me she was tired of living this way and wanted a change, at least for a while."

"What kind of change?"

"She wanted to move out. Wanted her own place. She didn't know for how long or if our situation would ever work out again, but she said she needed a change."

"So, what did you do?"

"I rented a little house for her on a month-to-month basis, and she moved out."

"When was that?'

"About three months ago."

"What happened then?"

Edward said, "I'll tell you what happened. She was messing with the wrong crowd, and she got herself murdered that's what happened. If she'd had a brain in her head and stayed with my brother, this would have never happened at all."

"Stop, She was my wife. I loved her then, I love her now. Don't do that."

Edward looked away as he said, "You know I'm right. She'd still be alive if she'd stayed with you."

"So anyway, I'd go see her at least once a week. We were on good terms. She even discussed some changes that would need to be made if she moved back in. We were actually making plans for her to move back home."

"When was the last time you saw her?"

"The last time I saw her was when she was lying on the bedroom floor in her rental."

"Tell me what happened."

Thomas looked down, hesitated for a moment, then said, "I went over to see her about a week ago. I knew it was late, but her lights were on. I knocked and there was no answer. I tried the door and it was unlocked which was somewhat unusual. But, I didn't think much about it. I walked inside and on the floor, near the door, was a letter opener. It appeared to have blood on it. I picked it up. Then I noticed small drops of blood on the floor. I called out to her, but got no response."

Tears started to stream down his face as he continued.

"I followed the drops of blood to the bedroom and saw her lying on the floor. Her eyes were open. When I touched her, she was cold and...she... was gone. I panicked. I left the house knowing there was nothing else I could do for her. I stayed home from work the next day, just remembering what we had and thinking about our life together. Apparently, a friend of hers she had met after we separated, went to check on her the next morning because she hadn't heard from her. She found her dead. They ran prints on the letter opener. Then they came to see me. They took me to the station and asked me if I'd been to see her the day before. I told them I had, but she was already gone when I got there. My fingerprints were on that letter opener so they charged me with murder."

Jack reread some of his notes, then said, "Why didn't you call the police when you found her?"

"Oh heck, I don't know. I've asked myself that same question time after time. It just felt like I wasn't even in this world. It wasn't real. To be honest, I don't remember leaving the house. It felt like it was all a dream, and I was going to wake up."

"Can you make bail?"

"No. Never."

"What's your situation at work? Do they know what's going on? Have you lost your job?"

"No. They said it would be there for me when I get out of here, assuming, of course, I'm found not guilty, which I'm not."

"What about attorney fees? Are you able to pay those, or do you need a court-appointed attorney?"

Edward said, "Between the two of us, we'll pay whatever your fees are. We have enough to pay you. Now, when can he get out of here and go back to work?"

Jack leaned back and said, "They've already indicted you, Thomas, so that's over. We'll enter a plea of not guilty. Then they'll set a trial date. I'll want to review some statements and probably waive the taking of depositions. We'll just have to wait and see who the witnesses are along with what they're going to say. It seems fairly simple, but obviously someone out there murdered your wife. We need to figure out who it was."

Edward said, "I'll tell you one thing, Mr. Attorney. It wasn't my brother. He don't have a mean bone in his body. He's never even stepped on a bug. It wasn't him and that's for sure."

Later as they drove home, Ann said, "Well, what do you think?"

"I have mixed feelings, I guess. The facts, at least at this point, are not too complicated, but what evidence they *do* have, certainly indicates he killed her. We're going to have to figure this out and come up with a plausible alternative, or we're screwed. I'll leave all the paperwork I have with you, if you wish, for you to review later this afternoon. We can talk about it at home tonight once you're finished reading the statements."

"Tell you what. Just keep them. I'll read them tonight. I don't have time to read them this afternoon. As I read them tonight, I can ask you questions while I go through everything."

"Are you going to have time to work with me on this?"

"I'll make time. I want to do this with you, I really do. I'll find the time. Has the guy got the money to afford both of us?"

"He tells me, between he and his brother Edward, who by the way, appears to me will be more difficult to deal with than our client, that they have the funds to pay our bill. I guess we'll just have to see how that works out."

"I can tell they are really close. His brother seems much more vocal, much more assertive than our client."

"I agree."

Once Jack left Ann at her office, as she reviewed her messages, Harold stuck his head in the door and said, "Hi, Ann. Where you been? I knew you were going somewhere with Jack, or something, I guess. But I can't remember where you said you were going."

She leaned back in her chair and said, "Today was the day I was to go with Jack to meet with that guy in Lebanon that's charged with killing his wife. Harold, Jack and I would like to try the case together. We'll each get our own fee, and of course I'll run mine through the office account just like I do everything else. You okay with that?"

"Absolutely. As long as you feel you have the time to take it on."

"I do. I'm looking forward to working with Jack on the case. He's a good trial attorney. I think I could learn a lot from him. Thanks. I just wanted you to know about it."

Later that afternoon, as she considered the time the Cline case was going to take away from her own practice, she ultimately concluded she was, in fact, very lucky.

She was certainly a rookie in every sense of the word. But on the one hand, she had Harold who was an old, established veteran of the traditional office practice, whom she could learn from. On the other hand, she now had Jack, a young, experienced trial attorney, as her teacher in the courtroom. She just figured that was about as good as it could ever get for someone like her, who was truly a complete novice in both those areas of the practice of law.

Chapter 17

It had been a week since the verdict had been rendered. Ann had used that time to carefully consider her next move. She had discussed the various possibilities with Jack more than he cared to discuss them. Yesterday, he finally said, "You need to figure this all out one way or the other and move on."

That statement provided the impetus she needed to finally come to a needed conclusion. The Kingston's, along with Matt Armstrong, were to meet together this morning in her office. Mr. Armstrong had arrived at an approximate figure concerning his fees based on what he concluded he would need to do. That, along with exactly what was expected of him, would soon be discussed.

Matt had called and told her he would arrive prior to the time the Kingston's would arrive, so they could discuss, objectively, and by themselves, exactly what would need to be done. Mr. and Mrs. Kingston were to arrive 30 minutes later.

Beth indicated Matt had just arrived. Ann told her to send him in.

"Good Morning. Matt Armstrong." He walked to the front of her desk, and extended his hand.

He was tall, well-built and handsome. She shook his hand, smiled and said, "Have a chair, Matt Armstrong. Thanks for coming today. By the way, you come highly recommended. I believe you most likely have a pretty good idea what we need done, but before Mr. and Mrs. Kingston arrive, do you have any particular issue with what they want accomplished?"

"Not really. I, of course, want to make sure the fee is acceptable and discuss every aspect of the investigation with them. But other than that, I know what you're looking for. I'll get right on it if they approve my approach."

They small-talked their way through the next 15 minutes until Beth informed them Mr. and Mrs. Kingston had arrived.

She took them all into the conference room and after Matt's credentials were discussed, Matt said, "It's my understanding you want me to investigate all three of them, correct?"

Ann said, "Yes. We have a feeling the situation with Randall may have happened before, but there is just nothing on the net that any of us can find out about any of them. That's why we called you."

"Mr. Kingston, are the fees acceptable?"

"Yes."

"Here's a contract setting out what I'm about to do in fairly general terms. Take a look at it and just sign at the bottom if it appears okay to you. Now, you do understand, I may have to pay a guy or two for information. You okay with that? Are you willing to pay whatever I may have to pay out-of-pocket?"

"Absolutely."

"I have a couple of cop friends in Louisville that might be able to get me information about them which I couldn't access myself, so it may be necessary to give them a buck or two just to grease the wheel. I'll figure that out when I get there."

"Have you been successful in running down people like this in other cases?"

He smiled and leaned back in his chair. "I can almost guarantee you I'll locate all the information you need about them. Now, whether it's what you want to hear, or whether I'll be able to uncover any other situations like Randall went through, is certainly up in the air. But I'll find out all there is to know about them before I finish. I just need to drive up to Louisville and start the process."

"When are you leaving?"

"I'll probably leave here about mid-week or so. This might take a trip to two and it might be a while before I finish, so don't expect the results the day after I start."

Ann said, "I've got some time before I have to file our motion for new trial. I'll probably take all the time that's allowed under the rules to file it and then talk to the prosecutor about holding off filing his response. I want to string this out and see what we can uncover, if anything, before the judge rules on our motion. I'm not sure that it will make much difference, but I want that motion lying there, without a ruling, until we hear from you,

Matt. So, do the best you can and do it as quickly as you can. I really don't know how much time I can squeeze out of the legal process involving that motion."

"Well, I have a feeling, based on what you've already told me, that your inability to find out anything about them in Louisville, even with your limited resources, most likely means they aren't from there. Now, that's not based on a damn thing, but I just have a feeling about it. If that's the case and I need to expand the investigation into another town or two, it might take a little longer, as you can imagine."

Ann said, "I understand. Just keep me updated, and I'll pass everything on to Mr. and Mrs. Kingston."

Late that afternoon, Mr. Dale walked in her office door and sat down. "What's the latest on the Kingston matter?"

"Good afternoon to you too, sir."

He smiled and said, "Sorry. Good afternoon. I'm not really on top of everything today, I guess. What's going on with the Kingston family?"

She hesitated. "You feeling okay? You look a little gray around the edges."

"Not really. I haven't felt good most of the day. I hope I'm not coming down with something. I probably need to go home and take it easy the rest of the day, but I got too much going on. Now, again, what about the Kingston's?"

"I got Matt Armstrong all lined up to do an investigation. Maybe I should have done this before, but I really didn't think it was necessary to go to the effort. I might have made a mistake and not called someone to investigate these three people *before* the trial started rather than now."

"Well, I never suggested it either and I was the one, at least initially, that was guiding you, so if you made an error, so did I. What's your thought process from here on?"

"I'm thinking if he comes up with something significant, we go to the prosecutor and tell him what we have. Maybe, as easy as he was to work with, we can work something out, based upon what we find. Then we can use it at the time of sentencing, or in how we handle our motion for new trial. It all depends, obviously, on what Matt finds out."

He stood and said nothing as he considered her statements, then said, "You know, that sounds like a really good idea. If he finds out nothing, of course you're right back where you started, but if he happens to uncover something, then you might get some positive movement from of the prosecutor. I really think you're on the right road."

"Should I have thought about this prior to the trial?"

"Maybe. Perhaps I should have too, but sometimes there are things like that that just slip through the cracks. It wasn't as if you did nothing. You did quite a bit of research on your own concerning those three and turned up absolutely nothing. You've got the ball rolling now. We'll just see where it takes you. Mr. and Mrs. Kingston are happy with what we've done so far and that's important."

"Thanks, Mr. Dale. I realize it's not time to lock the door for the day, but why don't you go home. I'll get everything closed up here. After all, that's one of the reasons you hired me—so I could help you. This is one of the times you appear to me you need help. Now, go home. I'll see you tomorrow morning."

"You know, I think I'll just do that. I don't leave here early very often, but it's probably best I do today. See you in the morning."

She could tell he was just having an off day. Today was the first time since she was employed that he had left the office without throwing out one of his awful jokes or laughing about something as he walked out.

Chapter 18

Ann turned the key in the office door lock at 6:00 a.m. The October sun hadn't even cleared the horizon, but there was work to do. She knew if she waited until later in the morning to handle the deskwork she needed to finish, the phone would be ringing, people would be walking through the front door, and she would indeed be fortunate to finish anything, let alone everything that needed to be done. At this hour, she could get a good start on the day. The majority of what she felt she needed to finish would be completed by the time the office became active.

Just prior to 8:00 a.m., when she heard Beth's key in the door, she had finished 90% of those items that needed attention. She would try to catch a moment between appointments to finish up the rest.

She heard Beth start down the hallway and looked up as she peaked around the doorframe of her office.

"Good morning, Ann"

"Morning. How was last night? Weren't you going to the Opry or something last night?"

Beth Thompson was unmarried, a couple of years older than Ann and still sowing a few wild oats. There were many mornings when she walked in the office with a hangover, most of the time undetected by Harold, but clearly obvious to Ann.

"Oh god, yes, but we changed our plans. There were six of us. We all had tickets, but we started drinking downtown before the show started and just never left our table. We were having such a good time, we just decided to stay put."

Ann laughed. "Whoa, that was a waste of good tickets, but apparently well worth the stay."

"It was. We had a great time. We'll take you and Jack with us some time. There's a small group of us that have known each other for years and really enjoy each other's company. We have fun together—nothing to drastic, but just enjoy living life day to day. I'll let you know when we're doing something special. Maybe the two of you can tag along."

"Sure, we'd love to, assuming the activity doesn't involve heights, or enclosed places. I'm a little claustrophobic, and he hates heights."

"I'll let you know. Looks like you have a full day. I'm surprised Harold isn't here. He normally arrives about the same time I do."

"He didn't feel well when he left last night. I hope he hasn't come down with something. If he has, you and I will be getting it before long."

"Yup, for sure."

It was near 10:00 a.m., and Ann had already finished with four appointments. She only had two more left before noon, but this afternoon was loaded with people. She had heard clients walk in the front door asking for Harold, but she still hadn't seen him yet this morning.

Just as she stood to walk out into the reception area to discuss Harold's absence, she heard Beth walking down the hallway. She walked into Ann's office with two hands full of tissues trying to keep up with the flow of tears from her eyes. She stopped in front of Ann's desk, and said, "I just got a call from Karen. Harold had a heart attack last night. They took him to Vanderbilt hospital, but it was too late. He died. Harold's gone."

Ann stood up while quietly trying to comprehend exactly what Beth had just told her. "No, there must be a mistake. You mean our…Harold…*not our Harold?*"

Beth just looked at her and said nothing.

Ann started to cry. She walked around her desk and embraced Beth, while trying to simultaneously comprehend the death of someone she so admired and cared for.

"Go out and lock the door. Put a sign on it saying we are closed for the rest of the day. Then call all those people that have appointments, and tell them they need to reschedule." She leaned back. "Can you do that, Beth?"

As she continued to wipe away the tears, she said, "I...guess...I can."

"Okay, you handle that while I call the rest of my appointments and change all of them."

Beth turned and walked out of the room. Ann, for just a moment, felt a rush of emotion start to consume her, but she immediately fought it off. This was not the time, nor the place. There would be time to grieve, but not now.

She started calling all her appointments, moving most of them into the future—some just a couple of days, some into next week. She then walked in Harold's office and checked his personal calendar to see if he was to be in court the next few days. It didn't appear he had anything, but she would check with the clerk's office later this morning.

She walked down the hall to Beth's desk, and between calls she said, "What did Karen say about coming here, about meeting with us?"

"She said she would try to stop by about four this afternoon. What's going to happen here, Ann? What's going to happen to this office?"

"Up to Karen, I guess. We'll just have to wait and talk to her when she has the time. Today, just answer the phone, and tell them someone will get back to them. Don't tell them he died. Just tell them someone will get back to them. We'll figure it all out after the shock has worn off and we've had a chance to talk to Karen."

She walked in her office, shut the office door, and immediately called Jack.

"Hey hon, what's up? Since you don't normally call me during the day, I'm going to assume you're just really, really missing me."

She started to cry.

"Hey, what's going on? Ann, what's going on? Are you crying?"

"Harold died last night. Apparently, he had a heart attack and died. I'm not sure what to do. I've done the things that I think need to be done, but I don't know what to do."

"I'll be right there."

He arrived about 20 minutes later. He met Beth and tried the best he could to console her. She had been with Harold for five years and was clearly having trouble accepting his death.

He walked down the hallway into Ann's office. She stood, and walked into his arms as she, once again, started to cry.

He yelled for Beth to come in and sit with them. As they all sat down, Jack said, "So what's happened here so far? What have you done since you heard?"

Ann said, "We've cancelled all appointments for the rest of the day. I checked his trial calendar. It appears he has nothing pressing for the next couple of days. I'll call the clerk's office and verify that later this morning."

"Is his wife coming down sometime today?"

"Yes, later this afternoon. Can you stay for a while, Jack? Do you need to get back to the office?"

"No. I told them to cancel my appointments. I'm here with you all day if you need me."

Beth said, "We do. We definitely need an experienced lawyer. Not that Ann can't handle everything, but this is a situation neither of us has been through. I'm really glad you're here."

The rest of the morning was spent answering the phone and going through open files that involved Harold. They needed to make sure the office wasn't missing an important deadline within the next few days.

Later that afternoon, Karen arrived. They sat around, remembering Harold, and discussing what to do with the office. Karen made it clear that the office was to remain open. They were to carry on as if he was still alive.

She told Ann to continue to collect the fees, then deposit the money in the office account. They could divide it at the end of each week.

The issue of ownership of the office was simple. Harold had told Karen if anything ever happened to him, the office was to belong to Ann, lock, stock and barrel. It wasn't to be sold to her; it was to be given to her. He told her she would have her hands full figuring everything out for quite some time. He didn't want her to worry about where the money to pay for the office was coming from.

Karen had agreed with him. She went on to say she wouldn't need the money anyway. They had done well.

Once both Karen and Beth had left the office, Jack looked at Ann as he said, "Quite a day."

"Yeah, it was. This wasn't exactly part of my plans for the next few years."

"I'm sure. You just lost your experience—your leadership in this office. You're going to have to adjust. You want to hire someone else to come in and work with you?"

"Absolutely not. I'll figure this out. I just need some time."

"Maybe this is the answer to that partnership issue we discussed. Maybe I should just quit my firm and move in here with you."

"Maybe so."

"I'm here whenever you need me, you know that."

Ann looked away and said nothing.

"You're really going to miss him, aren't you?"

As she started to cry, she whispered, "He was the best, Jack, he was just the best."

Chapter 19

Ann slept only a couple of hours all night, and was, once again, at the office before the sun came up. She hardly knew which way to turn. There was so much work she needed to finish *before* he died, and now…

Beth walked in a couple of hours later and prior to the time she normally arrived. Ann heard her lock the office door, then start walking back to Ann's office before she even took her chair in the reception area.

As she walked in and sat down, she said, "Good Morning."

"Morning, Beth. Well, how was *your* night?"

"Yeah, right. What night. I bet I didn't sleep an hour. I just kept thinking about the office and poor Karen. Whoa, life changed for us for sure, but my how it changed for her."

Ann stood. "I need to go get a cup of coffee. You want anything?"

"No."

As Ann walked back in her office, Beth said, "So what are your thoughts about moving forward?"

"That's what I thought about all night. I think what I want to do is look at every open file Harold was working on. Perhaps you can pull those. I'll work after hours to see what he was doing for the people he represented. The ones I think I can handle either alone, or with some help from Jack, I'll keep. The other cases, the cases I can't or don't want to handle, we'll just need to tell the client to find someone else. If we still have all or part of a retainer fee, we'll refund it, but I just don't feel comfortable trying to handle something I know absolutely nothing about. What do you think?"

"That sounds fine, but I think eventually you're going to need to figure out an identity for your office—some areas of law you really want to focus on. He was involved in a few things that you aren't going to want to be involved in. I think you probably need to narrow your practice down to a few specialty areas based on what you want to do and where you can net the most money."

"Good idea. I'll talk to Jack about that. Why don't you prepare a bill of sale so Karen can transfer the office and the contents to me and we can firm that all up. Then start pulling files. I'll look at them starting tonight. Have you got the motion in Kingston ready to file?"

Beth stood. "No. I'll get it ready."

"We've still got some time, but it's probably best if you get it ready first thing. Have you heard when the funeral is yet?"

"Day after tomorrow."

"Just put a sign on the door. Say something about his passing and that the office will reopen on Friday. I think I'll call Arnold. I'll tell him what's going on in the Kingston case and about Mr. Dale. I just want to make sure he'll work with me on that case as we move forward."

Beth hesitated, then took a deep breath. "Ann, I assume you want me to continue here, right? I mean, if you want someone else, certainly…"

"Don't say another word. I loved working with you *before* he died. Now that he's gone, I absolutely don't know what I'd do without you. Yes, I *want*… no, I *need* you to stay."

"Thank God. I worried about that all night. Thanks."

Ann stood and walked around her desk as Beth stood to leave her office. She embraced her as she said, "I don't know what I'd do without you, I really don't."

Beth smiled, and said, "That's one thing you're not going to have to worry about. I'll be here as long as you need me."

As she walked out the door, Ann speed dialed Arnold Leonard.

"Good morning."

"Morning, Ann. Wow, things have sure changed in your office. I was so sorry to hear about Harold. What a great guy he was, along with being so easy to work with."

"Thank you. Big shock around here that's for sure. We're struggling right now. That's one of the reasons I called you."

"What's going on?"

"As I mentioned, I'm going to file a motion for new trial in the Kingston case. I'll get it filed and within the timeline, but I need a favor."

"Sure. What do you need?"

"Can you hold off filing a response—just wait as long as you can? Then, if the judge gets on us about having it ruled on, maybe we can both ask him to give us a little more time. By extending the time, no one but my client would be harmed anyway."

"What's going on? Why the extra time?"

"You know, Arnold, I just don't think my client did anything wrong. I'm sure you hear that all the time, but I've hired a private investigator to research those three kids that say he did it. This whole matter stinks a little to me. I just need a little time to get to the bottom of it, one way or the other."

"Maybe you should have done that prior to trial."

She hesitated. "You're absolutely right. I made a rookie mistake. I assumed I was on the right side of the case and it didn't much matter what those three said. Won't happen again. But since it did, I just need as much time as you can give me. If I'm right and there are issues we need to discuss, maybe somehow we can work that into the ruling on my motion for new trial."

"Hmm. Interesting idea. You know, I had a bad feeling about that case from day one. Sure, I'll give you as much time as the judge will allow us. You're right. Not getting the motion ruled on promptly is really only hurting your client. And certainly, if you find something for us to talk about, I'll discuss it with you. I want what's right for the state *and* for the people involved—all of them."

"Great. Thank you. You'll get my motion. I'll be in touch as soon as I know anything."

"How are things in the office today—after his death?"

"That's another reason I need the extra time. It's a mess around here, and it's going to remain that way for a while. Thanks, Arnold."

She called Jack a few moments later.

"Hey, I just talked to Arnold."

"Was he receptive?"

"Yes. He's going to hold off on his answer to my motion. We'll both hold off submitting it to the judge for a ruling until Matt has had a chance to investigate. I'll go tell the judge what we're doing right after I file the motion and inform him Arnold approved extending the time for a ruling. That should get us about as much time as we need for Matt to do his job."

"You know, you and Harold should have probably…"

"Don't go there, Jack. I already heard that from Arnold. I know I screwed up and should have thought about doing this earlier, but hopefully we can remedy the mistake now."

"How's everything going in the office?"

"Good. We're just putting out fires right now. After the funeral, maybe Beth and I can sit for a moment and figure out how we want to handle all the work. When are you in court again on the Cline case?"

"Next week—Thursday afternoon. We have a conference with the judge to establish a timeline concerning his trial. You want to come along?"

"Yes. I figure I'll end up doing some work in Wilson County anyway, I might as well get my feet wet with you holding my hand. I'll put the date down on the calendar."

"That'll work. We can set a trial date while we're there so you will need to have your calendar with you. Then I won't have to be calling you and asking you if certain dates will or won't work. You can meet the prosecuting attorney and the trial judge. I've known the judge quite some time. He's kind of a prick, but he's a smart judge. No bullshit in his court. I don't much like him, but I respect him."

"I better go. I got four people waiting to see me. God, Jack this is insane. I don't have time to run to the bathroom anymore. Can't drink much coffee. Don't have time to pee. Gotta go. See you tonight."

As she took a deep breath, she considered what a strange situation she suddenly found herself. Once she left law school, she wanted all the clients she could get her hands on. The one issue that frightened the hell out of her was being unable to find clients. *Now,* she had so many clients she didn't have the time to finish all their work.

As she sat quietly, looking into space, trying to figure out which file to open next, she remembered what Mr. Dale said not long before he died…"one thing at a time Ann, one thing at a time."

Chapter 20

A cold late October wind whistled by as she walked, along with Jack, through the doors of the Wilson County Courthouse. Ann was glad to be able to pry herself free from the pressure of her office practice and take a ride, anywhere, anyplace, away from the issues she had been subjected to since Harold had passed.

Since his death, she had little time to think about Harold, or anything else that wasn't specifically office related. It consumed her. Whether she was going through files, talking to clients or returning phone calls, it was never ending, each and every hour of the day.

Unfortunately, the most important issue she handled during this week was Randall's sentencing. Pursuant to the statute, he was sentenced to prison. It was one of the most difficult moments of Ann's life. Going through the process only made her more determined to do what she could to make sure those she represented were exonerated and set free, rather than live through the hell Randall was about to endure.

They walked together down a long hallway and into the judge's chambers. There was already someone sitting, waiting for the judge to walk in. Jack soon introduced her to George Whitney, one of the prosecutors for Wilson County.

While talking amongst themselves, the judge walked in the door and took a seat behind his desk. He said nothing, as he opened the file and reviewed the contents. Tall, and athletic, he commanded the attention of all in the room, including her.

While in the middle of a sentence George was completing, the judge said, "Okay everyone, what are we doing here today? I don't have all afternoon. Let's get on with it."

George stopped mid-sentence, and said, "Judge, this hearing involves the case of State vs. Thomas Cline. His presence has been waived here today. We're here to schedule everything in anticipation of his trial. I believe you know Jack Connors from Nashville. He'll be representing the defendant along with Ann Jackson, also of Nashville."

"What's there to schedule? Surely, he's going to plead to the charge. What's there to try? I've read the minutes of testimony and this looks like a no-brainer. Don't you think this is a no-brainer, Mr. Connors?"

Jack smiled and said, "Don't think so, Your Honor. Not according to my client."

"Oh hell Connors, what'd you expect him to tell you—that he did it? Now, when do you want to plead him out?"

"Well, I get a little different story from him, so I'm thinking we'll probably just try it unless he changes his mind."

"Whatever. By the way, who's this young thing with you? I don't believe I know her."

"Judge this is Ann Jackson. Ann, this is Judge Rodney Dunn. Ann graduated this spring from law school and went to work in Harold Dale's office. He, as you might know, just died. She's taking over his practice. She's also my finance. We're trying the case together."

"Well, isn't that romantic. You two look so sweet together—and what a terribly romantic thing to do—try a case together. I'm impressed. Nice meeting you, Ms. Jackson."

"Thank you, Judge. Nice meeting you. Have we met before? I feel like we have."

"Didn't you just recently pass the bar? I don't associate with many outside the profession, so I highly doubt it. You don't look at all familiar to me."

"Okay, sorry. I'm looking forward to working with you on the case and hopefully working in Wilson County on a regular basis once I get on my feet."

He looked over the top of his glasses, smiled and said, "So you're going to be a trial lawyer, are you? That what you're going to specialize in?"

She hated this man, and she had barely met him. His smile was about as disingenuous as anyone she had ever met. "Right now, I'm just really trying to figure out *what* I want to do. It's been difficult with Harold's death. I'm just trying to figure out which direction to take. I do enjoy trial work so I'm thinking that may be my specialty."

He smiled. "I'll just be holding my breath to see what you finally decide. Now where the hell are we with this case? I've got about ten more to figure out before I'm out of here for the day."

Jack said, "Judge, I think we really just need a trial date. We've worked out dates for depos, and there isn't a lot left to do other than try this one."

"When do you want to do this? I've got some dates about 60 to 70 days out. Is that too soon?"

"I don't think so. What do you think, George?"

"That's going to put us near Christmas. That okay with you, Judge? Maybe the week before Christmas?"

"Hell yes, I love a good lynching in the courtroom during December. Let's go December 15th. I'll put it down for a week. That going to be enough time?"

George said, "It's not a difficult case. Yes, that's fine with me. If we need more time, I guess we can always reschedule."

"Sure, whatever. I really don't give a shit one way or the other. Anything else for you two men and this rookie?"

"Judge, just one more thing. Are you sure we haven't met before? You look so familiar, but I just can't place you."

He smiled. "What the hell did I just tell you? Now get out, all of you. I have important things to do here. I need you out of here to do them."

George went back to his office, and as Ann and Jack walked to the jail to visit with their client, Jack said, "What was all that business about meeting him before? Where'd that come from?"

"I don't know where it came from. He just looks somewhat familiar. I didn't think it would hurt to ask him, but I wish I hadn't now. I don't think he's going to be much fun in the courtroom."

"I've tried two cases with him. As I told you, he's a prick, but he's a fair prick in the courtroom."

"He married, have kids?"

"No, he's not married now. He's divorced, but he has a son. In fact, his son works in the clerk's office here in the courthouse. He's a little strange, but a good guy."

Once they reached the jail, Edward was waiting for them. Together, they waited for the jailer to bring Thomas to their table, and it was only a matter of minutes before he sat down with them.

After introducing Ann, all discussion focused upon the trial.

"We now have a trial date of December 15. That should leave us plenty of time to take depos and prepare adequately with the date that far away. Are there any witnesses you want to call on your behalf? I'd like to call a couple that can speak to your lack of violent tendencies. But the real problem with this case is that there is no witness that can put you somewhere else when she was murdered. You were apparently there about the time it happened. That in and of itself creates a small dilemma. Is there anyone else that might have some knowledge or know anything about the actual facts of the case?"

Edward said, "Me. I can testify she was a bitch. I can testify…"

Jack said, "Wait a minute. Can you testify as to anything that has to do with her murder? I don't care how you personally felt about her."

He thought for a moment. "I guess not. I could testify as to how great a brother he is, but as to the actual facts, no, I guess I can't."

"Thomas, was there ever any violence in your house? Did you ever strike her, or were the police ever called to your house for any reason?"

"Just once. It was about a week before she left. The neighbors called the cops because we were arguing to loudly, I guess. They never charged either of us with anything. They just stopped by, talked to us, and left."

"Yeah, well that's not going to help, even though they didn't make an arrest. They're still going to be able to show the two of you were having issues, which could have created a motive for murder. We just don't have much to use. We'll discuss everything when Ann and I get back to the office, then meet with you again next week."

Edward said, "I'll tell you one more time, just so you remember. He didn't do this. I know him like the back of my hand. He couldn't hurt another person if he was ordered to. So, get this figured out, you two. If he's convicted, you'll be sending an innocent man to jail."

On their return to Nashville, Ann said, "Boy that Edward and the judge make quite a pair. Put the two of them in a room alone and we could have ourselves quite an event."

Jack laughed and said, "We're going to have our hands full in court. I'm glad you're here to help me. One of us can handle the judge, while the other handles Edward."

But Ann wasn't thinking much about how to *handle* either of them. She was desperately trying to remember where she had met that judge. Somewhere, one day in their past, they had met, but she was damned if she could remember where or when.

Chapter 21

“What’s the situation with that Cline case in Wilson County? Is there anything I can do to help you with it?”

Beth and Ann were having an early morning conference, prior to unlocking the office door.

“No, I think we’re about ready. Depos are over, and the trial is only about a month away. There’s really not a lot to do. There are so few people for us to call as witnesses. There isn’t one individual we can call to have them testify Cline wasn’t in that house because he was, just not at the *exact* time she was killed. We’re going to have a couple of people from work testify as to his character, and of course his brother will testify, but we’re at a real shortage in terms of actual witnesses. Both Jack and I are worried about how this is all going to turn out.”

“What about his brother?”

“The guy just never quits. He goes on and on about the innocence of his brother, but provides us with nothing to use at trial. He’s really hard to control. I have no idea what he’ll do if the jury convicts. They’re best friends as well as brothers.”

Beth thought for a moment, then said, “Not to change the subject, but you don’t have any siblings, right?”

“No.”

“What ever happened to your father? Do you ever remember seeing him or being with him?”

“No. Mom never mentioned him. They weren’t married. Mom married a different man after I was born, but that marriage lasted only about a month. I kind of assume my mom was a little demanding when it came to men. From what I remember, she never stayed with one of them very long.”

“So, you and your mom had different last names?”

“Yes. She divorced the only man she married just a month later. I was never adopted by him, so we ended up with different names.”

"Did you ever know any of your family—have a relationship with any of them?"

"No, only Sally. I was moved around from foster home to foster home, and the only family member I ever heard from was Sally." Ann looked away, as she remembered those difficult years. She turned toward Beth and said, "Those were tough years for me, as you can imagine. Let's move on—let's talk about something else. How's the day look?"

"Good. I have appointments scheduled every 30 minutes. You have that conference call with that minister from Gatlinburg at ten-thirty and I left a half-hour open for you to talk to him."

"You coming to the wedding?"

Wouldn't miss it. Should be fun. That chapels right on the other side of Gatlinburg, right? It's right there on the left side of the road, correct?"

"Yes. Are you staying overnight or coming home?"

She smiled. "I'm staying. Never know who you might meet spending an unattached night in the Smokies. I'm staying for sure."

"By the way, did you cut Karen a check for her share of the fees from last month?"

"Yes. She's taken care of."

"You're doing that every time you cut one for me, right?"

"Yes. Her amount is, of course, dwindling as we move further away from his death, but I'll keep doing it until there are no more fees attributable to the work he was doing."

"Great. By the way, Matt Armstrong hasn't called, has he? Something really needs to happen in this Kingston case before long. I'm afraid one of these days the judge is going to call and tell me our time is up."

"As a matter of fact, Matt called right after you left for the day yesterday. Let me get him on the phone. We'll see if he's in his office this early."

She walked to her desk and a few minutes later informed Ann that Matt was on line one.

"Morning. I hear you called yesterday. Got something for me?"

"Yes, I do. Not much yet, but I can tell you one thing. They don't live and never have lived in Louisville, Kentucky. I can tell you that for a fact. That's the main reason I called. They're all three from Paducah. I haven't been there yet to figure out what the hell's going on, but that's where I'm headed next."

"You're kidding."

"No. So we're off to a good start anyway. I had a hell of a time getting my cop friend to come around. I finally bought him a few bottles of Jack Daniels and gave him five hundred bucks. That was just to get him to research the state records that weren't open to me and try to find out where they live. It was like pulling teeth, but I got the job done. I'll take off early next week and see what I can find out in Paducah."

"Great work, Matt. Keep me informed."

As she terminated the call, Beth walked in her office, just in time to hear Ann giggle.

"What was that about—that little giggle I just heard?"

"We're making some headway in Randall's case. Be sure and let me know if you hear from Matt, no matter where I am."

Beth left her office a few minutes later to unlock the door and start the day. Ann quickly called Sally.

"Have you about got all those things done I needed done for the wedding?"

"Oh my god, Ann, I am so excited. It's only a week away. I can't believe it's only a week away. Can you believe it's just one week away? I think about it day and night. This is going..."

"Sally."

"Ann, this is going to be..."

She increased the volume of her voice as she said, "Sally!"

"What?"

"Have you got everything basically ready to go?"

"Yes. Everything's done. All we have to do is show up. I got everything else ready to go. There's nothing left to do except show up. Oh, I am so excited..."

"Sally..."

"We are...*what.* What do you need...or want?"

"You still on those pills?"

"I take a few different pills. Which pills you talking about, Ann, because..."

"Are you still taking those pills you bought over the internet to lose weight?"

"Sure. Why? They're doing the job. I'm down 20 pounds. You can't believe how good I look because we haven't been together for a while, but you won't believe how good I look. You just wait…"

"Dump the pills and dump them before next week. I mean that Sally. Now you listen to me."

"Sure will. Well, thanks. I'm glad I called you. See you next week."

The line went dead.

Ann heard her next appointment talking to Beth in the reception area. She quickly called Jack.

'Hi hon, what's up?

"Jack, I just talked to Sally. She's gone overboard on those damn fat pills. I couldn't even hardly talk to her. I have no idea whether she's done what I told her needed to be done for the wedding or not."

Jack laughed. "Oh, come on. It'll be fine. She'll do what she needs to get do, and if she doesn't, we'll just figure it out when we get there."

"I mean it Jack, she's out of her mind."

"As I said, forget it. We'll clean it all up when we get there. Have you got your schedule handled for Tuesday and Wednesday? Mine's cleared. Is yours?"

"Yes. I have no idea how many from the wedding party are staying all night and into Thanksgiving Day."

"We are—that's all that matters. Let them do as they wish. It will all turn out just fine , now relax. I need to go."

The line went dead.

Ann told Beth to send in her next client. She leaned back, and quietly whispered, "Shit, shit, shit...this is going to be a fucking mess. This isn't…*Helllloo there, Mr. Johnson, have a chair.*"

Chapter 22

Neither said a word. The wedding was over. It had now been a couple of hours since its conclusion. Ann and Jack were stretched out, in bed, mindlessly watching the evening news with Lester Holt. The wedding dress covered the floor just inside the door. His underwear was draped over a lampshade. Her bra was hanging over the TV. The room was cluttered throughout with items they brought back from the wedding and which they tossed as they walked through the hotel door upon arrival. The bedspread was lying in a clump on the floor near the end of the bed.

They had each concluded they would remain celibate for the week leading up to the wedding, just so sex would perhaps be that much more exiting on their wedding night. It had necessitated Jack sleeping on the couch for a few nights leading up to the wedding, but he suffered through it, remaining true to their plan.

However, once the wedding was over, and they stood patiently in line, while the guests, especially those that would return home right after the wedding, wished them well, he had trouble keeping his hands off her. All the while, one of those thoughts uppermost in her mind was how long it might take her to drop the dress and jump in bed once they returned to the room

However, once there, the celebration hadn't lasted long. Going 'without,' for both of them, had turned into a curse, rather than a well-thought-out plan. After their clothes and the bed sheets had been tossed haphazardly through the air, it was the shortest sexual experience she had ever been through. Now, they lay watching the news, waiting for the party to begin.

With the conclusion of the wedding, came an overwhelming letdown and an intense desire to do nothing but sleep for the next six weeks.

"Great wedding"

"Sure was."

"Sally did good."

"She must have quit those pills. She was rational…or at least *more* rational, than she was the last time I talked to her on the phone. Unfortunately, I noticed she was eating everything she touched. For a while I was concerned about the tables and chairs. I'm just glad there was a steady flow of food, or I'm not sure anything or anyone would have been safe."

Jack laughed, as he said, "I think most everyone that was invited showed up."

She remained quiet, until she turned toward him, smiled and said, "You want to go again?"

"No offense, but I don't think I can move. I'm too tired to move, let alone move quickly."

"I understand. Frankly, thank god you said that. I was only trying to be accommodating. You know, we need to get ready to go to the dance. It starts in an hour."

"I know, but I can't get up. Sorry. You go alone and just tell'em I'm dead."

She sat up.

"Let's get dressed. Our guests will be waiting." She leaned down and kissed him. "I love you."

He reached out and pulled her down, near him. "You know, maybe we *should* do it again. I just feel we have a responsibility now that we're newly married."

"Okay, big guy, bring it on, but it needs to be quick. We got to get movin'."

"What a great event. I'm dead tired, as I'm sure you are, but what a great event."

They had just reached the eastern city limits of Knoxville on their way back to Nashville. It was a beautiful Thanksgiving morning and now time to return to the 'real' world. The break from the practice of law had, however, done its job. It had given both of them time to breathe—time to take a deep breath, even though it hadn't lasted long.

"You know, I love the Gatlinburg area. I just wish we could have stayed longer. Tell you what. The next time we have some free time or we're celebrating a special event, let's come back. Let's spend some time here. The next vacation we take needs to be here."

"How 'bout next week?"

"Funny. I have so much to do back at the office I hate to even think about it."

"I understand. I do, however, feel like we're at least ready for the Cline trial. Depos are completed. I'm comfortable with the approach I'm taking with each witness. You want to question any of them, or do you just want to second chair me?"

"I'm there to learn, Jack and that's all. I could handle a couple of them I guess, if you want me to, but I really just want to watch you. You're an established, well-regarded trial attorney. I want to watch you work, if that's okay."

"Certainly. But I think I'll have you handle a couple of them. We can discuss which ones when we get back to the office" He was quiet for a moment before he said, "I think it's time to start looking for a house, too. I have a little money saved up, as you know, and I just think it's time we look."

"Are you kidding me?"

"No. Are you okay with that?"

"Yes. Absolutely. That's the most exciting, positive thing that's happened to me since…well, since…okay since we just got married. But other than that, *yes, yes, yes*, let's look—as soon as we get home. Maybe tomorrow?"

"I'm a little busy tomorrow, as, I might suggest, are you. But we'll see what the day brings."

He hesitated, before he said, "You know, I think it's probably also time to start looking into a partnership. I'm ready to leave the firm. You have plenty of room in your office for another attorney. What do you think?"

"I think it's a great idea. I have people drop in and call every day that I just don't have time to see. And without doubt, some of your people would follow you. I think it's a great money-making opportunity and would work well for both of us. Do you think you can work with me during the day, then sleep with me during the night? Some people can't do that, you know."

"If I didn't think I could, I wouldn't have suggested it. I know you like I know the back of my hand. I never, ever get tired of being with you. Anyway, if it doesn't work, we'll make a change."

"I agree. I'll talk to Beth about it when we get back—see what her thoughts might be."

Ann had turned her phone off during the wedding dance. She had been hesitant to turn it back on. She knew turning it on would then begin the job she had been so happy to remove herself from for the last few days. But it was time for a reality check.

The first thing she noticed was a missed call from Matt Armstrong.

"I see Matt Armstrong called. I wonder if I should call him today, since it's a holiday."

"I would. Obviously, he needs to talk to you and knowing him like I do, he's like both of us—a holiday or a weekend doesn't stop our work. Call him."

"Hi, Matt. Did I catch you at a bad time? I see you called."

"No, no, not at all. I just had a little more news for you. I'm not finished yet, but I did have a little additional news I wanted to share with you."

"Okay, go ahead."

"I was able to spend a little time in Paducah the other day. I didn't get a chance to do all I wanted to do, but I did find out one thing. I had a chance to look at these kid's birth certificates. They may act like kids just out of high school, but they sure as hell aren't. Hell, two of them are 22, and that boy, that Johnny whatshisname, is 24. They may have come across as innocent 18 years old's, but they're far from that."

"Wow, that's interesting. Have you had a chance to figure out anything else yet?"

"I just can't find the right people to talk to. I've had a chance to talk to a few people that knew them, and I know there's something that just doesn't feel right about them. I can't get to the bottom of it, but I will. It's going to take a little time, but I'll get there."

"Just keep me informed. Good job, Matt. Keep at it."

He remained silent for a moment then said, "A little word of advice. Call me *before* the trial next time. I think I..."

"Just stop, Matt. I've kicked myself in the butt a thousand times for not doing that very thing. Next time, I will, believe me."

He laughed. "I figured you had that all figured out, but I just needed to do a little advertising."

She looked at Jack for a moment, then said, "You know, we may have another job for you. I'll talk to Jack and get back to you."

She terminated the call. Jack looked at her and said, "What job? 'We' may have another job for him? What are you talking about?"

"Maybe we should hire him to do some looking around in the Cline case. Apparently, they have the money to afford him. What harm would it do? We've sure as hell have hit a wall as far as our own investigation is concerned."

"Good idea. I'll talk to Thomas about it."

As they passed through Knoxville, she took a deep breath, considering how life had changed so quickly in the last few months—married, talk of a new house and a partnership. Then there was her dead boss, the trial she lost, a new trial in Wilson County, this asshole judge that looked like somebody, new clients, old clients...

She had hoped the trip to Gatlinburg would provide some relief, but it hadn't. She really wanted to tell Jack to just turn the car around, head back to Gatlinburg, and finish a *long* break she needed from the profession.

Chapter 23

"So, what do you think about that little craftsman on the west side?"

They both sat quietly while waiting for Judge Dunn and George Whitney to appear.

"I liked that townhouse down south, near the Gulch. Have we really got it down to just two? Are there any others you want to throw in the mix?"

"No. I think those are the two we need to consider. Financing is lined up on both of them, so I think it's just a matter of one of us caving in and going along with the other one."

Jack turned away as he said, "I don't like the sound of that. I know what happens under those circumstances. Unfortunately, for me, it's not normally good."

She smiled. "Let's just continue talking about it. We'll eventually come to a conclusion we can both accept. But I really think it better be sooner rather than later the way everything is selling in Nashville right now."

Neither said anything, until Jack said, "You act nervous. You concerned about the judge... or George?"

"You know, every time I think about this judge, I get butterflies. He scares the hell out of me. I don't know why, I really don't, but he really intimidates me."

As she finished her sentence, George walked in. After exchanging the normal pleasantries, Jack said, "After we get done with this pretrial conference, George, if you have a moment, I'd like to talk to you about a couple of the witnesses you're going to call. Do you have time?"

"Sure. I have as much time as you need, other than I need to be back at the office in about ten minutes."

Jack smiled and said, "I understand. This won't take long." He turned to Ann and said, "Do you mind me taking a few more minutes before we drive back, to discuss trial procedure with him?"

"Not at all. I got a couple of things I want to do while I'm here. Go ahead, and I'll meet you in the clerk's office."

"What are you going to…"

Judge Dunn walked in with a handful of files. "Good morning, everyone."

He took his seat, and as he did, he said, "Let's move along. I got a lot to do and I play golf at eleven. I love taking advantage of weather this nice in December. I do NOT want to waste a tee time, so let's move along. Are we ready to start this trial in what, three days? Is everyone ready to go? Why haven't you got your man convinced his best course of action is to plead, Connors?"

Jack smiled and said, "In response to your first question, Judge, I think we're all ready to proceed. In response to your second, he's not ready to plead."

"So, you're going to make us go through all this shit even though everyone in this room knows he's guilty? Really?"

"He says he's not. As you know, we're somewhat bound by his wishes."

"Whatever. Have you all reviewed the jury instructions? Do any of you have any questions about them?

"Judge, Ann and I are still looking them over, but by and large we think they're fine."

George said, "I agree. I don't see a major problem with any of them."

"There is one thing I need to tell you. There are going to be a few breaks in the action while we are trying this. I have numerous personal and professional matters which will need to be handled during the time we are trying this case. I just wanted to forewarn you now so no one is surprised."

George said, "What are you thinking, Judge? Are we going to have two, three or four breaks and for how long?"

"Probably two or three taking a couple of days to handle each time. I'll forewarn you the day before, but I did want you to know about them now."

"You're the judge. If that's how it's to be then that's how it's to be. We'll adjust accordingly."

"I agree, Jack. Not normally the way it's done, but we'll get by."

The judge smiled and said, "You should know by now *nothing* is normally done the way I do it. Anything else?"

Both attorneys shook their heads.

"Alright then folks, see you in three days. Now get out and send the next set of attorneys in."

Once in the hallway, Jack said, "The guy just always knows how to say the right thing at the right time, doesn't he?"

George smiled. "He's quite the deal. Jack did you want to sit down for a minute and go through witnesses, talk about how much time they might take, things of that nature?"

"Yes, I do. Ann so you want to sit in on this or not?"

"No. Go ahead. I think I'll go see someone in the clerk's office for a minute. Can you just drop in there when you're finished? It won't take me long."

"Sure."

Ann walked in the clerk's office and looked around. She had no idea what he looked like and there were a number of employees behind the counter. Finally, she said, "Ma'am, could you point out Mark Dunn? Does he work here?"

"Yes, he does. He's right there. Mark, Mark can you come over here a moment?"

He was tall and handsome, like his father. He appeared to be in his early twenties. She wondered if he was as big a jerk as his father.

"Hi, I'm Ann Jackson. I'm an attorney from Nashville, and we just got done with a hearing involving your father. Your father is Judge Dunn, correct?"

As he extended his hand, he said, "Yes, ma' am, that would be my father. Nice to meet you."

"Nice meeting you. I heard you worked here. Since I'm new to this area, I thought I'd just stop by and say hello, just introduce myself. My co-council and the prosecutor are having a short meeting so I am wandering around the courthouse until he is ready to leave. But I did want to stop by and at least say hello."

"Want a cup of coffee? I'm on break right now. We have coffee in the back room if you want to sit a spell."

She turned and looked out the door. As she reengaged in conversation, she said, "I don't see him coming after me yet, so sure, I have time."

They walked through the back door of the outer office into a smaller office with a few chairs situated around a table. He said, "Take a seat. You want anything in your coffee?"

"No, black is fine."

Fifteen minutes later, Jack poked his head through the office door and said, "Well, as usual I see you've found the coffee pot."

Ann said, "Yep. Mark and I were just getting acquainted. You ready to go?"

"I am." He extended his hand to Mark and said, "Morning, Mark. Good to see you again."

"My pleasure. Nice seeing you, Jack. Is your work done here for today?"

"Yes."

As all three walked to the front of the office, Mark said, "You two ready for trial? I see it's coming up in a few days. I already sent out all the jury notices."

Ann said, "We're ready as can be. I'll look forward to seeing you in a few days. Maybe we can have coffee together a time or two while the trial is going on."

"That would be nice."

As they drove back to Nashville after visiting briefly with their client, Jack said, "How was your visit with the judge's son?"

"He's really a nice guy. His demeanor, his attitude is far removed from that of his father. It's hard to believe he's his son."

"He has a great mother. She's left the area now, but she was a really nice lady. What did the two of you discuss?"

"Oh, not much really, other than his job, where he lives, why he quit college to go to work. He said his dad was mad as hell when he quit college, and wouldn't even recommend him for his job. He said he got it anyway, but it was without any help from his father."

"Well, that would be consistent—his dad's a jerk through and through."

I asked him a few questions about the judge. He told me there was a time his father lived in Nashville, but it was before he was born. So most likely, that wouldn't have been where I saw him."

"That still bothers you, doesn't it?"

"You know, I very seldom forget a face. I can honestly say that's one of my better traits. I don't forget people's faces."

"Well, that's good to know—I guess. Let's talk about what George and I discussed."

During the rest of their trip, they discussed procedure for trial, and what they needed to do to finish their preparation. But all the while, she thought of her conversation with Mark. Nothing he said today helped conclude the issue of where she and the judge had met, but she wasn't finished with him. Ann would be in Lebanon trying Cline's case for the better part of three weeks. Mark would most likely get sick of having coffee with her before the trial concluded.

Chapter 24

Ann stared at the ceiling as she tried to remember each morbid detail. The bedroom was only just starting to lighten up, so she knew it wasn't much after sunrise. She looked around—Jack had already awakened and most likely left for work. She knew she needed to get moving. But the night had taken so much out of her, it was going to take all the effort she could muster to push herself up and out of bed.

She relived sitting up in bed, in a sweat, and screaming just a few hours ago. Jack shook her and put his arms around her as she calmed down. But the damage had already been done. The dream had exhausted her. Even as tired as she was, sleep hadn't come easy. It must have been near five before she finally fell asleep, and now, a few hours later, unfortunately it was time to rise.

As she put her makeup on and fixed herself a light breakfast, she thought about Jack. He was truly her hero. He had to be tired of continually waking up with her as she relived the trauma time after time. The dreams had, however, become somewhat less frequent, but for all they had decreased in frequency, they had more than increased in intensity.

Last night was over the top. In fact, it had made her reconsider the possibility of once again seeking professional help. She had gone through it years ago, and figured once she quit, she would never need to return. But now, after last night, she thought she might have to reconsider that conclusion.

She arrived at her office just shortly after Beth had unlocked the door and taken a seat at her desk.

"Morning, Beth."

"Morning. Now, you remember you have no appointments for today, don't you? You wanted to use the day to work on that Cline trial. I cleared everything off the calendar. You haven't changed your mind, have you? I've got your calendar cleared from today all the way through the first of the year."

"Nothing today. As concerns the next few weeks, there will be a few days court isn't in session. The judge told us he needed to handle a few matters which would take him away from the trial. He said he would let us know in advance, as they came up. So, I'll let you know which days as soon as I know, and you can schedule appointments on those days, maybe in the mornings. I'll want the afternoon free to continue to work on the Cline trial."

The phone rang and Beth, before responding to Ann's comments, answered it.

She put her caller on hold. "It's Sally. You have time to see her today?"

"I'll make time. Just tell her to come in when she can—I'll be here."

Ann had just reviewed the Cline jury instructions one last time when Sally walked in her office door.

After she had poured herself a cup of coffee, Sally took a chair in front of Ann's desk and said, "What're you working on?"

"Oh, just these jury instructions for the trial I have that starts tomorrow."

"Jury instructions?"

"Yes. The judge reads these to the jury at the end of the trial. They explain to the jury what their responsibilities are in the case. They explain what the jury can and can't do in terms of convicting the defendant. It's both general and specific information concerning their conduct once they begin to deliberate."

"So how does the case look? Can I come and watch?"

"Both Jack and I are concerned. We haven't been given much to work with. Yes, you can come, but it's in Lebanon so you'll need to travel a few miles to get there."

"How's everything been since the wedding? What a great wedding that was. I've thought about it a number of times since we got home."

"Everything's good. Jack and I are forming a partnership after we get this Cline trial over and once the new year begins. I had a long talk with Beth and she's ready to go. We weren't sure she could handle the volume of work we may both put out, so we gave her the go ahead to hire additional secretarial help if she needs it.”

“Wow. That sounds great. Can the two of you work together? Do you think that’ll be a problem?”

“No. We’ve been working on this trial together. We’ve had no problem whatsoever. I think it’ll work out fine.”

“You look a little tired. You okay? You just look and maybe even act a little tired today.”

Ann looked away, hesitating a moment before she responded.

When she turned to face Sally, she said, “It was another long night.”

“Dream?”

She leaned back in her chair and looked out the window, as she said, “Yes.”

Sally said nothing, as Ann remained silent, deep in thought.

“But this one was different—really different.”

“Why. What made this one so different? I still think you need to go see someone about this—get some help.”

“I know you do, and I may just do that. This dream wasn’t like that. You know how there’s never a face on the guy—how I can never see a face?”

“Yes. What changed about that?”

“Last night he had one.”

Sally leaned forward in her chair. She whispered. “You’re kidding. You saw his face? Who the hell was it?”

Ann smiled. “The face was the face of a judge I just met.”

Sally leaned back and relaxed. “Yeah, well you know that’s a joke. Weren’t no judge killed your mamma, for sure.”

Ann said, “I know that. I think somehow, I just identify the judge who’s the one that will try the case tomorrow, as being evil, and dangerous, just like the guy that killed mom. He’s definitely a jerk, most likely misogynistic, definitely overbearing, but certainly no killer. How the hell I ended up with his face on the killer’s face I’ll never know. I know one thing though. I’ve decided I’m not going to back down from him.”

“Is he that bad?”

“I’ve only been with him twice, but both times he was an asshole. It’s his way or no way. I just let it go both times. My role in this trial isn’t very extensive. I’m just second-chairing

Jack and examining a few witnesses, but I'm not going to let the son-of-a-bitch bully me. I have no doubt that's what he does with everyone, including his own son, but that's not going to work with me. He'll probably throw me in jail before it's over, but I'm not going to let that happen—ever."

Sally's eyes widened, as she said, "You're kidding? That would be great. I'd come visit you. I have never, ever known anyone that's gone to jail for anything. I'll bring you stuff you need if you get tossed in the hoosegow. That's so exciting."

"Yeah, well hopefully that won't happen, but I decided early this morning, while lying there, awake after that dream, that I'm not going to take any shit from him. It's one thing backing down when in chambers, but I have a client to represent. He's not going to berate and belittle me in the courtroom without a response. I concluded that early this morning, and that's the way it's going to be."

Later that night, while discussing the trial, she disclosed to Jack some thoughts concerning her newly-developed approach before Judge Dunn.

He hesitated before he responded. "You know, I told you this guy is difficult. I don't mind you standing up for something if you think it's right, but remember you have a jury to consider. They're going to be watching everything you do, every move you make, and you don't want to piss *them* off, or turn them against you, believe me."

"I don't intend on doing that, but if I take issue with something he does, I'm not going to sit on my hands either."

"I understand. Just be careful, Ann. He's a mean, vindictive man, and you want to be careful when you're in his court. If you anger him in the courtroom, I doubt his anger will end when he walks out the courtroom door. Just be careful what you say."

She would listen as she always did. He was much more experienced, much more knowledgeable than her. But she would not back down again and that was that!

Then, there was the issue of his face on her mother's killer. While there was little doubt concerning how that all came about, and while she knew it was only a dream, she wondered if there was really more to it than that? She would consider that issue in more detail once the trial ended.

For now, she would stand her ground when it came to the dreadful Judge Dunn and consider her other interesting, but unrealistic issues involving him, once the trial had concluded.

Chapter 25

It had been many years since she had been this frightened. She was five-years-old and watched while a man killed her mother. Now, some 20 plus years later, she found herself nearly as frightened, even though the situation was much different.

She sat with Jack, waiting, along with the prospective jurors, for Judge Dunn to make his appearance. They had all been patient for over a half-hour as they waited for him to walk through the door from his chambers. Ann had no doubt his late arrival had more to do with a dramatic entrance than it did with business he was conducting in chambers.

She leaned over and whispered to Jack, "His highness is really using the drama card today, isn't he?"

"You don't know that. He could actually be busy—although I doubt it," he whispered back.

Thomas was pale with fear. His brother sat next to him, although he assumed the judge would make short work of that. Neither Jack nor Ann figured the judge would allow Edward to sit in front of the short wooden barrier separating the onlookers from the participants, but Jack had allowed him to sit there until the judge made him move.

It was another five minutes before his highness blessed them with his appearance. Once he took his seat, he gave the jurors some general information concerning their responsibilities and then explained the jury selection process. He was just ready to start with selecting jurors when he noticed Edward.

He looked over the top of his glasses as he said, "Now sir, whom might you be?"

Edward said, "I'm this guy's brother, Judge."

"Stand up."

"What for? Can't you hear me while I'm sitting? Believe me, my voice won't change much if I stand."

"Stand up—*and I mean now*."

Jack motioned for Edward to stand, which he did.

The Judge smiled as he said, "Now, what's your name?"

"Edward."

"Okay…*Edward*…from now on when you address me, you will address me as *your honor*—do we understand each other so far?"

"Sure…Your Honor."

"Okay, now Edward, you move on back behind the barrier there and sit with the rest of the observers. Just move on back and I mean *right now*."

"But, Your Honor, this here's my brother and …"

The judge looked at the officer seated in the courtroom, and said, "If he says one more word without moving behind the barrier, I want him arrested for contempt of court."

Edward looked down, turned around and walked to a bench seat behind the barrier.

"Thank you, *Edward*. Now, Mr. Prosecutor, you may begin selecting a jury."

The process on behalf of the state took the rest of the morning. Immediately after the noon break, jury selection on behalf of the defendant began, with Ann handling the questioning of prospective jurors.

She had reached her fifth juror, and stood to walk to the jury box where he was seated. The primary issue at this point, was to make certain that none of the prospective jurors either knew the defendant or his spouse and that they hadn't yet formed a conclusion concerning the defendant's guilt.

"Now, sir, again I would ask you if you have any thoughts or have come to a conclusion concerning the defendant's guilt or innocence as he sits there at the table? Do you have any thoughts about whether he's guilty or innocent as he sits there today?"

"No."

"None whatsoever?"

"Ms. Jackson, you've asked him, along with all the others you've questioned, that same question multiple times. Could you just ask it once and then move on? Would that be too much to ask?"

Ann quickly turned toward the source of the inquiry, and said, "Judge, I just want to make sure none of these people have already formed an opinion concerning the…"

"Oh, now Ms. Jackson, I *know* what you're doing, but from now on with each prospective juror, just ask them once, okay? Thank you."

She started to respond.

He leaned forward, looked over the top of his glasses and said, "No response is necessary. Just do what I tell you to do."

She looked at Jack, who sat dead still…and silent.

Ann took a deep breath, then returned to questioning the prospective jurors, taking great care not to ask the same question more than once.

As they reached the midafternoon break, Ann had completed questioning slightly over half of the prospective jurors. While sitting around one of the tables in the conference room, prior to commencement of proceedings for the remainder of the afternoon, Edward said, "That judge is really kind of a jerk, isn't he?"

Jack said, "He's the boss in there, Edward. He's the one that…"

"No, Edward you're correct. He's a jerk. But he's the one that controls the room and the one you must listen to." Ann leaned forward over the edge of the table, as the volume of her voice lowered, but the intensity increased. "Even though he may be the boss in there, he's still a son-of-a-bitch, as you have noted. He is one fucking bastard that you need to watch out for, because people like him…"

She suddenly realized what she was doing as she looked around at all three men, who were glued to every vile word about the judge that came from her mouth.

Ann regained control, sat back and said, "Just do what he says Edward, just do what he says."

While they were waiting patiently at the council table in the courtroom for the late afternoon session to begin, Jack said, "You really hate this guy, don't you?"

"Every time I'm around him, he pisses me off, and yes, I have now reached the point where I can't stand him. It's taking everything I have not to walk up behind that bench and just bitch slap the living shit out of him."

Jack's laughter quickly ended as the judge walked through the chamber's door and took his seat behind the bench.

Ann took the remainder of the afternoon quizzing jurors, but remembering not to ask the same juror the same question twice. The judge indicated at the end of the afternoon session they would continue picking a jury the next morning.

On their way home, once court had adjourned for the afternoon, and while discussing the day's proceedings, Jack said, "Again, Ann, you really need to be careful with the judge. He's so damn touchy, he'd just as soon throw an attorney in jail as look at him."

"I will Jack, I will, but you know, I think I have the right to handle my questioning of prospective jurors any way I wish, don't you?"

"Once the trial starts, it's all up to him, Ann. Whatever he says goes, and that's the end of the story."

The next morning, it took little time selecting the remaining members of the jury. By mid-morning the twelve that would listen to the evidence and come to a conclusion concerning the guilt or innocence of Thomas Cline had been seated. The judge gave them some simple instructions they would need to follow while jurors in the case, and it was now time for opening statements.

Once George had completed his statement, Jack stood to make his preliminary comments to the jury in a manner which he had refined and which had been effective as concerned past juries.

Jack outlined basically what he felt each of his defense witnesses would say and did so in some detail. Once he had reached the fifth witness he expected to testify on behalf of the defense, the judge interrupted his opening.

"Wait, wait, wait a minute, Mr. Connors. Are you going to go through each agonizing detail of the testimony of each witness you are going to call?"

Jack turned toward the judge, and said, "That's what I normally do, yes, Judge."

"Well, Mr. Connors, you're not in a normal setting now. Please summarize, in a sentence or two what the witness might say, and move on. I don't want to spend all day on your opening. Can you do that for us?"

"Well, I guess I can but…"

"Good, good then. Do it—starting right…*now*."

Jack continued to stare at the judge, but then slowly turned to the jury panel and quickly finished his opening. Once completed Judge Dunn took a fifteen-minute recess.

They had moved to the conference room and just sat down, when Jack said, "That son-of-a-bitch chopped off my opening. I have *never* had a judge do that—*ever!*"

Ann said, with just the trace of a smile, "Now Jack, just remember, he's the boss. Whatever he says, is just the way it is in his courtroom and that's the end of…"

"Oh, just hush. I know what you're doing. I know those were my exact words to you." He leaned back in his chair. "Guess it's a little harder to take when the shoe's on the other foot."

As they sat around the table waiting for the recess to end and the first witness to begin testifying, Ann thought back on the proceedings of the last couple of days. It hadn't started as she had hoped.

The judge was obviously going to closely watch everything both of them said and did. Hopefully what they did in his courtroom for the next few days would by and large be acceptable. It would be difficult enough to win the case on a level playing field, but it would become even *more* difficult with the judge criticizing every move the defense team made.

Chapter 26

It was *Deja vu* all over again, as they waited patiently for his highness to walk through his chambers door and start the day's proceedings.

Late yesterday afternoon, they had concluded the medical examiner's testimony. She had testified the victim had died as a result of a single stab wound to the midsection. She further testified Jean Cline had staggered into her bedroom apparently trying to reach her phone and died there, on the floor. There were no defensive wounds, or bruising of any nature noticed on her body, indicating to the medical examiner the stabbing had taken place in a sudden, unpredictable manner. She was also allowed, by stipulation of both parties, to testify that fingerprints found on the letter opener were those of the defendant.

There was little cross-examination of her by the defense. All the testimony she gave was based on information she had already provided both parties, and was not the type of evidence that was subject to speculation or conjecture—much of it was based on science and was irrefutable.

This morning they would begin the session with testimony from officer John Malloy, the individual that took the complaint concerning the noise issue which arose before the defendant and his wife had separated.

Ann had discussed, with Jack, the possibility of handling cross- examine of Officer Malloy and he had opined that she should—that it would be good experience for her. Once direct examination by the state had been completed, the judge said, "Cross by the defense?"

Ann stood and said, "Yes, Your Honor."

"You're going to cross-examine him?"

"I am."

"Oh, *this* should be interesting."

Ann could feel the blood rush to her face and her temper getting the best of her. She tried to suppress the words from tumbling out of her mouth, but she just couldn't help it, as she said, "And why's that, Your Honor?"

He looked over his glasses at her and said, "Just proceed. This isn't question and answer time. Proceed and I'll discuss it with you later."

"Sure Judge, that's just what I'll do."

Jack was sitting next to her. He reached over, grabbed her hand, and squeezed. She pulled away and approached the witness.

As she did, the judge said, "You mind *asking* me if you could approach? You know that's the proper procedure, don't you?"

She stopped. "Might I approach, Your Honor?"

"That's far enough. Proceed."

"Sure, that's just what I'll do."

The judge started to say something, but Ann started questioning the witness before the words came out. He let her continue.

"So, as I understand your testimony Officer Malloy, you talked to both the defendant and Ms. Cline, is that correct?"

"Yes."

"That was the first time you met them?"

"Yes."

"Did you visit with them separately?"

"Yes."

"As I understand your testimony, there was no physical violence involved—just a lot of yelling. Is that correct?"

"Yes."

"What did you determine as concerned previous physical violence between the two of them?"

"There had been none."

"And there wasn't this time either, right?"

"No."

"Was there any indication from either of them that the relationship between the two, might, at some point in time, turn violent?"

He thought for a moment before he answered. "Really, no there wasn't. I didn't feel it was anything other than a shouting match between the two of them. They both appeared to me to be nonviolent. I was not concerned they would harm each other."

"It had to have been a shock when you heard he had been charged with her murder."

The judge put his pen down and said, "Well now, is that a question or an answer, Ms. Connors?"

"*Was it*, a shock to learn he was charged with her murder?"

"Thank you, Ms. Connors."

"Yes, ma'am, it was a shock. I never expected that to happen."

"Normally, with others that you have investigated for murdering their spouse, was there at least *some* indication of violence prior to the killing?"

"Well, really there is no 'normal' concerning this type of crime, but most of the time, yes, there is at least some indication they could hurt each other."

"Was there with the Clines?"

He looked at the prosecutor, then back at Ann as he said, "No, there was nothing to indicate either of them would turn to violence."

"Nothing further, Your Honor."

"Any additional questions from the state?"

"No, Your Honor."

"Next witness."

The state then called Officer Ray Thomas to the stand. Through direct examination, he testified he was the one that arrived at the murder scene first and subsequently arrested Thomas Cline. His testimony on direct lasted until midafternoon.

Once direct examination had been completed, the judge looked at Jack and said, "Who's going to handle this one, you or the girl?"

As Ann started to stand, Jack said, "I am, Your Honor", and he quickly stood before Ann could say a word.

Ann sat back down as Jack said, "Now officer, as I understand the situation, you were unable to locate any other evidence at the scene whatsoever. It's my understanding the only item at the scene that pertained to the murder and could be considered as evidence was the letter opener, is that correct?"

"Yes."

"There were no other identifiable prints on the letter opener as I understand it, except for the victim, the defendant, and one print that couldn't be matched up to anyone else, correct?"

"Yes."

"Did you make any effort to determine whom that other print belonged to?"

"Not really. The defendant's prints were identified, there had been prior conflict between the two of them involving officers, they were estranged, he was seen leaving the house around the time of the murder—we felt we had all we needed."

"When you arrested him, did he resist?"

"No."

"Has there ever been any indication of violence as concerns the defendant, that you turned up in his past or that he has exhibited while in your custody?"

"No."

"Has the defendant ever admitted he had anything to do with her death, or that he was upset, or angry at her for any reason?"

"No."

"Nothing further, Your Honor."

The next witness, June Good, was a neighbor living next door to the rental Mrs. Cline occupied. She most likely wouldn't take much time. They had all agreed that at the conclusion of her testimony, court would be in recess until Monday morning.

Her testimony was short and straightforward. She happened to be up late the night of the murder and had seen Thomas drive away from the house.

Once direct examination was completed by George, Jack stood to cross-examine the witness.

"Ma'am I have just a few questions. Had you met the victim, Mrs. Cline?"

"Yes. She was really a nice lady. I liked her."

"Had you met the defendant, Mr. Cline?"

"Yes. I only visited with him a couple of times. I liked him. I just couldn't believe he killed her—she was such a nice lady."

Jack smiled and said, "Well, ma'am that's what we're here to figure out. It hasn't been established he killed her yet—that's what we're trying to sort out here today. Now, was there ever a time the defendant exhibited a temper, or any violent tendencies that you observed?"

"Well, no, not that I can remember. But I just wasn't around him or her hardly at all. I don't watch my neighbors much. I have better things to do with my time than watch my neighbors."

"Did you hear or see *anything* that night that might shed some light on what happened in that house?"

"No, nothing at all other than what I have already said."

"As I recall there's just an empty lot on the other side of the house that Ms. Cline was living in, correct?"

"Yes."

"No other homes across the street from her?"

"No."

"I have nothing further, Your Honor."

Court recessed after her testimony. They would reconvene Monday morning.

On the way home, Ann said, "Jack, I assume you and most likely everyone that's part of the proceedings, can tell it's taking everything I have, to remain in the same room with Judge Dunn. He's clearly a misogynist. He clearly hates everything I'm doing. I just have no idea how to handle him."

"You're doing fine. Just keep up what you're doing. You're not backing down, and yet you're not over the top with your comments or actions either. You're doing fine. You did a good job with that witness today. I'll probably have you handle Edward. I'll take our client and you can handle him. You up for it?"

She thought for a moment. "I think so. It's going to be interesting handling him *and* the judge at the same time, but I'll do what I can."

"I think the appropriate approach with Edward is to get him on and off the stand as quickly as we can. I'll talk to the prosecutor and tell him the purpose of Edward's testimony is strictly as concerns his relationship with Thomas and what he observed involving Thomas and his wife. I'll just tell him he should know that Edward loses his temper quickly—to be careful when he cross-examines him. You should be fine."

"It was a good thing you held me down when you did. I was ready to completely blow up. I had had all I could take."

"I know that. But it appears to me we're making a little headway in the case. I can't let you lose it in front of that jury."

She looked out the window. "I know that. I know that, Jack. I'm really trying to remain calm and cool about the situation, but he makes it tough. He really makes it difficult."

She would, however, exercise a greater degree of restraint from now on. She had taken the best he had to offer, and she had persevered. Ann concluded she had already lost one major case in her short career. She definitely didn't want to lose another one simply because of her inability to control her own temper.

Chapter 27

Saturday for Ann, normally meant relaxation—literally nothing on the agenda for most, if not all of the day. However, Sally had called midweek and wanted to go shopping. She needed a couple of new dresses for business purposes related to her husband's occupation. Ann had reluctantly agreed to go along.

Her frequent invitations to shop were becoming somewhat of a predictable, uncomfortable cycle. Sally would diet, lose weight and buy new clothes based upon her new-found, sheik figure. Then she would quit dieting, gain weight and want new clothes to cover her larger figure. Today was the fourth time Sally had altered directions in the past few months, and its constant reoccurrence would be a topic Ann would touch upon today.

After a couple of hours of looking, and buying, Ann suggested they walk to one of the coffee shops in the mall and relax for a while before proceeding onward, a suggestion Sally readily accepted.

Once seated, Ann said, "You know, you're stuck in this never-ending routine, don't you? You lose weight, you buy, you gain weight, you buy. Is this all some part of an overall plan, or is this all just an unplanned reaction to your never-ending cycle of gaining and losing weight?"

Sally laughed. "I guess I am becoming a little predictable, aren't I? One of these days it won't matter. One of these days I'll just move on up to about 200 pounds and forget about it. But until then, it's going to be a roller coaster ride". She winked as she said, "And a ride I'm just glad you're taking with me,"

"I hope you know that I, along with many others who call you their friend, don't give a shit whether you weigh 50 or 500. We all love you with all your faults, just the way you are. Certainly, today though, it's been good being with you and getting my mind off all that's going on. It's been a long week."

"So how are things with Jack?"

"Good. We're trying that case in Wilson County together. Just started this week. It'll probably continue for another few weeks."

"How's it going?"

"It's a tough case, but everything's going as well as can be expected."

"Are you actually participating in it? After losing that last case, will Jack even let you be a part of this one?"

She glared at Sally as she said, "Hell yes, Sally. You know, we all lose one on occasion."

"Well, I know, but you're like batting zero—you've never won a case. I would think he would want you to have a little more experience under your belt before you took on another one and screwed it up too."

"That Kingston case isn't over yet. Why don't you wait until it's really over to declare me the loser?"

Sally said, "Sure, sure I'll wait until then before I determine you lost. Good idea. By the way, you and Jack talked about kids yet?"

"You know, your mind is like a buzz saw. No matter what happens or what's said, you just keep on cuttin' those logs. Do you mean *having them*?"

"Yep."

"Hell no. I've just been out of law school a matter of months. My boss just died. I'm learning more about my relationship with Jack every day, which is a good thing by the way. I just inherited a law practice, which is hard to believe. Jack wants to start up a partnership which I am really apprehensive about, so *no* we sure as hell haven't even discussed starting a family."

Sally, as if she were releasing a secret she had just heard on the street, whispered, "Well, you know you're not getting any younger—you do realize that don't you."

"Don't even go there, Sally. Change the subject. How are your kids? They doing well? I need to stop by and see them. It's been a while."

"They're good. Growing like crazy. What about that partnership you talked about? Is that moving forward? When's Jack going to set up his practice with you?"

"We're hoping right after the first of the year. Beth is still trying to figure out how extensive the change is really going to be—she's still trying to determine whether we'll need additional help."

Sally looked around for a moment, then looked at Ann and said, "You know I have skills in that area. I..."

"Wait a minute, just wait a minute. You could no more keep up with us in that office than you could pilot a plane. You need to take care of your husband and your kids Sally, at least for the foreseeable future—just as you have been, just as you love doing. When they're out of the house, maybe we can talk."

"Okay, okay I have no doubt you're right, but if you need some part-time help, I'd be glad..."

"I'll keep you in mind."

"By the way, did you guys ever find a house you both agreed upon?"

"I told you we bought one, didn't I? I'm just sure I told you."

"No. As usual when it comes to the gigantic things in life you are involved in, you never tell me anything. Which one? Where's it at?"

"It's a small craftsman on the west side. I thought maybe the townhouse in the Gulch area was what I wanted, but Jack wanted this one. It took some time, but now I really think his choice was better than mine."

"That's great. We can help you move if you need us. So now, with a house, you might even be able to get a dog. I know you've mentioned that before, but it was hard to have one when you lived in an apartment. When do you close?"

"Middle of January. I can't wait. Yes, a dog is a distinct possibility." She looked away. "I haven't had one since...since..." She turned to Sally and said, "But right now I don't have time to even think about any of these things—way too much going on. The house was our Christmas present to each other. We're both really excited."

"I can imagine. Is it big enough for kids?"

"No, it's not—as if that, at this point in time, means anything. No it's not that big. We'll just have to look elsewhere if I get pregnant, which isn't in the plans for at least another couple of years."

Sally digested that pertinent bit of information, then said, "By the way, something I forgot to ask you earlier. Whatever happened to that Kingston kid? He still in prison?"

"Thanks for bringing that up. One of the worst events in my life—thanks a lot. But to answer your question, yes that's where he is. I filed my motion for new trial. The state hasn't filed a response, and the judge hasn't contacted either of us. I'm waiting for the investigator to contact me. He thought he was on to something the last time I talked to him, but as of yet, I've heard nothing."

"Not to change the subject, but, you know, I've thought about your wedding so many times in the past weeks. That was such an incredible event. The setting was beautiful, the food, the entertainment, it was all perfection."

"Don't worry about changing the subject with each new question you ask. I've become used to that particular character flaw of yours over the years. Now, in response to your most recent topic of discussion, yes, it was." She hesitated for a moment, then said, "That was a high light of my life. I love Gatlinburg. I love everything about it. We would spend a lot of time there if we could."

"Gets pretty cold there this time of year. Probably just want to go during the summer months."

"I don't think the season would make much difference to us. Even if it's cold, you could start a fire in the fireplace, grab a good book and curl up until you had to cook a little food. Or, you could walk the shops most of the day, come back late in the afternoon, crank up the fire, and get cozy while it's warming up the room."

"You make it sound like heaven."

"For me, that's what it is." She looked away, as she said, "The next time we can get away, whether it's a special occasion or just a vacation, that's where we're going—back to Gatlinburg."

Chapter 28

Ann had scheduled a meeting for this morning at 8:00 a.m. The judge had decided he had something more important to do than start his week with a murder trial. As a result, he had determined they would not reconvene until Tuesday morning, which left this morning open. She sat in her office waiting for Beth to arrive, and for Jack to finally get off the phone and find his way to her office.

It was pretty obvious who *didn't* carry any clout around here. She wasn't sure who the office boss was, but clearly it wasn't her. They were both already late for the meeting *she* had called. Maybe next time they needed to have one, she could somehow, subtly suggest that one of *them* call a meeting so they might get this shit all straightened out. Maybe they would both be on time if one of *them* called it.

Beth walked in the front office door five minutes later.

She yelled, "You two want to get a cup of coffee and then come on in?"

Jack peeked his head around her door frame and said, "What for?"

"Dammit, Jack I told both you and Beth I thought we should sit down early this morning and discuss where we're at. We got a break from the trial, but I have appointments starting at ten and lasting all day. Now, do you want to have a meeting or not? What do you want to do?"

"Sure, sure I'll meet with you. Let me get Beth."

He heard some whispering in the reception area and figured they were discussing the fact they had both forgotten the meeting. Ann's conclusion was confirmed once they began a discussion concerning why Beth was late.

"Sorry, sorry, I couldn't get out of my apartment building or I would have been here on time. Sorry."

"Oh really. What happened?"

She hesitated, clearly shocked her boss wanted the details.

"Oh, you know, just things happening…just stuff going on. You know."

"Just sit. *Jack, where are you?*"

He walked in, sat down, and said, "Okay boss, what's up?"

"Glad you could both make it. I want to make sure we're all on the same page here. As of the first of February, we will change the name to Connors and Connors. The accountant is making the necessary changes to a partnership rather than a sole proprietorship, correct Beth?"

"Yes. He has everything under control. I'll need to set up new bank accounts before then and provide our new number to them. I'm also changing the letterhead. I've lined up someone to put the appropriate name on the door. I think most everything else is ready to go, Ann. There are going to be a few things we need to handle as we go along, but I think we'll be fine. I have a new girl set to start the first of February. If the business grows like I think it will, we're going to need a bigger office. I'll put the new girl in the back, until we figure out what we're going to do."

"Great. Any thoughts, Jack?"

"Not really. Sounds like Beth has it under control."

"I think we really have a busy day. So, Beth, why don't you go ahead and open up while I talk to Jack about a couple of things."

Beth quickly stood. As she left the room, Jack said, "What's up? What do we need to talk about? I need to get back to my other office. I've got a ton of stuff to do. I'm just starting to get everything finished up there."

"Have you talked to the title company lately? Are we all ready to close on the house?"

"Yes, we've done all we need to do except provide our money. They said as soon as all the costs were figured out—our share of closing costs—things of that nature, they would email a closing statement and we could wire the funds. That's probably not going to happen until near the end of January. Don't worry about it. I'll handle that. Just know that everything is on course for a closing the first of February."

"We haven't talked much about actually moving, but since we don't have to move furniture, since most of it stays with our apartment, I assume we can line up a couple of pickups and move what's ours by ourselves, correct?"

"Yes. A couple of guys at work said they would help. It shouldn't be a big deal at all. We're going to have to buy what else we need, but I figure you and I can handle that between now and the first of February."

She smiled. "I can't wait. I just can't wait."

He stood. "You finished with me? I need to get to work."

"Sit for a minute, will you? What about the trial? Are you feeling okay with where we're at?"

He sat, as he said, "Not really. We just don't have that big kick at the end I wish we had. We just don't have anyone to say they were with our client about the time of the murder, or anything that really creates that question for the jury as to whether he really did or didn't do it. That concerns me."

"It does me too. And something else that bothers me is the testimony concerning that other fingerprint on the letter opener. *That really* concerns me. Who else would there have been in that house that would have messed with a letter opener unless it was to stab her? If we take our clients word that he didn't do it, then that fingerprint most likely belongs to the murderer."

"They apparently tried to run it, but had no match. And, of course they really didn't care whether it matched up or not, because they all believed they had the right man. But I'm not sure there's a damn thing we can do about it now. What are we going to do now? It's a little late in the game."

"I don't know much about trial practice yet, but I just figured it was never too late if you're on the right side, and I really believe we are."

"So, what do you want to do?"

"You heard me tell Matt Armstrong I might have another case for him, didn't you? I think we should ask Thomas if he'll pay the bill, or if Edward will, so that we can have Matt look into this."

"He may not have the time to do it. Of course, as slowly as this trial is going, we may not be finished until next May. By the way, I'm considering filing a complaint against the judge if he delays this much longer, especially if he delays it as long as he said he's going to. There's no reason for this. But, as concerns an investigation, if Matt has the time, if he can get right on it, and Thomas will pay the bill, let's get it going. We have nothing to lose."

"Okay, I'll try to get ahold of him yet today. If he's working on our case up in Kentucky we may have an issue getting him back here to work on this case, but I'll find out what his timetable might be. Obviously, if he can't start until after the first of the year, we're out. I'll check with him and we can talk about it tonight when we both get home. What do you think about getting someone else if he can't do it? Do you know anyone else?"

"No. I've never used anyone but Matt, and to be honest, this is probably not a good time to line up someone new. I just hope he can do it for us."

Jack stood as she said, "I'll see you tonight."

She stood, walked around the front of her desk, and kissed him. "You know Jack, I have a feeling someone else was in that house. I feel like if we can somehow figure out who that fingerprint belongs to, the complexion of the whole case may change. I just hope we can figure something out soon, because I'm really concerned that without some new evidence, Thomas is going to find himself in amongst a society of criminals that will eat him alive. If he's found guilty, I'm afraid no matter how long his sentence, as timid as he is, and considering those animals he'll be living with, he'll never make it out of prison alive."

Chapter 29

The trial continued on Tuesday morning. The state introduced testimony from a couple of additional police officers who testified concerning their involvement in the investigation. Both offered little as concerned significant evidence. But apparently the prosecution felt their testimony was necessary and, as a result, both Jack and Ann were obligated to listen and object, if need be.

The morning proceeded slowly, as she listened to testimony that was not going to break or make the state's case, all the while waiting for a return call from Matt Armstrong. As noon approached, Jack leaned over and whispered, "What should we do over the noon hour? You want to stay in the conference room with our client or should we let him go back to his cell and go eat somewhere ourselves?"

"Let's stay with him. I'm still waiting for Matt's call, but let's go through all of that with Thomas, so when Matt does call, we know where we're at."

That seemed to suit Jack. Once the judge indicated they would take their noon recess, the four of them walked into the conference room across the hallway.

As they all sat down around the table, Ann said, "Thomas, we need to discuss a matter with you involving the case which hasn't been discussed. Once we explain, Jack, maybe you can go get these guys a sandwich. I have something else I need to do before we reconvene."

"What do we need to discuss, Ms. Connors?"

"Well, Jack and I have been talking, and even though we're well into the trial, it's moving slowly enough that we believe we have time to hire an investigator to look into this a little further."

"Really? Why now? What's changed?"

Jack leaned back in his chair, and said, "We're really concerned about whose fingerprint, other than yours, was on that letter opener. We have a feeling it might belong to the murderer."

"But they made it clear they had no match. If they couldn't figure it out, why do you think we can?"

"Thomas, we don't think they tried. They had you. You were the most likely. They stopped investigating when you were arrested and they felt they had all the proof they needed."

"So, what do we need to do?"

"At this point, the question is can you pay for the guy to do the investigation. Do you have the money to pay him?"

"Do you really believe this is necessary?"

"Yes. We believe, strongly, that this is an important issue. Now, that doesn't mean the investigation will turn anything up, because it certainly may not, but we feel it's important enough to pursue."

Thomas thought for only a moment, before he said, "Yes, sure, go ahead. I have the money. I've been able to accumulate a little money because we never had children and we lived very frugally. I guess this is important enough to spend it on."

Ann stood and said, "Great. I'll get right on it. Jack, if you want to get something for them to eat, I'll meet you back here before court reconvenes."

"Where're you going?"

As she walked out the door she said, "See you in about an hour."

While walking toward the clerk's office, her cell buzzed. She pulled it from her pocket and noticed it was Matt Armstrong.

"Matt, thanks for returning my call."

"No problem. I'm still in Kentucky. I've got a lot of news for you. I should be home tomorrow."

"Great. That's not why I called, but that's certainly good news. I need to know if you can squeeze in a quick investigation for us. I've talked to our client, he can pay the bill, and it's urgent that it be done asap."

"Oh, hell I don't know. I've been gone and I know my desk must be a mess. Can we meet tomorrow or Thursday?"

"The case I want you to investigate is being tried as we speak, but we're off tomorrow. Can you come to my office? I'll have Jack there—maybe around ten or so?"

"I'll see you then."

Ann walked in the clerk's office and said, "Is Mark working today?"

As she finished her sentence, Mark walked out of the back room. "Someone mention my name?"

"Hi, Mark. We're on noon break. You have time for a cup of coffee. I just wanted to get away from it all for a few moments."

"Absolutely. Come on back. Janice, I'll be back here with Ann for a few minutes. Can you handle everything while I'm with her?"

She nodded her approval. Ann walked into the back room, grabbed a cup and filled it up.

As she took a chair, Mark said, "How's the trial coming along?"

"Oh fine. We seem to be taking quite a few breaks, but your dad's the boss, so we just kind of go with the flow. Hopefully we'll finish before spring."

Mark laughed. "Yep, if dad's the presiding judge, there will certainly be no other boss but him."

"You have any siblings Mark, or are you, like me, the only one."

"Just me. They had me and that was the end of having kids. I think I was one and done. After they had me, they didn't want any more."

Ann laughed. "You go to school here?"

"Actually, I did. Dad lived in Nashville for a while before I was born, but he moved here, met mom and I've lived here all my life."

"Why did your dad leave Nashville?"

"You know, he's never mentioned anything about it to me. Mom told me he got in a little trouble there. Nothing that amounted to much, but after that happened, he left and moved here. That was all she ever said."

"They been divorced long?"

"Quite a while, yes, I'd say maybe ten years. He didn't treat her very well. She finally said she'd had enough and took off.

She lives in California now. I talk to her most every day. I'll probably move out there in a few years, once I get a little money built up."

"You live at home?"

"Yes, I do, but that too is going to change before long. I really don't want to live with him any longer. He's a little difficult to live with."

"You know, I'm certain I've met your dad somewhere. That's why I wanted to talk to you about him. It's driving me crazy. I never forget a face…ever…and I've met him, but I cannot remember where. It'll come, but for now I'm just at a loss."

Ann spent the rest of the noon hour visiting with Mark. The conversation flowed easily between the two of them until it was time for her to return to the conference room.

Once she arrived, she told Thomas the investigator would meet with her tomorrow morning. They would then hopefully hire him to do the job. Either way, she would let Thomas know what happened later in the day.

The state rested right before noon. It was time to introduce evience on behalf of the defense. The first witness would be Edward. She would examine him. She was somewhat anxious about trying to handle him and the judge at the same time, but it had to be done, and she would get it done or die trying.

Chapter 30

And so it began.

She would need to force the words from her mouth. She needed something to drink. She needed to try once again. *This time*, if her voice failed to cooperate, she would need to ask Jack to examine Edward Cline. "Please…please… state your name."

"Edward Cline."

"And where do you reside, Mr. Cline?"

"Here, in Lebanon."

"How long have you lived here?"

Slowly, but surely, she was returning to the land of the living. She had been so nervous about examining him, she had almost forgot what to do.

But now, now that she had started, it wasn't so terrifying. She continually glanced at the judge waiting for him to make some type of caustic comment. But he seemed content to let her run with Edward, hoping, she assumed, she would just hang herself without any intervention from him.

After some additional, irrelevant, but necessary, foundational questions, she slowly moved toward the reason for putting him on the stand in the first place.

"Are you related to the defendant in this case, and if so, how?"

"He's, my brother."

"Do you have any other siblings?"

"No, it's just the two of us. It's always been just the two of us—in many ways."

"Now, Mr. Cline just answer the question Ms. Connors asks you, nothing more."

"I can do that, Judge, but I just felt that was something she should know."

"I understand. Again, answer what she asks you. We don't need to know what *you* think we should know."

Edward turned and looked at the judge with distain. Quickly Ann asked her next question.

"Are you older or younger than your brother?"

"I'm a year older."

"Can you tell us how Thomas ended up here, in Lebanon, if you know?"

"I suggested he move here. I like it here. They were moving, so I suggested they consider Lebanon."

"And by 'they' I assume you mean his wife and himself, correct?"

"Yes. I was close to both of them. I felt Lebanon would work for them as it has for me."

"Again, Mr. Cline, answer only the question you are asked, nothing more. This is the last time I'm going to tell you."

Edward turned toward Judge Dunn and said, "Look. How is this story going to be told if you keep cutting me off? I need to explain the details she doesn't ask about, it's that simple."

The judge first looked at him, then turned toward Ann and said, "We're going to take a fifteen-minute break. When we come back, if he offers any more of an answer then is called for, and by the way, I will be the one determining that, not you, I'll throw him in jail for contempt. Do you understand?"

"I do, Your Honor."

"Good for you." He looked at the jury and smiled as he said, "Court's in recess for 15 minutes. When we reconvene, you will be allowed to continue to listen to the testimony of Edward Cline. How much of it you end up hearing will be up to him."

Once back in the conference room, Ann looked at Edward who was pacing back and forth near the windows, and said, "Do you understand what he's saying, Edward? You can't say anything beyond what it takes to answer the question I ask you. I'll eventually get around to asking you questions which involve everything you want to say at some point or other, but in that room it's his rules, and he's made it quite clear you're breaking one of them. Do you understand what he's saying to you?"

He stopped and faced her. "Hell yes, I understand. But I need to get this story out. I need to explain why Thomas couldn't have been the one that did this and why he doesn't even deserve to be charged. That jury needs to know. That son-of-a-bitch sitting behind that big desk of his, needs to know."

He started pacing again.

"You're never going to get your story out, or tell the court how you feel about your bother, if you continue the way you are. He'll throw you in jail and have a hearing concerning whether or not you were in contempt a week after this trial ends. We need you to do this and do it right. Doing it right means following his rules."

He stopped walking as he turned to look out the window.

He whispered, "This is just so unfair, so unfair."

She walked up beside him, and said, "I know, I understand, but we have no choice. If you're going to testify and get your story told, we need to follow the rules while we're in his courtroom. There's no other way this can be done."

He hesitated briefly, before he said, "I understand."

Upon reconvening and upon Edward's return to the stand, questioning him went much smoother, with the judge finding it unnecessary to intervene.

After asking a series of questions which were designed more to make sure Edward was comfortable in his chair, rather than provide meaningful testimony about the case, Ann said, "So Edward, tell us about your brother. How's your relationship with him? Have you ever noticed a propensity for him to be violent at any stage of his life?"

"Never."

"Describe, if you would, his demeanor."

Ann was somewhat concerned the prosecutor would object to this whole line of questioning. She was also concerned the judge would be inclined to sustain the objection. But when he failed to object to the initial testimony offered by Edward, she decided to continue on until someone stopped her.

"He's always been a wonderful brother, a good husband, a friend to everyone who needed one. This whole situation with his wife is just so far removed from anything he would have done at any point in his life. I don't know who did this horrible thing to her, but it couldn't have been my brother. He would never, ever, hurt anyone and certainly not his wife."

"What type of relationship did you observe between the two of them?"

"Great."

"Please explain."

"Obviously they were having a few problems near the end, but it was nothing they couldn't have worked out if she had lived. All of us have marital problems at some time in our lives. They did too, but they would have worked things out if she had lived. That's just the kind of relationship they had. They worked things out, whether it was what they were having for supper, or whether it was to move to Lebanon. I never saw my brother raise his voice, let alone hurt anyone."

After a few additional questions concerning their relationship, she deferred to George for cross-examination.

He stood, as he said, "How often would you see the defendant and his wife before they moved here?"

"Oh, I don't know—maybe a couple of times a year."

"So, during that time period, you really had no idea what was going on inside their home on a day-by-day basis did you?"

Edward thought for a moment before answering. "No, I guess not. I didn't live with them."

"You're aware of the altercation they had when the police were called, aren't you?"

"You mean the one right before she moved out?"

"Yes."

"Well, he just said they were having some problems. Then later, she moved out, but that's about all I know."

"Was that type of activity, and by that, I mean arguments or problems between them and her moving out, normal?"

"No, it wasn't normal."

"So wouldn't you agree then, that something had changed— that something must have happened to have caused that radical a departure in their relationship?"

Edward looked away, hesitating before he answered.

"I don't know."

"His wife had *never* left him, had she?"

"Not that I know about, no."

"So, the couple you knew in the past, and the relationship you were aware of, somewhere along the way had changed, is that a fair statement?"

"I guess, yes, I guess so."

"And would it be fair to say that the change may have resulted in her death? Is it fair to say that whatever caused this change, might have generated feelings between the two of them that resulted in this violent act, and caused your brother to do something you would have, in the past, never thought possible? *Could* that have been the case?"

Again, Edward looked away.

The judge said, "Answer the question, Mr. Cline."

"I guess it could have. But I'm telling you no matter *what* happened, my brother could never have killed another human being, never."

"Nothing further, Judge."

On redirect, Ann asked a few more questions concerning Edward's response to questions asked by the district attorney, but nothing that resulted in an earthshattering answer.

Later, on their way back to Nashville, Ann said, "What'd you think of Edward's testimony?"

Jack said, "I don't believe we can rely on it to work any miracles for us. What'd you think?"

"I thought it would turn out better than it did. No, I don't think he really did us any favors. I think he did what he could, but George's cross didn't help. All in all, it's pretty clear to me Thomas better be convincing when *he* testifies. Because if he isn't, unless Matt can come up with something at this late date, I'm afraid it's going to take a hell of a lot more than you and I can provide, to keep him out of jail for the rest of his life."

Chapter 31

Ann sat at her desk, wondering where to begin. Court would not reconvene until 1:00 p.m. tomorrow, and then, because of Christmas, would not reconvene until the following Tuesday. Both George and Jack had commented how unusual it had been that the trial was continued as often it had been. Of course, as Jack had discussed with her, it really made no difference to them—at this point, the more time they had, the better.

But George was incensed at the time it was taking to try the case. He made it clear he would file a complaint with the bar association concerning the judge's actions in stopping and starting the trial as many times as he had.

Matt Armstrong indicated he would be in her office at 8:00 a.m. Ann had no doubt he would be on time, as he was the last time she met with him.

She heard Beth walk in the front office door. As soon as she sat down, Matt arrived.

Ann messaged Beth to send Matt in.

"Morning."

"Morning, Matt. Have a seat. Cup of coffee?"

"No thanks. I don't have much time. I have too many things I need to do. The office was insane while I was gone."

"Okay then let's get right to it. First of all, what about Randall's case?"

"Well, that was an interesting trip—the one I took to Paducah."

"What happened?"

"I already knew when I got there, that we had a conflict in the facts. I already knew they had lied about where they came from and about their ages, so I knew something just wasn't right before I ever hit town."

"I think I spoke with you right after you had figured that out. You told me then that something was wrong."

"Correct. So, when I got to Paducah, I started nosing around and found out those three kids were inseparable when they lived in Paducah. I drove by the homes where all three lived. They were all from households that weren't well off financially. I couldn't find out much about any of them, until I talked to one of my cop friends. He told me the department had heard some rumors about that Cartwright girl, along with one of the banker's sons that lived in town."

Ann leaned forward in her chair. "This is starting to get really interesting. Go on."

"So, I went to the bank and made an appointment with that kid's father. When I met with him, I told him what I was doing, and also told him that I had heard something about his kid and this Cartwright girl."

"What'd he say?"

"He walked over and opened his office door. Then he told me to leave. I told him to relax, not to worry, that I would keep everything in confidence. He still asked me to leave. He said he couldn't talk to me about anything."

"Did you leave?"

"Didn't have a choice."

"What'd you do then? Because at this point, we have nothing more than we did, other than they lied about their age and residence."

"Just wait. About ten that night, I got a call at the motel. I had told the banker if he changed his mind, to call me at the hotel, but that I was leaving for home late the next day. I told him if he needed to contact me, to do so before I left town."

"How did he respond?"

"He told me had talked to his attorney at length, and his attorney told him to call me and tell me everything. He said this Cartwright girl had contacted him about a year ago. She told him his son had raped her and she was filing charges."

"*You are kidding? Had* he raped her?"

"Not according to his son. He had been with her, but there was no sex involved whatsoever. The banker told her to wait before she filed charges. She told him she would wait for a couple of days. Then she was going to the police."

"What'd he do?"

"He called her back a few days later. They agreed on a figure. He paid her off. Then later he heard she, along with those two boys that testified for her here, left town together. He just felt, because the town wasn't that big and because of the publicity a rape trial would generate, being the president of the bank, he couldn't afford to let her file the charge."

"Holy shit, that's exactly what she did here—that the *three* of them did here. The only difference is here they never were given the opportunity to blackmail Randall's parents, and in Paducah they were. I'm assuming everything just got away from them here and they ended up having to go through the trial."

"Exactly."

"So, she's clearly a liar and she lied on the stand. She said nothing like this had ever happened to her before. She flat out lied about that."

"When I told the banker the story concerning what was going on here, he was livid. But I did get him to agree to sit tight until I contacted him. Both he and his son will testify or do whatever is necessary to stop the three of them."

"Well, I think the next thing we better do is meet with the prosecutor and tell him what we know. Hopefully, we can work something out with the judge and get this all stopped before it goes any further. I'll contact him, then contact you as to a time you might meet with him."

"That will work. Now, what about this case you have going on in Lebanon. By the way, when are you going to start calling me *before* the trial starts?"

Ann laughed. "Really, I didn't think we were going to need your help in this one, but some issues have come up we're a little concerned about. We're just not sure if you can help us."

"Tell me about it."

Ann took a sip of coffee, set her cup down, leaned back and said, "Our client is charged with murdering his wife. They were estranged, and she was murdered in the home she was living in."

"Is this in Lebanon?"

"Yes."

"Her husband was seen coming out of the house that night. She was stabbed with a letter opener which had his prints on it."

"Okay, now that's probably not a good thing for your side."

She smiled and said, "Very astute, Mr. Armstrong. Let me finish. The letter opener had his prints, her prints, and one other print that was never matched up with anyone. I think they probably did a rush to judgement—the couple was estranged, he was there near the time she was murdered, his prints were on the murder weapon. They just figured it was him, and to be honest, why wouldn't they."

"Sounds to me like it's a done deal. What do you need me for?"

"That other print—that other print on that letter opener. There's little doubt in my mind our client didn't do it, and if there's someone else's print on that letter opener, it most likely belongs to our murderer."

He shrugged his shoulders. "Maybe—maybe not. Again, what do you want me to do?"

"Ask around. See if maybe there were other people coming and going from that house and who they might be."

"But really, if the cops can't match up that print, what good is it going to do?"

"Let's take things one at a time. Can you help us? And remember we're in the middle of his trial. Time is short."

"Can he pay me?"

"Yes. He's already agreed to pay whatever your fees are."

"I guess I can put off the other work I'm doing and concentrate on this for a few days But I'm not going to promise you anything."

"I understand. Now, I don't know much about the neighbors concerning either house, but that might be where you want to start. Also, his wife seemed to have developed some new friends after she and her husband separated so you can take a look there too."

"I'll do what I can, but I'm still a little confused about how this fingerprint is going to fit into the mix. Let me see what I can find out. I'll probably start later today. Also, what's the next step in the Kingston matter?"

"I'll contact the prosecutor. Maybe we can set up a meeting with myself, you and him. We'll just see what he says and how he wants to proceed from here."

Matt left shortly thereafter.

Later that afternoon, Jack who had been in court in Nashville, returned to the office. He wanted to know about Matt—could he help with the Wilson County case—what he found out about the Kingston issues.

She told him about the new information concerning Randall. He was surprised and pleased with the change in direction the case had taken. She also told him Matt was starting on the Cline matter later today and would keep in touch as he moved through the process.

Jack was glad Matt was starting immediately, but was also quick to point out the chance of coming up with something at this point in time, was extremely slim.

She suggested, from now on, it might be appropriate if he would provide her with an opinion or fact which she *didn't already know*, rather than wasting her time *pointing out the obvious*.

Chapter 32

"You know, I hope you're not as easy to read in court as you are in your office. You look really tired."

Beth said it with a smile, but Ann had no doubt she was right.

"I didn't get much sleep last night."

"Out late?"

"No."

"I didn't think you were planning on being out last night. You normally tell me when you're doing something fun, something unusual during the evening, and it's not normally during the week. Dream again?"

"Yes. It was a bad one, too."

Beth walked away from Ann's office door. When she returned, it was with a cup of coffee. She walked in, sat down and said,. "Were you up all night?"

"No, but I might as well have been. I think falling asleep for just a couple of hours after waking up is worse than just getting up and staying up."

"It must have been pretty vivid."

"It was. What concerns me is that they seem to be happening more frequently. I don't understand. Sometime, when I get a minute, I'm going to go back to my shrink and visit with him."

"I don't know if you realize it or not, but these seem to be happening in conjunction with court. I've noticed you seem to have them the nights before you go to court. Maybe it didn't happen so much during Randal's trial, but I've noticed now, when you do dream, you normally have a court date in Lebanon the next day."

"Well, that judge probably subconsciously scares the living shit out of me. I know he does consciously, and I can't imagine it's any different subconsciously. Last night, though, added a new dimension."

"What do you mean?"

"I told you that one night I saw his face on mom's killer, right?"

"Yes."

"Last night, he talked to mom before he knocked her to the floor, which has never happened before. His voice sounded just like the judge's voice. Somehow, in my mind I'm identifying Judge Dunn as her killer. I'm really not surprised. Judge Dunn to me is the worst of the worst. As you know, I can't stand him. Apparently, my subconscious has decided to make the judge and the killer one and the same."

"You going to be okay? I mean, you're going to appear before him this afternoon."

"I'll be fine." She looked away, thought for a moment, then said, "I just hope someday, one of these dreams identifying the killer, whoever he is, comes true. I would really like to meet up with the son-of-a-bitch face to face…just once, some day."

She remained silent for a moment, then turned toward Beth, smiled, and said, "Sorry. Sorry, I was somewhere else for a minute there. Now where was I. Oh, Jack is handling the direct of Thomas. So luckily, I don't have much to do. Good thing. I'm so damn tired I can't see straight."

"State your name for the record."

"Thomas Cline."

"And Mr. Cline you're the defendant in this case, aren't you?'

"Yes, I am."

"You kill your wife?"

Thomas looked down before he raised his head and said, "No, I didn't."

Ann saw the judge look up at Jack after he asked the question. Obviously, that ultimate question and resulting answer normally came after considerable lead up. Jack changed his strategy and surprised everyone including Judge Dunn.

"Ever been in trouble, Thomas?"

"No."

"Tell us about your relationship with your wife. Let's break it down. Prior to coming to Lebanon, were you ever separated?"

"No. We were married 21 years and were never apart for any reason."

"Ever another man or woman in either of your lives?"

"No."

"Ever need marriage counselling?"

"No."

"Other than the one incident right before she moved out, have the police ever been called for any reason involving the two of you?"

"Never."

"You have any children, Thomas?"

"No. It's always been just she and I. That's the way we wanted it."

"Why'd she move out?"

"I really don't know. She just said one day she was unhappy. It never went any further than that. I quizzed her about it a number of times. She always just said she needed some time to think things through."

"You ever strike her?"

"Never."

"She ever tell you what she needed to 'think through?'"

He whispered softly, "No, she never did."

"Tell us what happened the night in question."

"I was alone at home. I wanted to see her. I knew it was late, but I didn't figure that would matter. I wanted to see if we could discuss her coming home."

"Go on."

"I got there late in the evening and knocked on the door. No one answered. It was open so I walked in."

Ann looked at the jury. They were glued to his every word.

"I called out to her, because she wasn't in the living room. I looked down and there was the letter opener on the floor. I picked it up because it looked like it had something on it. It was blood."

"Go on, Thomas. What happened then?"

"I walked into the bedroom and saw her lying on the floor. I dropped the letter opener, walked to where she was lying on the floor and touched her. She was…cold… and clearly gone."

"Did you kill your wife, Thomas?"

"No."

"What happened then?"

"I walked out of the house and drove home."

"You remember the drive?"

"No."

"What'd you do when you arrived home?"

"I sat down on the couch and cried."

"Did you call the police?"

"No. What good would that have done, she was dead."

"Didn't you think reporting her murder to them as quickly as possible so they could start investigating, was important?"

"Why? I didn't care who did it. She was dead. That was all that mattered."

"Was there anyone you were aware of that might have been upset with your wife—anyone that might have wanted to harm her?"

"No."

"Had you had a recent argument with her?"

"No. In fact we were getting along so well she had talked of coming home. I was going to talk to her that night about doing that very thing."

"Have you ever had a physical confrontation with anyone?"

He looked away, then looked down as he whispered, "No."

"Did you kill your wife, Thomas?"

He never even looked up, as he whispered, "No."

"I believe that's all, Your Honor."

"Cross, Mr. Whitney?"

"Yes, Judge, just a few questions—this will be short and sweet. Mr. Thomas you and your wife apparently had enough issues between the two of you that she felt it necessary to move out, is that correct?"

Thomas hesitated. "Well, yes she moved out, but I didn't have any issues..."

"Your answer is 'yes'. That's all I asked for. Now, the two of you were separated when she was murdered, correct? In other words, you had not resolved your differences to the point where she had moved back in with you, right?"

"Well, that's why I went over there that..."

"Now, Mr. Cline, please just answer the question I asked you. You had *not* resolved your differences to the point she had moved back in with you, is that correct or not?"

"No, not at that time, but as…"

"Nope, nope that's good enough. You answered the question. As I understand the medical examiner's testimony as to the approximate time of her death, you were there, in the house the night she was murdered. Is that also your understanding?"

"Objection, Your Honor, the jury can figure that out from the testimony already introduced into the record."

"No, no I'll let him answer. Were you there the night she was murdered, Mr. Cline?"

"I guess so, based on what the medical examiner said. Yes, I guess I was, but I didn't…"

"That's fine, thank you, Mr. Cline. Now, your finger prints were on the letter opener, right? They were on the murder weapon because you handled it, right?"

"I handled it, yes, so I'm sure my fingerprints were on it."

"You have no idea who might have killed her because she had no enemy's—no one you know of that might have had a reason to kill her, correct?"

"No, I don't have any idea who might have wanted to kill her."

George stood. "With all those facts clearly against you, you're still here today to tell this jury you never killed her?"

"Yes, because I didn't."

"Look at the facts, Mr. Cline. Just consider your testimony here today, and then you tell us why this jury shouldn't find you guilty. Consider all the evidence against you, then you tell me why this jury shouldn't find you guilty. There's not one shred of evidence pointing toward someone else is there?"

Thomas looked out the window.

"Answer the question, Mr. Cline. Why should anyone look anywhere else, but at you? Can you give us one reason why they should look anywhere else based upon the testimony, *from you*, that's been presented here today?'

Thomas turned, looked at the prosecutor and said, "No, I can't."

"Neither can I, Mr. Cline, neither can I."

The ride home was extremely quiet. Jack had tried to clean up some of the testimony on redirect, but clearly, at least to Ann, the damage had already been done. Thomas looked and acted about as guilty as one could.

Hopefully Matt would come up with something soon. Because based on what she had just heard and observed, if the jury were sent out to deliberate tomorrow morning after only the testimony they heard through today, the state wouldn't have to worry about paying for their noon meal. They would, without doubt, come back with a unanimous guilty verdict long before the clock struck twelve.

Chapter 33

Jack sat on the living room couch, watching some new game show on TV. She lay, with her head in his lap, drifting in and out of sleep, as he continued to mindlessly watch the conclusion of the show.

She whispered, "What a great Christmas."

"Yes, it was. Pretty quiet, but that was just what we needed. We honestly didn't need a lot of family or friends this year. It's been crazy enough. This was a great weekend just to relax and enjoy each other."

She never opened her eyes as she said, "We've certainly done that."

"Sex, good food and time away from work—hard to beat. What have you got on for tomorrow?"

She said nothing.

A few minutes later, he said, "You asleep?"

"Nope, just relaxed. I'm to meet Matt at Arnold's office to see what his thoughts might be about Randall's case."

A few minutes later he said, "You ready to go to bed? Can you open your eyes long enough to find the way?"

"Will you carry me?"

He laughed. "Is there some kind of benefit for me if I do carry you, or must I do it out of the goodness of my heart?"

"You carry me, you'll be happy you did."

He shut the TV off, and said, "I'll carry you like you've never been carried before, even with this bad back. Now get up so I can get a grip on you."

She smiled, opened her eyes, and stood up. He lifted her up, as she said, "Have I told you in the last half-hour how much I love you?"

"Not really," he said as he laid her on the bed. "But you're about to have a chance to show me. Now get those clothes off— or do I have to do that too?"

Ann arrived at Arnold's office about 15 minutes early. She didn't figure she would need to wait long and she was right. Matt walked in precisely at ten o'clock and they followed Arnold's secretary into his office where he offered both of them a seat.

"Arnold, I don't know if you've met Matt Armstrong before, but he's a private investigator I like to use that lives here in Nashville."

Arnold rose, offered his hand, and said, "I don't think we've met."

Matt stood, shook his hand and said, "I think you're right."

As they both sat, Ann said, "I mentioned to you I was having the Kingston situation investigated a little further and Matt took care of that for me. I think you'll be interested in what he uncovered. Matt, you want to take it from here?"

"Sure. I know Ann told you I was going to do some investigating concerning the case and I did. She got me started a little later than I would have liked, but we've had a discussion about that, and I doubt she waits that long again before engaging our services."

Ann said, "A hard lesson to learn, but I'm coming around."

Both men smiled and Matt continued as he handed Arnold a file. "I have assembled this information concerning everything I did while on the case, which you can read later. For now, I would like to just verbally discuss what I've learned while investigating the situation."

Arnold opened the file, briefly glanced at the front page, then looked up at Matt and said, "That's fine with me. Go ahead, continue."

"Well, the first thing I did was drive to Louisville, where all three said they had come from. After doing some preliminary research I discovered not one of the three came from Louisville. They all three were from Paducah."

Arnold looked at Ann and said, "They all three said they were from Louisville. They all three committed perjury."

"Mr. Leonard, that's only the beginning. The next thing I determined is that their ages aren't what they testified to. They aren't teenagers, they're all three over 20."

"They then, once again, committed perjury. I need to make a call..."

As Arnold started to reach for his phone, Matt said, "Wait. I haven't even got to the good stuff yet."

"I can only imagine. Go on."

"Okay, so I leave Louisville, and drive to Paducah since I had discovered that was where they all three were from. Once I get there, it took a day or two, but I learned this had all happened before."

"What had happened before?"

"This whole scheme. They had done exactly the same thing with a kid who was the banker's son, in Paducah. The only difference is he paid them a large sum of money to just go away. But they didn't get that far with the Kingston family. This case was different in that they went ahead and filed the charge because Randall wouldn't even discuss a payoff. He was charged before they really ever offered to make it all go away. Although she tried to reach Randall a number of times, he would never answer the call."

"Were they paid the money in Paducah?"

"Yes, and as I understand it, although the banker wouldn't say how much, it apparently was quite a sum."

"So, we have the exact same set of facts here as we had in Paducah, but here, it all backfired. They got no money, and as quickly as everything happened, they felt compelled to see it out to the end. Is that what I'm hearing?"

"Exactly. I figure they just concluded at some point in time they would approach the kid with an opportunity to make this all go away. But that never happened, so they felt obligated to complete the criminal case. Now, the banker and his family are willing to do whatever is necessary to prosecute these three or do whatever they need to do in order to make sure it never happens to someone else."

"Didn't that Cartwright girl testify this had never happened before?"

Ann said, "Yes, she did."

"So, she's perjured herself all the way through her testimony."

"Yes, she has, Arnold."

The prosecutor looked out his window, clearly deep in thought.

After a couple of minutes, Ann said, "How do you want to handle this?"

"That's what I'm trying to figure out. These three are good at what they do and exceptionally good liars. I just want to make sure whatever we do, we get them, all three of them, and stop them from doing this again."

"I'm afraid if you give them any indication of what's going on, they'll all three run. They were pretty bold in their approach concerning both these situations and obviously won't hesitate to do or say whatever they need to do to get what they want."

"I think I'll have an officer file charges here for perjury. Then I'll call the banker in Paducah, tell him what we're doing, and ask him to consider filing against them up there. Once that's done, I'll get them in here and the four of us will have a little discussion. I don't want to call them and tell them to go in to the police station because I'm afraid they'll run before we can get our hands on them. If I ask them to come in *here,* first I'll see what they might admit. Then we can take them from my office to jail and not risk them running before they're picked up."

"Can I get Randall's family in and explain what's going on— maybe tell them that we may be able to get him out of prison before long?"

"Certainly. I'll file a response to your motion for new trial. Then I'll talk to the judge about the best path to take to get him out of prison and the charges dropped. Matt, you did a hell of a job. You're to be commended."

"Thanks."

Arnold stood and extended his hand. "Thanks for coming in today. I'll take it from here and keep you informed."

Both Matt and Ann stood, as Matt shook his hand.

Ann said, "Just let me know what I need to do."

"I will, Ann, I will."

Once they had left the building and were standing outside, Matt said, "I'm ready to start on the Cline case. In fact, I've already read most of the paperwork in his court file and researched Thomas on the net. I just need to start doing the legwork. That I plan to do starting tomorrow morning."

"Okay, just keep me informed. We're back in court tomorrow morning in Lebanon, so if you need to reach me, I'll be there."

"I'm going to talk to all the neighbors tomorrow."

"Matt, you did a great job. Now, see what you can do for us with this Cline case. We really feel the guy's innocent, but the facts are just going to be hard for us to beat. Jack and I are both concerned he's going to be convicted if you can't come up with something."

He smiled as he said, "Oh sure, just put the pressure on. I'll do what I can as quickly as I can and contact you when I know something."

"Good luck. We'll both keep our fingers crossed."

Chapter 34

They sat quietly as both Ann and Jack reviewed the jury instructions that would shortly be read to the jurors. The judge had prepared all 42 instructions. Now it was up to the attorneys to either agree with each and every one, or make their record as to why they didn't agree.

Finally, Edward broke the silence when he said, "Okay, what the hell are those things you're looking at. You've been reviewing them all morning, making your little marks here and there, as if they were the difference between life and death. What are they?"

Ann looked up and smiled. "I don't know that they're the difference between life and death, but they're pretty darn important."

She took about half of the sheets of paper in front of her and shoved them across the table toward both Thomas and Edward. They started to look through them page by page.

A few minutes later, Edward looked at Ann and said, "Okay, neither of us know any more now than we did when I asked about these. Come on now, what the hell are they? Tell me in layman's language."

Jack said, "These are the courts instructions to the jury—all 42 of them. They are the basis upon which the jury comes to a verdict. The court will read these to the jury right before we give our closing statements. Then a copy will be given to the jury to use and follow while they deliberate."

"Where do they come from? Who makes them up?"

"The judge does, but we have the right to suggest instructions or to offer changes. Look at number two. That's the one that tells the jurors that the first thing they should do is select a foreperson. It's just an organized set of rules that the jury needs to follow as they come to a verdict."

"I assume there's one in there that says they should find him not guilty, right?"

"There is. Look at number 37. It provides, basically, that if they don't believe, beyond a reasonable doubt, that he committed this crime, they should find him not guilty."

"How long does this all normally take? I mean how long could they deliberate if they don't come to an immediate conclusion?"

"I've seen them take weeks. There is no norm here. It just depends on each individual jury. In this case, we also need to keep in mind how much time this case has taken to try. We weren't able, partially because of the holidays and partially because of this judge, to try everything in one consecutive time frame. This trial has been extended out over a period of time. It's going to take the jurors a while to piece everything together."

"What if everyone can't agree as to one or more of these instructions?"

"The judge makes the final ruling concerning any objections."

As Jack finished his sentence, there was a knock on the door. Jack opened it, and the court attendant told him the judge wanted to see the attorneys in chambers.

When they walked through the chamber's door, George was already seated and still reviewing the set of the same instructions Ann and Jack had just both been reviewing.

"George has a problem with numbers 18 and 27. Look them over and tell us your thoughts. He thinks those may need to be altered as a result of that Supreme Court case handed down a couple of months ago."

Both Ann and Jack sat down and pulled numbers 18 and 27 from their paperwork.

Jack said, "Judge I don't know anything about that case. They are both fine with us."

"Okay, look, it's almost eleven now. I need to be out of here by three. I never, ever figured the three of you would take this long to approve these standard instructions. I'll give you 'till noon to research it. I'll let the jury go and tell them to be back at one. At that time, you're either going to approve the instructions, or propose a change which I'll rule on and that's the end of it. I'll then read them to the jury. Then George, you can do your closing statement, and we'll reconvene tomorrow at one, since I have a conflict tomorrow morning. The defense can give their closing statement then. Once that's done, we'll submit it to the jury and get this thing over with. Now all of you get out."

At precisely 1:00 p.m., the judge walked back into the courtroom. The jury was in the jury box and all the attorneys were seated at the appropriate council table.

"Gentlemen, are we in agreement with the instructions?"

George said, "The state is Your Honor."

Jack stood and said, "Yes Judge they're fine."

The Judge proceeded to read all 42 instructions to the jury and informed them they would be given a copy of the instructions to follow while they were deliberating. George gave a closing statement which lasted almost a full hour.

The judge sent everyone home and told them to return tomorrow at 1:00 p.m., at which time the defense would give a closing statement and the case would be submitted for deliberation.

"The Kingston's are here. Should I send them on back?"

"Yes."

She stood as they walked in her office and said, "Good afternoon. Please have a seat. I have some news to tell you and I wanted to tell you in person rather than over the phone."

Both were clearly hanging on her every word as they took a seat and waited for her to begin.

"As you know, we hired a private investigator to look into all of those issues that involved Randall. He's now come back with some interesting facts which I felt, at this point, you should know. I've also made a copy of Matt's file that's been given to the prosecutor for his review."

Through the next hour, Ann revealed the results of Matt's investigation. With each new fact, the worried look on their faces slowly diminished as both started to smile.

At the conclusion of her review of everything Matt had submitted, Bryce said, "So, where are we? What's going on at this point? Is it all over?"

"No, unfortunately it's not. Arnold is reviewing everything. But I believe he's going to concur with our motion for a new trial, and then dismiss. However, there are a few things he needs to do first. I'm sure he'll want to confirm the facts contained in Matt's report. I believe he's going to get all three of them in his office and discuss it. Then, he wants to get the charges filed against them before he does anything else, so we need to wait and see what happens. But I can tell you one thing. We're really close to ending all this. I just hope it all works out like it appears it could."

They had just finished supper, and were cleaning the dishes off the table, when Jack said, "Have you heard from Matt concerning the Cline case?"

"No. I assume this is going to take a little time. He hasn't been working on it very long."

"I changed my mind about filing that complaint against the judge."

"Why?"

"Because the extra time we've had in trying the case has been the only thing saving us. It's only because the son-of-a-bitch is so self-centered and keeps putting his own life ahead of this trial, that we got the extra time to do this investigation. If it hadn't been for that, we would probably already be appealing his conviction to the Supreme Court. He's definitely done us a favor, without knowing it of course."

"Yeah, don't tell him. The prick would certainly find a way to offset it—he'd do something to penalize us if he thought he had done us a favor. I dread appearing in his court again. But I suppose, since I plan on practicing in Wilson County, I'll need to suck it up and take whatever he dishes out."

Her phone rang. She looked at the caller's name. "It's Matt."

"Hi, Matt. What's up?"

"You in tomorrow morning?"

"Yes."

"I need to see you first thing."

"Why, what's happened?"

"Not now. I got other things I need to do. I'll see you about eight."

"Okay. See you then."

She terminated the call.

"What'd he want?"

"He wouldn't tell me. He wants to see me first thing in the morning."

"He wouldn't give you any idea?"

She looked at him and curtly said, "No." She shoved the food left over from supper into the refrigerator, as she said, "I got a feeling it's going to be another sleepless night for me. Either the dreams or that phone call will keep me up tonight for sure."

Chapter 35

Ann finally just got up and out of bed. She had been wrong concerning her overall assessment involving what was currently keeping her awake at night. It wasn't the dream, and it wasn't the judge or any other *singular* issue. It was *everything*. It was Randall, it was George, it was the judge—it was *everything* that had kept her awake until somewhere around 3:00 a.m.

At that time, she fell into a restless sleep for a couple of hours, woke up, then decided to quit fighting it and go to work. It would take her an hour to get ready and drive to the office. She figured she might as well make the best of her time. She could complete at least a couple of hours of work before Matt walked in—there was certainly plenty to do.

The overall plan today was to get as much office work completed as she could before noon, then drive to Lebanon with Jack. He would give his closing statement and they would wait with the Clines while the jury deliberated.

She turned her office light on after she had locked the front office door behind her and turned off the light in the reception area. She then dug into a pile of work that needed to be reviewed.

Beth arrived shortly before eight and Matt walked in immediately behind her.

"Hi, Matt. You sounded stressed last night."

"I was. I had a lot going on before I started this project for you. This was thrown in on top of everything else, so, you're right, I was a little stressed."

"Sorry about the urgency of the project, but, if possible, we wanted you to do it and nobody else."

He sat down, as he said, "I understand. Let's talk about Cline."

"Go for it."

"You know I haven't had much time on the job yet, but I've found out a couple of things that I felt you should know as soon as possible. Normally, I take it slow and do what I can to insure I come to one and only one conclusion concerning each case. I haven't done that in this case. It wasn't possible to move slowly, or to take my time. I do however, have some information which I felt, because of the circumstances and the ongoing trial, you need to know right away."

Ann leaned forward in her chair. "This sounds serious."

"You can be the judge of that. First of all, have you driven by the Cline's house? Now, by *their* house I'm talking about the one they both owned and lived in. Do you remember how it's situated?"

"In what respect?"

"Well, of course, the houses along the street aren't far away from each other, which leaves neighbors on both sides with potentially a clear view of who comes and goes from the Cline house."

"Yes, I know they aren't far apart. Did that help?"

"Did you ever drive around the back of the Cline house?"

"No."

"There's an alley which runs the length of the block. Off that alley, there is a single car garage which belongs to the Cline house."

"Okay. I didn't know that. How is that relevant?"

"The people on the south side of the Cline house have no window facing toward that part of the Cline property. They can't see out back toward the Cline house and garage. If you walk up their steps you walk directly into their kitchen and there is no window facing toward the Cline house. However, that's not the case with the neighbor on the other side. They have a screened-in porch facing the alley, which gives them a pretty good view of the driveway and the garage."

"Go on."

"I talked to the owner of that house and she saw plenty."

Ann moved forward in her chair, hanging on every word he said. "What'd she see?"

"Over a period of time, she noticed one person showing up, always after dark on a regular basis, but only after Thomas had gone to work. He would drive into the garage, apparently to hide his car, and then walk into the house, once again, always after dark. She was able to make out the persons features, because there was a utility pole with a light on it, by the alley near the garage. Besides that, Jean always left the porch light on every night the individual showed up. She could identify his features every time he showed up."

"Why didn't she tell someone about this person? Obviously, they were a person of interest."

"She said while the Clines were living there as a couple, she didn't really know them that well. They hadn't lived there all that long, and she just wasn't going to get involved in that type of situation if the guy wasn't supposed to be there. After the killing, the cops immediately arrested Thomas. Both she and her husband are very mild-mannered and very laid back. When the cops arrested Thomas, they figured that was that—they had the guy and they didn't need to tell anyone anything."

"Did she know who the person was? Could she identify him?"

"No, not for sure. But she said he did look a little like Thomas. His actions were also similar to the actions of Thomas."

Ann leaned back in her chair as she processed what he had just said. "You're not telling me…"

"Let me finish. Yesterday, while you were finishing up, I waited in the back of the courtroom. You didn't see me, and I said nothing to you, because I had a job to do. I was, of course, able to tell which one was Thomas and which one was the brother, so I walked outside, and when the brother…"

"His name is Edward, Edward's his name."

"Okay, when Edward came out, I used my phone to take his picture. I then went back to the neighbor and showed her his picture. Edward was the one that was seeing her. I don't know for how long, or what the nature of their relationship was, but he's the one that's been driving in the garage, after dark, and seeing her."

"Oh…my…God."

"I wouldn't have come to you so quickly—I would have taken my time, and continued to investigate, but I felt you needed to know this ASAP."

"I can't believe it, I just can't."

"Now, you understand it may *not* have been him, Edward, that murdered her, but he was in and out of the Cline house a hell of a lot of times while Thomas was working. I have no reason to believe it stopped when she moved out, and plenty of reason to believe Edward was the *reason* she moved out."

Ann looked away, as the continued to process the facts.

She turned toward Matt and said, "Do you know anybody in the Lebanon police department that you can trust?"

He smiled. "I know people everywhere, especially in Nashville and the counties surrounding Davidson county, where I do so much business. Why?"

"If I can get a print from Edward, can you have someone compare it with the one on the letter opener? They have the one from the opener on file. Do you think you could get someone to see if it matches one from Edward?"

"I *know* I can. You get the print; I'll get it compared to the one on the letter opener. Better hurry though. It sounds to me like the trial's about over."

Jack drove up to the front of the their office. Ann opened the car door to get in.

"You're not going believe this. I talked…"

"Shut the door."

Ann stopped in mid-sentence, reached out and grabbed the door handle, after starting her conversation without closing it.

"You're not going to believe…"

"Fasten your seatbelt. I don't want to hear that dinging seatbelt sound all the way to Lebanon."

She fastened her seatbelt.

"Can I talk now?"

He smiled as he said, "Let me take a quick look and see if you're ready for the trip."

"Shut up. Just shut up. I met with Matt this morning. You're not going to believe what he told me."

"You're probably right, but go on anyway."

"You're never going to believe who was seeing Jean Cline and apparently on a regular basis."

"Oh, really. Who was it?"

"Edward Cline."

He said nothing. By then, they were close to the interstate access ramp. As he approached, he suddenly turned into a

McDonald's. He pulled into a parking spot in their parking lot and stopped the car.

Jack looked at her and said, "What the hell did you just say?"

Chapter 36

Both Ann and Jack had concluded they must remain quiet concerning Matt's investigation. They needed Edward's print, and they needed it before the jury convicted a man whom it now appeared had been arrested in a rush to judgement.

Ann told Jack she would figure out what to do about the print. He just needed to present a closing statement that got Thomas off, so all of this investigating and concern over who actually committed the murder would be unnecessary—there wouldn't need to be this insane urgency to determine who actually killed Jean Cline.

Jack agreed uncovering who actually committed the murder shouldn't be hurried. But it was also clear that trying to find the magic words for a closing statement which would convince the jury to find Thomas not guilty, was going to be extremely difficult.

They met Thomas and Edward in the courthouse conference room after deputies had escorted Thomas there from his cell.

"So, what happens today?"

"Well, Thomas you actually don't have much to do today. After the state gives there closing statement, I need to give ours, and the jury will then retire to reach a verdict. My closing won't take too long, so I'm thinking the jury will start deliberating by three or so."

It was hard for her to keep her mouth shut. She just wanted to glare at Edward and say, *'Did you really kill your brother's wife?'* It took all the restraint she had not to accuse him—just get to the bottom of the issue right now. But she contained herself—she knew she needed to, or they, most likely, would never get a good print from him.

"You think they'll come back with a verdict yet today?"

Jack said. "I hope not. Juries that come back that quickly are normally inclined to convict. No, I want them out a couple of days, taking time to consider all the evidence and then hopefully finding you not guilty. We'll just have to wait and see what happens."

"I'm a little afraid to ask, but what happens if they find me guilty? Do I go straight to prison?"

"Pretty much. I'll file a motion for new trial and eventually appeal your conviction, but there's not much to appeal here, Thomas. The judge has been correct in most of his rulings. Even though the trial has been delayed so many times, and most all of the delays were caused by the judge, those delays actually worked to our benefit. So there's not much we can do about that either. We'll just hope they find you not guilty and we don't need to worry about all those post-conviction issues."

The court attendant knocked on the door. He told them the judge was now ready to proceed. They all stood, walked across the hall, and into the courtroom.

A few minutes later, the judge walked in, and opened court for the afternoon. He then nodded at Jack as he said, "You may present your closing statement, Mr. Connors, after which I shall submit the case to the jury for deliberation."

Jack stood and walked to the front of the jury box. He first verbally reviewed all the facts from the defendant's point of view.

Once that was completed, he said, "Now, let's consider the evidence that we feel is most relevant to the case."

"The first thing you need to consider is the demeanor and nature of the defendant as concerns his ability to kill anyone, or *anything* for that matter. You saw him—you observed him testify. Now I ask you, can you really, with a clean conscience, conclude that soft-spoken gentle man you heard testify, has the mental toughness to stab someone to death—to stab to death the woman he obviously loved more than life itself. I would suggest there was no way he could stab to death the woman that was obviously the love of his life. He just doesn't have it in him. I believe that was obvious from his testimony, his demeanor on the stand."

"Now I realize you have no idea what he's like when he's not on the stand, but the testimony *about* him speaks for itself. You never heard one shred of evidence from anyone, at any point in time, indicating he had a violent nature or had a mean bone in his body. I ask you to consider that during your deliberations. His demeanor, and the nature of the testimony given about this man, provided not one shred of evidence that he was capable of committing a crime of this nature."

Quietly, he walked to the other end of the jury box, as he said, "Do you remember the testimony of the officer who told you someone else's print was on that letter opener? Whose was it? Was it the murderers? No one goes around just picking up a letter opener. You pick it up for a reason. Why wasn't that followed up on by the officers?

"I'll tell you why. They had Thomas. That was all they needed."

"They made no attempt to figure out to whom that other print belonged. We submit that print was in fact the murderer's print. What effort would it have taken for law enforcement to continue their research a few more days? You know the answer to that question as well as I—*very little*. They could have tied that issue down, figured out who it belonged to, *then* arrested her killer. But they elected not to because they thought they already had their murderer. At least in *their* minds they did. They made a big mistake. They should have stayed at it until they determined to whom that print belonged to."

"Now, keep in mind folks, there was absolutely no direct evidence in this case. It's all circumstantial. And in that respect, what evidence do we really have? It was his wife—she was murdered. He was at her house sometime after the murder—no one places him there at the exact time she was murdered. His prints were on the letter opener—the reason for which was explained. That's it. There's nothing else. There's no other evidence. You cannot say with a straight face someone else *couldn't have killed her*. It's all too wide open. The facts do *not* establish his guilt. They are indicators he *could* have killed her, but not that he *did* kill her. There is a significant difference between 'could have killed her' and 'did kill her.'"

Quietly, he walked behind the council table, standing beside Thomas, putting his hand on his shoulder.

"You'll be given a copy of the instructions the judge has previously read to you. In them you will find an instruction concerning finding the defendant guilty beyond a reasonable doubt. That instruction is vitally important. That instruction is the one you must use to find Thomas not guilty. Always keep in mind that if there is a question or doubt in your mind, you must acquit him. You can't simply say, 'Well, I'm thinking because he was charged, he's guilty.' That's not enough. You can't say, 'Well, he was married to her, he probably killed her.' That's not enough. You can't say, 'Well, he was probably there around the time she was murdered.' That's not enough. To find him guilty in this case, you must find that, contrary to his nature, contrary to his own testimony, contrary to the fact that they found someone else's print on that letter opener, contrary to the fact no one saw him do it—contrary to all those facts, we just *think* he's guilty."

He walked to the front of the jury box. "That's not the way this works, folks. If you aren't convinced beyond a reasonable doubt based on the facts you heard from that witness stand, then you *must* do the right thing—you must find him not guilty as charged."

Immediately after finishing, Jack sat down, George was allowed a short response, and the judge submitted the case to the jurors. They marched out as those at the defendant's council table held their breath.

A few minutes after the last juror walked through the courtroom door, Jack, Ann, Thomas and Edward walked back into the conference room, where they would wait until the jury was released for the evening. Ann had no idea whether they would return with a verdict before supper. She assumed if they did, it would be one of *guilty*.

By 6:00 p.m., when they hadn't yet returned, the judge released them for the evening and told them to return at 9:00 a.m. the next morning to resume deliberations.

Jack and Ann drove home for the evening, and as they did, each remained silent, both clearly immersed in their own world and their own separate thoughts.

Near home, Ann said, "I need to figure out how to get Edward's print."

Jack said, "I just thank God they didn't come back with a guilty verdict yet this afternoon."

They traveled the remainder of the trip without either saying another word.

Chapter 37

Ann had better things to do than sit and stare at the images on her computer. But Arnold Leonard had taken the time to set up a computer with a camara facing the three individuals that would hopefully provide them with the information the prosecuting attorney needed to let her client out of prison. She would be able to see everything that went on in Arnold's office and was more than anxious for the show to begin. The three had agreed to be in his office at 9:00 a.m. today.

Arnold had provided them with a substantial amount of misinformation concerning issues involving posttrial obligations, which the trio had accepted as valid and which carried with it the necessity of meeting with the prosecutor in his office. He had three law enforcement officers sitting in the reception area awaiting further instructions from him once they arrived.

A few minutes prior to nine, his secretary indicated they had just walked in. He told her to send them all in. He also told her to tell the officers not to leave his office under any circumstances, which she indicated she would do.

He stood as they walked through his office door.

"Morning, morning, have a chair. Good to see the three of you."

As they sat, Charlene, whom he had assumed from day one, was the leader of the group said, "What's going on? We all thought the trial, and this case, was over. Isn't he in prison, where he belongs?"

Arnold smiled and said, "He sure is. He's right where you put him. I want to thank you all again, for hanging in there and remaining so strong while the trial was proceeding. You were great to work with, and all three of you were good witnesses."

Charlene said, "Is that it? Is that the only reason you had us come in?"

Arnold smiled once again, as he said, "No, not really. You see, after the trial, but luckily before it was time to finally conclude the proceedings, Randall's attorney felt a little additional investigating might be in order."

Charlene said, "Investigating what or who? What about? The jury convicted him. That's the end of it, right?"

"Not really. She had an investigator first determine if you were actually from where you said you were from. You weren't—none of you. I certainly don't need to tell any of you where you're from, but, contrary to your testimony, you're all from Paducah. You don't have to answer or respond to that, we already know."

Ann smiled as she watched Johnny Stark began to squirm in his chair.

"The next thing he checked into was your ages. He found out you are all over 20 and certainly not fresh out of high school, as we were all led to believe you were."

"What the hell does our age have to do with anything?" Charlene stood, looked at the other two, and said, "Come on, let's get out of here. We got better things to do than screw around with this old bastard."

Arnold also stood, as he elevated his voice, and said, "Sit down."

She continued to stand her ground.

"Did you notice those officers sitting outside—in the reception area? They are for the three of you if I need them. *Now, sit.*"

She thought for only a moment before she took her seat.

"I know you're really going to be interested in this part of the investigation. While in Paducah, the investigator ran into a banker that lives there. He told him that you, the three of you, were involved in a scheme to bilk him and his family, out of a lot of money by indicating his son had raped you. He told us instead of going through that, he paid you off so you would keep quiet. Is that true?"

Johnny started to say something, but Arnold stopped him before a word came out of his mouth.

"Don't say another word. Don't any of you say another word, at least not yet."

He messaged his secretary, asking her to send two of the officers in his office.

As they walked through the door, Arnold said, "There have already been charges filed in Nashville against all three of you for perjury. Charges for what you did in Kentucky have also just recently been filed. All of those charges are felonies and carry prison terms." He turned toward the officers and said, "One of you advise these three of their Miranda rights, so we can carry on here."

One of the officers then advised them they had been charged, and cited the appropriate sections of the law. He then proceeded to advise them of their Miranda rights.

"Thanks, officer. Now please have a chair, while I have one last conversation with these three."

"Do any of you have anything to say about the charges or what's going on?"

No one said anything.

"Look, here's the deal. If one of you wants to admit what happened, and turn state's evidence, I'll give you a break. Probably a pretty good one. Or, if you want to leave with the officer now, you can. You can go get yourself a lawyer and we can try all three of you. Then they can take you to Kentucky and try all of you again on their charges." He sat back in his chair and said, "Up to you. First one to admit everything and agree to testify is the winner."

Charlene said, "Liston, you old asshole, you can't prove a thing. Certainly, they'll have to extradite us to Kentucky which we'll all three fight. I'll get the best lawyer in Nashville and he'll…"

"Officers, just take all three of them away. I got better things to do then listen to her line of bullshit. See you in court, folks."

Both girls stood, as did the officers. Charlene looked at Johnny and said, "Let's go. We can beat this shit. Let's get out of here."

Johnny looked at her and said, "I've listened to you for the last time. I got a few things to discuss with this gentleman. You two go ahead and go."

"Why you rotten son-of-a-bitch. I outta rip you a new one you…"

"Take both of them out of here."

Once they had left the room, Arnold said, "Okay son, what do you have to say?"

"What kind of deal you offerin'?"

"Will you testify against them?"

"Yes, I will. This was all Charlene's idea. I'll testify against her, for sure. Thelma, she's not too smart. She just came along for the ride—because Charlene told her to. So, while I can't really blame her much, or say much about her involvement, I'll testify against the one that started all this and whose idea it was to start with."

"If you'll plead to a reduced charge and then testify, I'll do what I can to make sure you get probation, no jail time."

Johnny hung his head, deep in thought. Finally, he looked up, smiled and said, "Sounds good to me."

"What happened?"

"This was Charlene's idea from the beginning. So was what we did in Paducah. She organized it all. She first put the one together in Kentucky and it was so easy, we decided to move on down here and do it one more time."

Ann whispered, "We got'em,"

Arnold said, "This one wasn't so easy?"

"No. It was different from the beginning. The kid was really a nice kid. It really was hard for both Thelma and me to do that to him. The kid in Paducah was a little prick so it was easy to take him and his old man, but Randall was a nice kid. There were two or three times both Thelma and me wanted to pull out, but she kept pushin'. All of sudden we were too far in to get out. They wouldn't pay. She tried to contact Randall to talk to him about paying and us dropping the charges that had already been filed, but he wouldn't talk to her. It just got to the point where we couldn't back down, and she just kept pushin' us."

"I'm going to have this officer take you to be processed. Unless you can bail out, you'll remain in jail until the time of trial. While you're there, during the next few days, write everything down you just told me. We'll get everything set for trial unless they plead. Once the trial is over, you'll be released upon the terms you and I just discussed. You understand?"

"Yes." He looked away. When he turned to reengage in conversation, he simply said, "Thank you."

A couple of hours later, Arnold called Ann.

"So, what'd you think?"

"Well, first of all, thanks for setting up the camera. Secondly, I don't think it could have gone much better."

"Just so you know, this case has become a real irritation for me. I hate liars. Especially liars like these three, who did whatever they had to do, to get what they wanted for their own benefit, and ruin the life of a good kid. I agree with you in that the meeting couldn't have gone any better. Your boy is definitely off the hook."

"Thank God. Thank you, Arnold."

"I've gone ahead and called the judge. Since this is all for your benefit, I assumed you wouldn't mind me doing it ex-parte. I told him I would file a response to your motion for new trial, concurring with the motion. He can then sustain it, and I can go ahead and file a written dismissal of the case against Randall. That should get him out of prison and finish the case against him once and for all."

"How long will it take to get him out?"

"I'm thinking maybe a week or so. It shouldn't take long."

"Do you care if I get his parents in here and tell them?"

"Absolutely not."

"Thanks again, Arnold, I'll call them right now."

Chapter 38

She put her pen down as she heard Bryce and Martha Kingston walk into the reception area. Matt hadn't arrived yet. She would wait for him and see all three at the same time.

Her cell rang. It was Jack—a call she had been anticipating. He was sitting with Edward and Thomas waiting to hear from the jury. She only hoped this call wasn't to tell her they were ready to render a verdict.

"Hi, what's going on? The jury render a verdict yet?"

"No, we're still waiting. They wanted one of the instructions concerning the lesser-included offenses clarified. But other than that, we've heard nothing."

"Did you eat lunch with the two of them, or go somewhere else by yourself?"

"No, I didn't eat with them. I'm walking back to the courthouse now. I wanted to get away for a while. I was with them all morning, trying to small talk our way through the hours. It got a little tough late in the morning."

"You didn't use your subtle form of cross-examination on Edward, did you? I hope you didn't give him any indication we were on to something here. I've seen you use that *subtlety* before Jack, and it's not pretty. It's too damn easy to see through—you're pretty obvious when you try that. We can't give him…"

"Just stop. No, I didn't do that. Thanks to you telling me that over and over, I now know that's not my one of my better traits. Like I said, we just small-talked our way through the morning. And I suppose we'll do the same thing this afternoon. The judge told me if they hadn't come to a verdict by three, he was sending them home for the night, so once I am done with them here, I'll probably go back to my office for a bit before I see you at home."

"Okay. Better go. The Kingston's are waiting for me."

Ann heard Matt walk in the front door as she terminated the call. She told Beth to send the three of them on back to her office.

As they walked through her door, Martha said, "Hi, Ann. What's going on? Have you heard something?"

Ann said, "Have a chair. Yes, I have. Matt, why don't you explain what your investigation turned up."

"Well, I first went to Louisville to try to find out what I could about all three of them. That turned up nothing, because they didn't live in Louisville. They were all three from Paducah."

Bryce said, "Then they lied, because they said they were from Louisville."

"Oh, that's only the beginning. I also determined they were not the age they said they were—they are all three over 20, and certainly not the innocent, recently graduated high school kids they professed to be."

"Well then, they lied again," Bryce opined.

"Just getting started. Once I went to Paducah, to make a long story short, I found a banker that eventually opened up to me. The same thing that happened to Randall had happened to him and to his son. The difference between your situation and their situation was that he paid them off. He couldn't handle the damage a trial might cause, so he just paid them off."

Margaret said, "You have to be kidding. So, they lied about all that too—about it never happening to Charlene before? What happened next? Where are we at?"

Matt said, "Ann, why don't you take it from here."

Ann smiled. "Glad to. We turned all the information over to Arnold. He in turn, filed charges here against all three of them, and had charges filed in Paducah. He got all three of them in his office and placed them under arrest. Johnny has now admitted everything as part of a plea bargain and they're all three in jail."

Martha, now sitting on the edge of her chair, said, "Okay, okay, okay, so what does all that mean for Randall?"

"Well, it means he's getting out, and real soon—just as soon as the judge can sign the order. I would say he'll be home in a week or so, maybe sooner."

Both Margaret and Bryce turned toward each other. He stood as she started to cry. She stood, and he held her in his arms, neither saying a word.

Finally, as each sat down, Bryce said, "Ann, Matt, how can we ever thank the two of you enough?"

Ann said, "I'm just sorry it took so long, and that you ever had to go through any of this in the first place."

"We just wanted it done with Randall exonerated. It didn't matter how long it took. Now, the two of you have done that. That's all that matters."

Ann wanted to remember this moment—to somehow capture the exact moment she actually won her first case. It had taken awhile, it resulted in a tough learning experience for her, but in the final analysis, she won—and the feeling of exuberance was unmatched by anything she had ever experienced.

They remained only a few more minutes and then left her office, telling Ann they would wait to hear from her as concerned the particulars involving Randall's release.

"We did good, Matt."

"Yup, that investigation turned out like you'd like to have all of them turn out—on a positive note."

"You know, I can't thank you enough for putting this ahead of the other cases you were working on. You went above and beyond."

He smiled. "Just remember the next time to call me *before* the trial starts. It really works out better that way."

"I know, I know, and that's just what I'm going to do."

"What's going on with the Cline case?"

"We're just waiting for the jury to come back. I'm hoping they take a while so we can figure this all out. Now, if I get you something with Edward's fingerprint on it, how long will it take to compare it to the one on the letter opener?"

"I'm thinking I can get the results the same day or maybe the next if you happen to get me the print late in the day. It won't take long. The cop that handles that process owes me. It won't take long to compare the two prints."

"I don't suppose it matters what they take the print off of either does it? I mean, about any kind of surface will work, right?"

"Yes. Obviously the smoother the better, but most any surface will do the job."

"I'll be going with Jack to Lebanon tomorrow morning to sit with both Edward and Thomas while the jury deliberates. I'm thinking I'll have a print for you by ten or so. Can you meet me outside the front door of the courthouse around that time?"

"Yes. If I get it that early in the day, I can probably have something for you before nightfall."

"Okay, let's plan on that. If anything changes, I'll let you know."

Later that night, she was sitting at the kitchen table when Jack finally arrived home from his office.

After he had leaned down and kissed her, she said, "No verdict yet?"

"No. They reconvene at nine tomorrow morning."

"You want something to eat? There's some left-over pizza in the frig. If you want something else, I can make it for you."

He walked to the refrigerator, took out the box of pizza left over from the previous night and shoved a piece in the microwave.

As he waited for it to heat up, he walked to the table, leaned on one of the chairs and said, "What in the world are you doing?"

"Cleaning off my iPad."

"I've never ever seen anyone clean off their iPad cover before, especially using a cleaner of some kind. Why are you doing that?"

"I don't want anything on it. I want it spotless. I don't want your prints on it, my prints on it, or anyone else's prints on it. In fact, I don't want *anything* on it, period." She looked up at him, smiled and said, "Thus, the reason for my cleanliness."

"I'm really sorry, but I don't understand,"

"You will tomorrow morning. Believe me, you will tomorrow morning."

Chapter 39

Ann was beginning to think there was some truth to Beth's belief that her dreams were most likely to occur the night before she was to appear before Judge Dunn.

As they drove to Lebanon, she reviewed what had been a very short night of rest for her.

It had started innocently enough. She continued to prepare her iPad for the next morning, and Jack, overly tired from the day's activities, went to bed early. She followed, but it was two hours later.

About 3:00 am, she woke up after having sweat through her night shirt. Jack shook her to stop the dream and to bring her back to reality. Sleep had been difficult the rest of the night. After she fell asleep, she hadn't slept a full hour before it was time to get up.

"You okay?"

"I'll be fine. It was just a long night—again."

"I know, I was there. You going to be okay today? It was hard waking you up this time."

"I'll be fine. Thanks for putting up with me."

"You're worth it. Glad it doesn't happen every night though."

"Last night was a bad one. It wasn't only frightening, but it was confusing."

"What do you mean confusing? I don't understand."

"Well, of course it's no longer unusual that the killer has the face and voice of Judge Dunn. I've come to expect that. But there was something about a box, or something…a box. I don't know. I couldn't figure it out."

She was quiet for a few moments until she turned to Jack and said, "You don't think putting the judge's face on this killer has any meaning do you? I mean, it seems strange that's all I see now, when I dream, is his face. It's really starting to bother me."

He turned slightly toward her, while continuing to keep an eye on the road, and said, "You mean, do I think he's your mother's killer? No, Ann, I don't. I think you think of him as a demon, and he may be, but no, he's not your mom's killer. Now, let's change the subject. You never have told me how the meeting turned out yesterday with Randall's parents. Every time we started to discuss it, something else came up—and then I went to bed a little early. How'd that go?"

The change in subject matter was effective. She was able to move away from the issue of her sleepless nights, at least temporarily. But she knew it wouldn't last. The discussion concerning Randall and his parents was a bright light in the middle of a difficult morning. She was anxious to discuss how happy they both were, and the conversation concerning that issue lasted most of the way to Lebanon.

But she just couldn't shake the thought that perhaps there was some truth in her dreams, or at least in some portion of them. Maybe it was worth looking into a little further. She knew it was a longshot but maybe she should carry on a little investigation of her own.

This *box* issue, though, really had her puzzled. It had come out of nowhere, and that's where it remained—nowhere. She had no idea what, if any, significance it held, either to her or to the killer.

The judge had just sent the jury out to continue to deliberate. The foreman had made it clear they were having trouble coming to a conclusion, which was exactly what Ann and Jack wanted to hear.

Judge Dunn questioned the foreman, indicating his concern they hadn't already come to a verdict. The foreman indicated they just had two or three people that were not in agreement with the rest of them. They were working on coming to a conclusion as soon as they could.

Ann figured a hurried conclusion would most likely not be one they would like. She figured time was growing short. If they were ever going to figure out what happened that night in the home of Jean Cline, it better be soon.

Once they were seated around the conference table, after they had small-talked their way through the first half-hour, Ann looked at Thomas and said, "Matt, your investigator, may be making some headway."

Edward looked at Ann, and said, "What kind of headway?"

Ann had deliberately seated herself on the opposite side of the table from Edward.

She said, "There's one man that seemed to be in or near Jean's home on a number of occasions while she was living alone. I have a picture of him for you both to look at and determine if he looks familiar."

She stood, walked to the other end of the table and carefully took her iPad out of her briefcase. She handed it to Edward. She could have slid it across the table, but that might have defeated the purpose. He took it from her, sat it down on the table and opened it.

"Does the guy behind all those people look familiar to either of you?"

Edward turned the iPad so Thomas could see the picture.

Last night, Ann had found a picture of an old friend and had already pulled it up for both of them to look at. She knew without a doubt, neither of them would know him.

Both men looked carefully at the picture.

Finally, Edward said, "I've never seen him before."

"Either have I," Thomas responded.

Edward closed the iPad and slid it across the table to Ann. She carefully picked it up and returned it to her briefcase.

"Is that all he's come up with?" Edward asked.

"Yes, so far. But he's not done yet either. He's devoting his full attention to it. Hopefully he'll come up with something soon."

"What happens if they come to a decision before his investigation turns up something?"

"That's going to be a problem if they find you guilty. Obviously, we're fine if you're found not guilty, but if you're found guilty before Matt comes up with something, we're going to have a problem." Recalling the advice of her now deceased mentor, she said, "Let's just take this a step at a time. Let's run with what Matt's doing and think positive about that, *and* about the fact they may find you not guilty. We'll figure out what to do if they find you guilty, and Matt finds nothing, when and if that becomes our new reality."

Edward said, "If that's all he's come up with, maybe we should just terminate his services. If some picture of a man neither of us has ever seen before is all he's got, is he really worth continuing to pay him? Thomas, I wonder if you should just terminate him and let the chips fall where they may, with the jury."

Thomas turned to Ann and said, "You know, I think he's probably right. Why go to the extra cost if that's all he can come up with?"

"Let's give him a few more days and then terminate him. He hasn't had much time to work on this, so let's just give him a few more days."

Edward said, "Whatever. I just think we should end his services now. He sure as hell isn't helping."

As Ann stood, she couldn't help but consider Edward's comments. He had made an intelligent move trying to terminate Matt. If Edward killed her, having Matt on the case was something Edward certainly didn't want.

Ann picked up her briefcase and excused herself for a moment. She walked outside and met Matt, waiting for her near the front door.

As she approached, she carefully pulled the iPad from her briefcase and held it out to Matt using only her thumb and index finger on the very edge of the unit.

"Now, before you take this, know that I have touched it a couple of times this morning, but the only other print on there is Edward's. So, take hold of it carefully."

He took out a handkerchief he had in his back pocket and carefully took the iPad from her.

"I'll get this right to them. I may have an answer before tonight. Otherwise, it'll be sometime tomorrow. I'll let you know when I know."

"Okay, Matt." She smiled. "Don't lose it. That iPad could be the difference between life and death for a couple of people sitting in the courthouse conference room."

He smiled, "I'll handle it with kid's gloves."

Chapter 40

As they drove to Lebanon the next morning, Ann wondered if Matt was having trouble pulling the print off the computer or in comparing it with the print they took from the letter opener. She had heard nothing from him during the remainder of the day yesterday, nor last night.

As they waited for court to open, Judge Dunn sent his court attendant to their conference room indicating he wanted to see the attorneys in chambers. Thomas wanted to know why the meeting was necessary. Neither attorney had an answer.

George was already seated when they walked in the room.

As Jack took a seat, he said, "Is there a problem? What's going on, Judge?"

"This jury is taking too long to come to a conclusion."

George said, "Are they having issues? Did they contact you for some reason?"

"No, but in my opinion, there must be a problem. Any jury in the world would have found this man guilty in the blink of an eye."

It had taken all of Ann's self-control to hold back during prior days while in court with this judge—to hold back her anger and contempt for someone who seemed to have unknown issues with both she and Jack. She had finally reached her breaking point.

"Why's that, Your Honor? Upon what do you base your opinion?"

He turned and stared at her with contempt.

"My opinion, sweetheart, is based upon the fact that the defendant had one competent attorney who presented a piss-poor defense, *and* had an associate rookie attorney who clearly doesn't know her ass from a hole in the ground." He smiled. "That's the basis for my conclusion."

"You know, we didn't have much to work with, Judge. Your conclusion seems to me a little harsh."

The judge rotated his swivel chair around to face her.

"In my opinion, my comment was extremely diplomatic Ms. Connors. You may have had little to work with, but you sure as hell didn't use what you *did* have, to its best advantage. You presented a horrible defense, and if I were you, I'd probably look for another profession if what you provided the last few weeks is the best you got." He smiled that same condescending smile once again. "Of course, that's just one man's opinion, but I've been known to be right a few times during my legal career."

She leaned forward, smiled and said, "You know, I would agree with a portion of your statement."

"Oh, really? And which portion might that be?"

"The portion that indicated you were right *'a few times.'* All that time we've spent in court with you, I would have to admit you were right *'a few times.'* Of course, I'm assuming you are saying *'a few times'* is just a short step higher than 'seldom', because to me, that's about where you belong on the 'being right' scale—just slightly above *'seldom.'* I haven't practiced in many judge's courts yet, but if you're an example of what the judicial system has to offer as a judge, I can see right now I'm going to need to join a committee that believes in overhauling the whole system—*Judge.*"

George had left the room immediately after the discussion between Ann and the judge began, leaving Jack as the only potential moderator.

As Judge Dunn leaned forward to respond to Ann, Jack said, "Judge, wait. Let me have a talk with co-council outside, in the hallway, for a moment if you don't mind."

He grabbed Ann by her blouse sleeve, pulled her up, and toward the doorway. She resisted all the way, but he finally got her out in the hall.

He whispered, "Okay, what the hell are you doing?"

"I can't take that misogynistic, antagonistic bastard anymore, Jack. He's everything I abhor in life and I cannot take him calling both of us incompetent. He's completely out of line—I just couldn't take it anymore. I'm sorry if I embarrassed you, but I said what I felt needed to be said, and I'll do it again if he pulls that shit on us one more time."

"Okay, now you listen to me. You go back down to the conference room and sit with the guys. I'll handle whatever the judge wanted to see us about."

"Oh no, Jack, if you're going back in, I'm going with you."

"Goddamn it, Ann, you listen to me. I'm no longer your husband as far as this conversation is concerned. I'm chief council in this case. I'm not asking—I'm *telling* you to go sit with our client. Now get your ass down the hall before I have *my* client fire you."

She so badly wanted to argue with him, but she knew he was right. At this point, it was in their client's best interest that she back off. She said, "Whatever. I'll go if you think that's what's best."

"Oh, it's what's best all right—what's best for you, *and* our client."

She walked back to the conference room and waited for a phone call from Matt and for the return of her husband. Jack walked back in the room a half-hour after she had arrived.

"What happened?"

"Oh, he chewed on me and criticized you most of the time, but he's can't understand why the jury can't come to a conclusion. He's going to give them another day and then call it a hung jury."

"I assume George will try it again, won't he?"

"I asked him. He told me he would have the case back in court as soon as he could get it on the calendar."

Edward said, "So if this jury can't come to a conclusion, and the judge releases them, we have to go through all this again?"

"Yes, Edward, that's exactly right. Now, you have to understand it's a win for us in a few ways. If Thomas isn't found guilty, then the jury will have told us that we have a pretty good case. So, when it's retried, we will have, by then, talked to a juror or two, and found out what their thoughts were about the case— what was good, what was bad—and improve on it the next time. All is not lost just because he isn't acquitted this time around."

They waited until late in the day, when the judge called them into the courtroom to release the jurors until tomorrow morning. Once they left the courtroom, the judge, on the record, made it clear he would give the jury one more day, and if there was no verdict by the end of tomorrow's afternoon session, he would release them, declare a mistrial, and the state could do as they wished—either retry or dismiss.

On the way home, Jack said, "You know, you were out of line today."

"Sorry you feel that way."

After her response, he initially said nothing, but a few miles down the road, and a few minutes later he said, "You don't agree?"

"No. Jack, I can't let him run over us—or maybe I should say, over *me*, day after day after day. I've taken all the shit from him I can. If he throws me in jail, so be it. I realize now, no matter what interaction we have, he's the type of person that will always rub me the wrong way. I can't help that, and I suspect neither can he. But I also can't let it go. It's the way I'm made. I don't think you and I should try anything together in his court again. If I end up in front of him, if I need help, I'll look elsewhere, and I think you should do the same. I have no desire to embarrass you, or to affect the final result in your cases, but I am who I am, and I can't change that because you're my co-council. I'm sorry, I really am."

"I'm not trying to change who you are, so don't misunderstand what I'm trying to say. But you're going to need to learn there's a time to shut up and a time to speak up. The great majority of the time, when you're in front of a judge, any judge, it's best you keep still, just try your case and go about your business. I know that's going to be hard for you to learn, because you have always, ever since I met you, said what you believe and what you believe in. But I'm telling you when you're in court you just need to be careful. You're no longer in charge. Someone else is. You just need to be really, really careful—that's all I'm saying."

Later that night she thought about his words. They were spoken by someone who, first of all, was well experienced in the courtroom, and second of all, had nothing but her best interest in mind. She needed to tone it down when she was before a judge, and she would start doing that immediately. Well, just as soon as she moved on to another case and another trial, she would start that. She *knew* she needed to change her approach *starting right now,* with the trial she was currently involved in, but Judge Dunn would indeed make it difficult.

As she continued to assess her relationship with the judge, her phone rang. It was Matt.

"Hi, Matt. What'd you find out?"

"Sorry it took so long. The guy had a couple of other jobs he needed to finish before he could handle mine."

"Was he able to come to a conclusion?"

"Yes."

She hesitated, waiting for an answer. Finally, she said, "Okay, what conclusion did he come to?"

"Well, I'm not sure if this is good for you or bad, but the print on the computer and the print on the letter opener were a match. Both prints belong to Edward."

Chapter 41

As they were approaching Lebanon, Ann could only hope this was the last time she made this trip for quite some time. Today, most likely the trial would end, one way or the other. She could then put this 'rookie experience' behind her, and not return to Lebanon until she was more experienced, seasoned, and ready to handle Judge Dunn as a professional, leaving her personal feelings in the hallway outside the courtroom.

Ann and Jack had both discussed the fingerprint issue, and tossed around different ideas on how to handle this major development, although they had come to no conclusion. While they were both excited the print belonged to someone other than their client, there were still a number of ways this could all play out.

"Okay, so you have your ideas, I have mine. After discussing most of the alternatives, what do you think is best, Jack? You are way more experienced in all this than I am."

"Here's what I think we should do. First off, I don't believe we should reveal any of this to Judge Dunn until we know for sure what position all the parties are going to take. We need to be careful and get our ducks in order. I think we probably should talk to George and just explain what's going on. Hopefully, he will jump on board with what we want to do, and then we can go from there. When we tell Edward, I defiantly want a cop there to arrest him. Hopefully once we confront him, he'll admit, we can have him arrested, and George can dismiss the criminal case against Thomas. That's how I would like the whole process to unfold."

"That sounds like a good approach to me."

Upon reaching the conference room, they were told by Thomas that the judge had sent the court attendant to inform the attorneys they were needed in chambers.

Ann said, "Should I go? What do you want me to do?"

"The judge said 'attorneys' and I assume he meant both of us. You can leave if there are problems."

She hesitated, uncertain as to what she should do.

He continued looking at her, impatiently awaiting a response.

"I guess I'll go with you. Yes, Jack, I understand what you said to me, and yes, Jack, I'll walk out if I get in trouble by opening my big mouth again."

Thomas said, "You get in trouble with the judge?"

Jack said, "No, no just a little misunderstanding. It's no big deal."

As they walked down the hall, she said, "Do you still want to keep this fingerprint issue quiet until we can discuss it with Edward and Thomas?"

"Yes."

When they reached the chambers door, they noticed George was already waiting, along with the judge.

Once seated, Judge Dunn said, "I'm going to end this trial today if they don't come to a verdict."

Jack said, "Sounds fine to us, Judge."

"I assumed it would. Again, for the life of me I can't believe they haven't reached a verdict. Maybe the next jury will, once it's retried. George, are you going to try it again?"

"Yes, just as soon as we can get it on the docket."

Ann said, "Judge, will you be the presiding judge if it's tried again?"

He slowly turned toward her, and said, "Will that make a difference?"

"Yes. If you are, I won't be involved."

"Oh really. And why's that?"

"I just think it's best if our paths don't cross—at least for the present."

She could see Jack change positions in his chair. He was already uncomfortable.

"So, you apparently feel the same way I do? Well, that's great. I always like it when both parties in a relationship are able to think along similar lines, if you know what I mean."

She leaned forward in her chair and said, "I know *exactly* what you mean. Now, let me tell you how I really feel—*Judge*. You…"

Jack grabbed her by the shoulder, stood her up, and said, "Go. Get out of here. Go keep the brothers company."

This time she had no response. She jumped up, grabbed her files, and walked quickly out the door. This time she didn't care what any of them thought, including her own husband. This man irritated her without saying a word—by simply being in the same room.

She was done. Jack could handle it all from here on. There was little left to do. He could handle it all. If it were retried, if Judge Dunn presided, she was out. Jack would need to find someone else to second chair the trial. If a different judge presided, she would help, but otherwise her time with Judge Dunn was over.

Jack walked in the conference room shortly thereafter and motioned for her to follow him. As they walked down the hall, he said, "I have George in one of the other rooms down here, and I want us both to visit with him concerning what we've come up with. You think you can visit with him and not get into a fight?"

The twinkle in his eyes told her all she needed to know.

"You jerk, don't even go there with me."

He laughed and was still laughing when they walked in the room.

Jack and Ann sat down with George and told him their story. They told him about Matt, whom George had previously met, and had worked with. They told him about the fingerprint on the letter opener that now had been identified as a print belonging to Edward. They told him how the neighbors had identified Edward as the individual going through the back door of the Cline house on numerous occasions, making sure to hide his car in the Cline garage each and every time.

When the story was complete, George said nothing. He stood, and walked to the window, starring out at the street, with hands on hips, looking at nothing in particular and clearly deep in thought.

After a few moments, he turned and said, "It appears to me the cops clearly charged the wrong man. I guess we need to figure out how to handle things from here."

Jack said, "You know, I think we should tie this down a little further. Let's see if, before we do a thing, we can get Edward to confess. Let's wait until Matt gets here, presents the facts to both Thomas and Edward, and then see if we can get him to confess. That would really make all our jobs just that much easier."

George said, "I agree. I'll wait here. You let me know when Matt gets here. I'll then sit with you while you confront Edward. I want to follow the tone of the conversation, essentially to learn if I'm going to need to try Edward next. If he wants to admit, I'll have an officer give him his Miranda warning and we'll go from there. If he doesn't, I'll just have him placed under arrest, we'll throw him in jail, and figure out what to do with Thomas at that time. If he does admit, I'll probably just drop the charges against Thomas yet this afternoon. There would really be no reason to leave those charges pending against him."

"That makes perfect sense to me," Jack said.

Matt arrived a half-hour later, as usual, on time. He tapped on the conference room door, and Jack let him in. He was followed through the door by a cop, who stood just inside the door, near the wall and near George, who took a seat at the table.

"What's going on here?" Thomas asked. "Why are they both here?"

"We have some information for you, Thomas. This was information Matt uncovered so we felt he should be here to answer any questions. You'll understand why the other two are here when he finishes."

Matt walked across the room, shook Thomas's hand, then pulled up a chair to within a few feet of the conference table, sitting with his files in his lap.

"Okay, to start with, I questioned neighbors around Jean's house, as to any unusual people coming and going. Mrs. Thurgood never noticed much, but the neighbor on the other side did. Before Jean died, that neighbor indicated there was one particular person coming to and going from the house on a regular basis. He would pull around in back and pull into the garage, walk inside and leave at some point in time, later that evening. It was always the same man. She identified Edward as that person."

No one said a word. Slowly, everyone turned toward Edward.

"What? I don't know what…Thomas I have no idea what…"

"Wait, Edward. Before you say anything else, let me finish. We got a fingerprint off the computer Ann handed you yesterday. We then compared that print with the print on the letter opener. They were a match—they both belonged to you. You're the one that killed Jean Cline, Edward. Your brother, Thomas was not involved in any respect."

Chapter 42

No one spoke. No one moved. Finally, Thomas said, "Edward, I don't understand. What's going on here?"

Edward looked away, but said nothing.

Matt looked at Thomas and said, "He would drive his car in the garage, so no one knew he was there. He was clearly having a relationship with your wife and wanted to make sure you never found out."

Again, Thomas looked at Edward for a response. Edward remained silent, avoiding eye to eye contact in any respect.

Matt continued. "The letter opener had his print on it. Now, who goes around just picking up a letter opener? He picked it up because it was available, and because he needed something to hurt her with. He may not have wanted to kill her—that's probably his defense. But he was there the night she died, and he's the one that caused her death, there's no doubt in my mind about that."

Again, Thomas looked at his brother for a response or a denial.

Edward looked down, took a deep breath, and then turned toward his brother.

"I'd been seeing her for quite some time—ever since you first moved here. She told me the marriage was over—that was the only reason I was seeing her. But I also knew how you felt about her, so I didn't want you to know. At least not yet, not until she told me the marriage was really over, the paperwork for a divorce had been filed, and things had settled down."

Thomas looked away, as he said, "You could have told me. I would have understood. You didn't have to see her behind my back, Edward."

No one said anything, until Matt broke the silence as he said, "What happened the night she died, Edward?"

He looked away. It was a long 90 seconds before he told his story.

"Everything was fine when I first got there. We had a drink, and we were talking on the couch. But then she told me she was thinking of going home, moving back in with you, Thomas. I tried to change her mind. I didn't want to lose her. I loved her too much to lose her. We started to argue. We had never had an argument before."

He hesitated, as he struggled with the remainder of his story.

Edward looked down and said softly, "The argument grew really heated. She stood up and pulled me up off the davenport. She pushed me away as I tried to hold her. It became much more physical. Again, I just didn't want to lose her. As we started to struggle, I just lost my head. I became incensed that she would even think of leaving me for…for…"

"For me, Edward? You became incensed because you couldn't understand her *leaving you for me*?"

George said, "Now just wait right here. Before you go any further, not even knowing for sure what you are going to say, I think I better advise you of your Miranda rights. You have the…"

Edward put up his hand, and stopped him. "Don't I have the right to waive them rights or something like that? I want to get this off my chest. I've held all of this inside long enough. I waive you reading that crap to me. I want to say what I want to say and get this over with."

George said, "That's up to you, Edward. Go ahead then.

"As we continued to struggle, I kind of fell back and as I did, I felt the letter opener on the end table and in an instant, I had stabbed her. She was able to walk away. I knew she was hurt real bad, but I didn't know what to do. I threw the letter opener down on the floor and left."

No one said a word, as everyone continued to process the information just provided.

Ann said, "Why did you let Thomas take the blame? You know how much he cares for you. You know how fine a man he is. How could you do that?"

"I didn't feel they had that much on him. And as the trial progressed, I really figured maybe he would get off—that neither of us would have to worry about it."

"So, you would have let him go to prison for something you did?"

"I guess I just never thought he would be convicted. I never considered what might happen if he was actually convicted."

After another few seconds of silence, George said, "Officer, take him into custody. You know, Thomas, after hearing the whole story, you're probably only looking at manslaughter, which is a far cry from murder. It's a much less serious crime than your brother faced, and while you may do time, you won't do near the time Thomas would have if he had been convicted of murder."

Edward stood. The officer walked forward to take him away. As he approached, Thomas said, "Wait."

He stood up, walked up to his brother and put his arms around him as he said, "I'll be with you every step of the way. We'll get through this together. I can't lose you too. You're all I have left."

Ann started to cry, as did Thomas. They all watched as they took Edward to be processed and to, most likely, occupy the cell his brother would soon vacate.

Once they had left the room, George said, "Let's all go tell the judge what happened and see how he wants to handle the proceedings from here."

Ann said, "I'm sure this will be interesting. He should be a real joy to deal with—as usual."

George said, "Let me handle him. I'll be glad to do the talking."

"And I'll be glad to let you."

The three of them walked into Judge Dunn's chambers as he was reviewing a file. He looked up and said, "And to what do I owe this interruption? What do you three want?"

As they each took a chair, George said, "Judge we've had a strange turn of events. Just within the last hour, as a result of some fine detective work done by a private investigator hired by Ann and Jack, the defendant's brother has admitted he murdered the victim. The investigator uncovered plenty of evidence, all of which points toward him and just now, in one of the conference rooms, he has admitted everything. We have him in custody. I'll most likely charge him with manslaughter."

"Well, isn't that interesting. Sounds like that crack police force you have working for you didn't initially do their job, did they?"

Ann said, "Judge, in their defense, they probably did what any other police force would have done. They went the direction the evidence took them, they arrested the most likely suspect, and that was it. I don't blame them. And by the way, if you remember, we told you from the beginning he was innocent—you know, while you were continually telling us to plead him guilty."

Jack started tugging on her hand about half way through her soliloquy.

"Well, aren't we blessed with someone of such wisdom at such a young age? God bless you, my child. Now shut up so the rest of us can figure out what to do."

Ann sat up on the edge of her chair, and in an elevated tone, showing a clear disgust for the man sitting on the other side of the desk, said, "What we *need* to do, Judge, is release the jury, dismiss the charge against the defendant and get out of here. That's what we *need* to do, in case you can't figure it out."

The judge looked at Jack and said, "Do you want to continue to practice before me—in my courtroom?"

"Certainly."

"Then get your wife out of here, or I guaranty neither of you will ever practice before me again, do you understand?"

"I do."

Jack stood, and said, "Let's go."

"Now wait a minute, I have a right to…"

"You have no rights in here at all—only those he gives you, and he just terminated whatever remaining 'rights' you had left. Let's go. *Now*."

She stood and walked out ahead of him into the hallway.

Once they were far enough down the hallway the judge could no longer hear their conversation, she said, "What the hell are you doing? I have just as much right to be in there as anyone else in the room."

"Goddammit, no you don't. I warned you, Ann. Just go in the courtroom and wait. We'll be in shortly. He can't stop you from being in there."

She whirled around and walked through the courtroom door.

A few minutes later, Jack brought Thomas into the courtroom, and they both sat down at one of the council tables. Shortly thereafter, the courtroom attendant brought the jury in, and they were seated. Judge Dunn then walked through the chambers door and took his seat.

"Ladies and gentlemen of the jury, we've had an unusual development. Someone else has admitted they committed the crime the defendant was charged with. Law enforcement has determined that individual is, in fact, guilty of the crime, and as a result, the charges against this defendant have all been dismissed."

You could hear a murmur throughout the jury panel, as they quietly discussed the turn of events.

"You are hereby released from any further responsibility concerning this trial. Thank you for serving. The clerk's office will contact you when you need to return again. By the way, not that it matters, but just for my own information, what were the numbers concerning the last vote you took just before you came in here?"

The foreman stood, and said, "Well Judge, it's interesting you should ask. We were just ready to come in and tell you that we had finally come to a unanimous conclusion for the first time since we started to deliberate. It was 12-0."

"Which way?"

"Guilty."

They drove home in virtual silence until Jack started to smile as he said, "You know, I'm really sorry about today...at least about the part where I had to haul your ass out of chambers."

"That's not funny, you jerk. That's just not funny."

"Yes, it is. You were funny. My god, I've never, ever seen you that angry. But damn it, Ann, you have to pick your battles. I looked at you one time, and there was literally smoke coming out of your ear. All I could see was the one ear, so I assume it was happening on the other side too...just smoke coming out..."

She started to laugh. "You pissed me off so bad—I don't even want to think about it."

"Hey, it came out fine. We won. Doesn't matter how you get there, just as long as you get there. We did what we needed to do and you were a huge part of the process."

"Yeah, just go ahead and kiss up to me, you jerk." She started to snicker. "I was so mad I would have killed that son-of-a-bitch if you would have let me."

"Believe me, you're not telling me anything I don't already know."

"You were probably right in what you did. I probably owe you one."

"You do." He smiled. "You can just repay me tonight when we get home."

Chapter 43

Ann tried sleeping late the following morning. Prior to graduation from law school, on occasion, and upon reaching a level of achievement she was proud of, she would reward herself by sleeping in. But that had all changed since she started practicing law.

Even though she had eventually prevailed as concerned the first two important trials of her life, her days of sleeping as a reward for reaching a new level of achievement, were over.

As she lie there, trying to dismiss all those issues awaiting her attention, she finally just quit trying to avoid their continual intrusion into her normal process of falling asleep and got out of bed.

She left home before Jack even woke up, arriving at the office about an hour before she knew Beth would arrive.

Ann had reviewed a number of phone calls and messages concerning new appointments, when she heard Beth walk in the front door. After reviewing a few items with her and making sure she was fully aware of the day's activities, she decided to call Sally. Contact with her lately, because of everything that had happened in the practice, had been limited.

"Morning, Sally. Got the kids handled for the day?"

"Ann, how are you? Good Lord it's been forever."

"I know. I miss talking to you. It's been pretty crazy here.I just haven't had a chance to contact you. How are the kids?"

"Good, good. I tried calling the office a couple of times, but you were tied up with that case in Wilson County. How'd that all turn out?"

"Interesting you should ask. We hired a private investigator and he found out that our client's brother had been sleeping with our client's wife. His print was also on the murder weapon. When we confronted him, he confessed. All the charges against our client were dismissed."

"You're kidding me! Wow, what a way to end everything. Well, that's a good win for you and a great conclusion for your client."

"Yes, he was happy to say the least."

"So, do you have time to get together today?"

"No, not today. What are you doing over New Years?"

"Not much really. Maybe we can get together New Year's Day. By the way, whatever happened to that other guy: Randall what's his name? He still in prison?"

"You know, as a matter of fact, they're letting him loose. We determined those three witnesses that testified against him, had done this very thing before, up in Kentucky. This was all just one big scam. They're going to release him anytime now. In fact, he may be out already. Thank God. That one was really bothering me."

"So, after two major trials, you are on the top side of both of them?"

"Let's just say our clients are no longer incarcerated."

"I'd say you were a winner in both. Good for you, Ann, good for you."

Ann had been a little perturbed when Sally continually asked about "the client in prison". It felt good, without finding it necessary to brag, when she was able to set the record straight. They talked for a few more minutes, then agreed the four of them would get together on New Year's Day—maybe watch a bowl game or two and just relax.

Later in the morning, Beth buzzed her, and said there was someone here she would want to see. Ann walked out into the reception area and found Randall Kingston waiting to see her. She embraced him and asked him to walk back to her office for a moment if he had time.

As he sat, he said, "I can't stay long. I have a number of things I need to do."

"It's just so good to see you. I wasn't sure I would see you in this setting for a long time once you were sentenced."

"I know. Once I ended up in prison, I lost hope. I had no idea when I would ever get out. Not only did that worry me, but considering the people I was living near, and around, I really questioned whether I would *ever* get out *alive.* Thank you for finding a way—for finding a way to get me out of there."

"I'm just so sorry you ever ended up there in the first place."

"As you found out, those three were pretty good at what they did. They were stone cold liars and certainly able to turn my world upside down."

"I'm just glad the investigator was able to uncover what he did."

"You just did what you needed to do to get me off. Didn't matter how long it took. The point is I'm here with you today, and I owe that to you for what you did for me. I'll never forget that, ever."

He stayed for another hour as they discussed his immediate and future plans for life. Finally, he stood, she embraced him, and he told her no matter what happened in his life, if he ever needed help, concerning anything, it would be her door he walked through.

Thomas Cline had also stopped by to see her a few days ago. Even though his brother was facing the consequences of his actions and would be in jail for quite some time, Thomas couldn't help but display his happiness with the way it had all turned out. His job was still available, and he was very much looking forward to living a simple, normal life. As he left, he asked her if it was alright to stop in from time to time, just to see how she was doing. She told him to stop in as often as he wished—she would love to remain in touch.

Once Randall left, she sat, alone, thinking about both men, about how involved she had become in their lives, their families, and their problems. How quickly it had all changed. Just a week ago, she was very concerned about the future of both men.

Now today, both of their lives had turned on a dime, and each of them were thanking her for getting them out of their dilemma.

Hopefully, both cases would be the beginning of a long line of success stories that she could remember and reflect upon as she continued to practice law. She had no idea, just a few short weeks ago, either case would turn out the way it did.

She had concluded losing was no longer an option. She learned a little about herself while representing Randall and Thomas. If she had accepted defeat in either the Kingston or Cline case, when everything looked desperate, they would both still be in jail. In the future, she would indeed have an issue accepting defeat in *any* case, until absolutely *every available option had been pursued*.

Chapter 44

New Year's Eve was unremarkable, which was just as Ann and Jack had planned.

They had done nothing but prepare a few late evening snacks, watched TV, and discussed both the Kingston and Cline trials. Each continued to remain exuberant about the final results, anxious to review what went wrong and what they had concluded was done properly.

They were both sleeping by 11:00 p.m., and Jack was still sleeping at seven-thirty the next morning.

Not so with Ann. She had been awake since shortly after three. This time she hadn't awakened Jack. This time she had somehow managed to wake up on her own prior to creating all the noise she normally created when having one of *those dreams.*

As she sat, by herself, looking aimlessly into space, Jack walked out of the bedroom, and said, "How long you been up?"

"Since about three-thirty."

"Another dream?"

"Yes."

As he walked into the kitchen he said, "You didn't wake me up this time."

"Nope. This one was different. The subject matter was the same, but the overall dream was different. Not so much violence. I woke up on my own and wasn't so much in a frenzy as I normally am. Guess the amount of violence that's normally contained within those dreams isn't directly proportional to the amount of sleep I get after they're over. Even though this one wasn't so violent, I still couldn't go back to sleep."

He sat down on the couch with her, picked up the remote, and turned down the volume on the TV.

"What was it about?"

She looked away as she took a sip of her coffee. After remaining silent for a moment, she said, "I don't honestly know."

"Does the killer have the same face as Judge Dunn? Is that still going on?"

"Oh yeah, that hasn't changed."

"So, what happened?"

"I really don't know. Again, it was something about a box, some box. I still haven't figured out for the life of me, what the hell I'm looking for. There was a box in front of me, and all of a sudden, he was standing over my shoulder. I never looked at him. I just kept looking through items in that box. Then I'd stop, like I was thinking about something, then I'd start looking through the box again."

"Did you ever find anything?"

"No. I just don't understand. It's no longer only about him. It's about something else. I mean, the nature of the dreams has changed. I could never make out a face. Now, I can see a face, even though it's apparently the wrong one. The dreams have never, ever, included anything, but the murder. Now, here I am looking through some fucking box, for some fucking thing—for something or other…I just don't get it. It's so frustrating for me, Jack. I just wish it would all end."

"Definitely time for you to see a shrink."

"I know, I know. I'm planning on making an appointment this week. But that didn't help much last night. Don't you think it's strange though, that I continue to see that judge's face as the face of the murderer? I am really starting to wonder if there's something to this. I wonder if I should somehow follow up on it."

"How the hell are you going to 'follow up' on that? Are you just going to go up to him and ask him if he killed your mother 20 years ago? Come on, Ann, there's nothing to it, believe me. It's coincidence and clearly caused by the fact that you met the judge, he's a prick, you couldn't get along with him, and now you've placed his face on the face of your mother's murderer. That's it. No more, no less. How the hell could he be her murderer? There's just no way."

"You may be right, but it just seems to me, out of all the pricks I've met since mom died, particularly in law school, he's the only one I see in those dreams. Don't you think that's a little strange?"

"No. He's clearly the *biggest* prick you've ever met."

She laughed. "You've certainly got that right. But I think it's strange. I don't know what to do about it."

He frowned and looked down his nose at her.

"Okay, okay, obviously I can't do *anything* about it, but I've come to the conclusion there's somehow a connection. I'm not sure what it is, but there's a connection, Jack, there's a connection." She remained alone with her thoughts for a moment, before she said, "Let's change the subject. Where are we at on the partnership? We haven't discussed it at all the past couple of weeks."

"I talked to Beth about that a couple of days ago. I guess everything will be ready about the first of February. The new girl starts then, and all the tax paperwork is scheduled to take effect then."

"So, as of the first of February, it will be Connors and Connors?"

"Yup, it sure will."

She kissed him. "Couldn't be more excited. Professionally, are you ready for the change?"

"Yes. Most everything I'm working on in my other office will be completed by then. Those matters I'm working on that can't be completed by then, I'll just turn over to someone else."

"Great." She looked away, thought for a moment and said, "What about the house? Have you heard anything from anyone about it?"

"Nope. The last I heard was they would let me know the amount I needed to wire in about three weeks."

"When do you want to start looking for furniture?"

"Maybe next week we should start. That work for you?"

"Yes." Again, she remained quiet, deep in thought.

She turned toward him, and said, "You know, Jack, I've never been happier. This has all worked out so well. I mean, I miss Harold, but I guess it all worked out for us in the long run. We work well together—we have been so successful in what we've done together—I couldn't be happier."

"Nor I, Ann. We definitely work well as partners, not only in our personal relationship, but in the practice. I felt many times during the trial, that what I was weak at, was your strength, and vice versa. Now, what about a little breakfast. You cookin' or am I?"

She said nothing, continuing to stare into space.

"You still believe, even after my incredible powers of persuasion, that the judge may be the murderer, don't you?"

"I don't know that I actually believe *that*, but I think somewhere in my subconscious, there's a reason for all this, that's all. I'm just not smart enough to figure it all out. But I still think somehow, he's involved, yes I do."

They were to be at Sally's home around 3:00 p.m. She had a couple of hours before they were to be there, so she decided to go to the office, look through a few more messages and check her appointment schedule for the rest of the week.

As she looked through her list of appointments, she leaned back in her chair, and thought, once again, about the dreams. One reoccurring fact continued to bother her and this one had nothing to do with the identity of the murderer. Obviously, there was a box, a box...

She started to smile. *She remembered a box*—maybe *it* was the box that was continuing to find its way into her subconscious mind.

After her mother died, she had boxed up those personal items that to her, at five years of age, were important. She put everything in a box, a box that looked amazingly like the one in her dreams. She hadn't opened it since she had filled it. Ann could never make herself look through it because of the intense sorrow she felt every time she considered looking through those items that were so important to her at that age—at the time her mother was so violently removed from her life.

But now she was certain—she was certain *that* was the box she continued to see in her dreams. It was probably insignificant, but it was time to open it—time to consider all those physical items that would again remind her of that horrible event, but were, in addition, a part of her persona, a part of who she was today.

Maybe, after such a lapse in time, she could now look at those items without the flood of emotion she felt during each and every one of those nightmares—*maybe*.

Chapter 45

Even though she had convinced herself that the *box* with her possessions was *the box* she was dreaming about, and even though she really did want to look through it, they were still obligated to those preplanned social events the remainder of New Year's Day.

Certainly, it would be there tomorrow. In addition, it wasn't as if she was giddy about going through all those items again—pulling up all those old memories one more time. Most likely, her efforts would amount to nothing more than a waste of time anyway.

They spent the waning hours of New Year's Day with Sally and her family, not arriving home until after 9:00 pm. She had thought about leaving Sally's early—driving to the storage unit where both she and Jack left all their unnecessary items when she moved in with him. But she was tired and just couldn't see the necessity of the trip at that late hour.

The next morning, once at the office, she reviewed her schedule for the day. There would be time near noon to drive to the storage unit. She needed to make sure that time period remained open and not full of appointments.

As Ann was about to tell Beth she needed to see her, she appeared in her office doorway with a cup of coffee in hand.

Beth leaned against the doorframe, and said, "How was your New Years? You drink him under the table on New Year's Eve?"

Ann smiled and said, "No. It was very quiet in our home. We did go to Sally's on New Year's Day, but that, too, was quiet. There's enough excitement and drama here during the week to carry over through those holidays. I don't need more of it when I'm home. What'd you do?"

"Oh, my newest boyfriend and I drank a little too much, but nothing we both couldn't handle. We went out for a while early in the evening, then just crashed at his place the rest of the night."

"I was just going to message you. Don't fill in those open time slots later this morning with appointments. I have to be out of the office for a while today."

"Okay. Anything important?"

She leaned back in her chair and said, "No, not really. I just need to look through some of our items we placed in our storage unit."

"I know you been having a lot of dreams lately about your mom. Do these 'items' you're referring to have anything to do with your mom—with her murder?"

"They might. Probably a complete waste of time, but I need to go through them and that's the best time today to get it done."

"Apparently you're still dreaming?"

"Oh yeah. I'm afraid that's not going to end anytime soon."

"You've never mentioned it, but I assume you've seen all kinds of professionals for help, haven't you? I mean, is there nothing you can do to stop the nightmares from continuing to reoccur?"

"Unfortunately, no. At least that's what I'm told. And yes, I've seen shrinks from the time I was five, until I went to college. I stopped then. The nightmares didn't seem to be as severe. Really, they haven't increased in intensity until just recently—until I met that idiot Judge Dunn."

"Did any of them help you remember anything relevant?"

"No. To be honest, initially I couldn't hardly remember a thing. I had what they called *repressed memory*. Oh, I could remember a few minor details, but the trauma of it all prohibited me from remembering everything that happened. As time has passed, there are moments when I see something, or smell something, or there's a sound I hear, that brings part of it back. But it's never been enough to really figure out who did it."

"Did they try hypnosis?"

"A couple of times. It was in the year's right after it happened. There just wasn't enough to go on. I did recall a few more facts, but there was just never enough to figure out who it was."

She looked away, hesitated, then said, "To be honest, I've been pretty good for a long time. In the past few years, I would have an occasional nightmare, but nothing I couldn't handle—until recently. It's all been much worse in recent weeks. I keep seeing this box. I have no idea what it means. I do have a box of my things I had as a child, but I haven't looked at what's inside forever."

She looked at Beth and said, "So today I'll take the time out of a rather busy schedule to go to that storage unit. I'll go through my things and try to figure out if there's something I've missed."

Beth looked down for a moment before she continued. "You know how much I respect you." She looked up and smiled. "You've had so much to overcome during your life, but you just keep hanging in there. You're my hero."

Ann smiled. "That's nice of you to say, Beth, but I'm no hero, believe me. I've just faced a few more adverse situations then most people and, as you know, quitting is not an option in this world. You just keep moving along and hope to hell it all turns out right."

"Even with these two cases both of which it looked like you were going to lose, you just kept hanging in there, until they ended up like you wanted them to. You know, I've worked for people who would have lost because they just gave up—just couldn't see it through like you did. Your perseverance, your determination, saw you through both cases. I just want you to know I'm proud to work for you."

"Thanks Beth, that's nice to hear. I'm glad you work for me also. We work well together." She heard someone walk through the front office door. "Apparently, we just got busy. Let's go to work."

Beth smiled. "Sounds good, boss. I'll mark off the time."

Ann drove to the storage unit later that morning. She parked, unlocked the storage unit door, and rolled it up, out of the way.

They had basically filled the space. The front end was packed, with only a narrow path leading to the back, which was where she remembered she placed that small, cardboard box.

Along the back wall, she found what she was looking for under a number of old blankets. Ann had left those there when she determined they just wouldn't fit in with Jack's décor, and which were unnecessary, but which she was unwilling to throw away.

She picked up the box, and carried it to the front of the storage unit. She placed it on the hood of her car while she closed and locked the storage unit door, then placed it in her car and drove back to the office.

It was noon. Ann had to unlock the door to get in. She locked it behind her, walked back to the quiet sanctity of her office, placed the box on a chair, then pulled a chair around to face it.

Ann opened the interlocking flaps and looked down on those items which, some 20 years ago, had seemed so very important to her.

The first item she removed was her blanket. She had to smile as she held it to her chest. She never, ever went to bed without it. The first thing she grabbed upon waking each morning was that blanket, and most days it remained exactly where she was until it was time for bed, at which time it was again, lying by her side.

Ann laid it down and looked back at the remaining contents, next pulling out her teddy bear. It too, was an important element of each night's bedtime process, never going to bed without that teddy bear by her side.

Under the teddy bear, she found her three dolls. Her mother had given her all of the dolls, and she couldn't count the number of times they—the three dolls, Ann and her mother—had had a tea party. She laid them down carefully on her desk, thinking how much joy she would have in giving them to her own daughter someday, even though they, most likely, would be outdated.

Ann once again looked in the box. What she found next, brought tears to her eyes. A dog collar and rubber dog bone belonging to Rags, were near the bottom of the box. She picked them up and held them to her chest, remembering the night his life was cut short by the bastard that killed her mother. That memory was almost as difficult to recall as her mother's murder.

She wiped away the tears, then placed the items alongside the other memories on top of her desk.

The only remaining item laying in the box, at the very bottom, was a picture within a medal frame. She reached down, and picked up the frame containing a picture of her mother and herself, taken immediately prior to her mother's murder, remembering vaguely the day it was taken.

Ann stood it up on her desk, then looked down into an empty box, hoping, praying, there might be something left at the bottom which might have caused the increase in intensity of the dreams she continued to have concerning the container she had just emptied.

She stood and walked behind her desk, still having no idea why she had been drawn to it by her subconscious.

As she stared at the items, absolutely nothing about any of them, shed any light on those dreams. Ann walked to the back room for a cup of coffee. As she walked back through her office door, she continued to stare at the items on her desk.

She sat down as she once again recalled that night. Ann reviewed everything from the moment she heard the noise in the living room until the police walked in. She remembered being in the closet and looking through that crack between the door and the door frame, watching him…watching him walk across the room, and …

What was he doing? What did he do? She had *forgotten* what he did. *He reached down, and took hold of that picture frame.* That was the moment he knew someone else lived there with her mother! He looked her direction, then the cops came and he ran.

She sat up in her chair and looked at the frame. She had forgotten he had picked up that frame. How could she have forgotten that? What the hell was wrong with her? Could there be a print he left on the frame? Could it still be there? She had touched it. Could touching it now, or touching it when she had, years ago…picking it up and placing it in the box, have obliterated his print?

Ann stood and walked to the front of her desk. Carefully she placed everything, but the frame, back in the box. She then, using a tissue, picked up the frame, slid it into a large brown envelope and placed it in her bottom desk drawer.

As she took the box containing all its contents but the frame, to the back room, she considered what should do next. She had to know if the frame contained a print and if it did, if it matched anyone's print now contained in the law enforcement data banks.

She had no idea how to proceed. As she walked back to her desk, she started to smile. There was one person who would know how to proceed from here. Matt Armstrong had helped her get out of two difficult situations already. Hopefully, she could call on him one more time—this time to help her solve a mystery that had dominated her life for almost a quarter of a century.

Chapter 46

Ann called Matt's office, but had been unable to reach him. He was out on business and most likely would not return the rest of the day. She asked his secretary if he had time available tomorrow. She indicated he did. Ann scheduled an appointment with him, at her office, tomorrow morning at 9:00 a.m. She was anxious to meet as soon as possible, but tomorrow morning would need to be acceptable—she had no other available option.

Is it possible the judge was, in fact, her mother's killer? How could that be even remotely possible? Even though she knew it was highly unlikely, she would pursue *both* issues—the fingerprint on the knife and the possibility the judge might be the killer.

As she considered what additional information he might need for Matt, she wondered if the judge's son might be able to provide her with any additional facts that might prove helpful. Obviously, she wouldn't divulge her purpose, but perhaps a visit, in the name of friendship, might shed some additional light upon issues concerning the judge's past.

Her appointments would preclude any contact with him this morning, but immediately after the noon hour, she would drive to Lebanon, hoping Mark Dunn had time to visit with her.

As she cleaned up some pressing matters that needed her attention, she heard Jack walk into the reception area and ask if she was busy. A few seconds later he walked through her office door.

"Hey hon, how about lunch? You have time?"

"Hi, Jack. Lunch? Can't today. I've got a few things I really need to get done before this afternoon, but I'll certainly take a rain check."

He sat down as he said, "Really? You're turning down lunch with me—the love of your life—the man who, contrary to most men you might have hooked up with, loves you more than he loves himself? What's so important?"

She was reluctant to tell him what she had remembered about the frame. She hadn't told him last night. She was concerned he might, for some reason or another, be upset because she was spending her time on unresolvable issues that occurred so many years ago. He had been less than receptive as concerned her pursuit of issues involving her mother's death in the past. But she ultimately concluded it was going to come out eventually one way or the other, so it might as well happen right now.

"Oh, I thought I might go see Mark Dunn—you know, the judge's son. I want to ask him a few more questions about his father. Won't take long, but there are a few things I need to do here before I go see him."

"Questions about what?"

"Oh, just some questions about the judge's illegal activities in Nashville and a time line as to when they might have occurred. It's no big deal, but I have a little extra time during the early afternoon so I thought I'd go have a cup of coffee with him."

"You're kidding. Ann, why don't you just move on, like the rest of us do? You know, it's been almost a quarter of a century. We have our own lives, our own issues to look forward to together. Can't you just forget the past and move on with me— together with me?"

She could tell this conversation was heading the wrong direction and she really didn't want this to end up in a heated argument. They seldom argued about anything and, at this point, there was little substance to argue about anyway.

"You're probably right. I'll think about it. Maybe I won't go."

Neither said anything. Finally, he stood, and said, "You're going anyway, aren't you?"

"I don't know. I may. Don't get upset, Jack. I won't be long if I do go. I'll be home in time for supper."

"Whatever. I just hope one of these days you can put that issue behind you and live in the present instead of continuing to fight with your past. Maybe the nightmares would end then. Maybe we could both move on with our life together, rather than having this issue always hanging there, never knowing when it will come up again, at which time we *always* end up having to regurgitate the whole event over—and over—and *over*. I'll see you at home."

"Jack wait…"

He was out the door before she could finish her sentence.

Ann walked in the Wilson County Clerk's office just after 1:00 p.m. She walked up to the counter and asked if Mark was working. A few minutes later, he walked out of the back office and toward the front counter.

"Hi. I thought your trial was over. What're you doing here?"

"Hi, Mark. Oh, I had a few people I needed to visit with in Lebanon, and while I was here, I thought I'd just drop in and see if you had time for a cup of coffee."

"I do. Come on back."

During the following 15 minutes, they talked mostly about the trial and how it ended. She didn't want to immediately dive into the intended purpose for her visit, concerned he would wonder what her motive might actually be. But after a long quarter of an hour, it was time to, at least subtly, address the reason for which she was there.

"Your father is an interesting study."

"Never thought of him as 'interesting' I guess. I just thought of him as my father and little else. What do you mean, 'interesting?'"

"First of all, I assume none of this conversation will go any further. I don't want him mad at me. I plan on being in his court many times before either he or I give up the practice."

He laughed. "If we are going to talk about him it would probably be good if what *either* of us says never gets back to him. No, you don't need to worry about any part of what we say getting back to him."

"Thanks, Mark. As you already know, he's a tough old bird in court. Is he the same way at home?"

"Pretty much. He's always been difficult to be around, unless he's had a drink or two. Then he's a little easier to be around, but not much."

"You said he and your mother were divorced. Does he date? Are there any women in his life?"

"Oh, there are until they find out what he's really like—then there aren't. He's reached the point around here where his reputation precedes him. There aren't many left that want to go out with him."

"Was he tough on your mother?"

"Yes, both verbally and physically. She loved him, but she just reached the point where she couldn't take it anymore. I'm still close to her. As I told you, I plan on leaving here in a few years to live near her in California."

"Does he have any friends—people he confides in?"

"No, not really. Oh, on occasion, he'll go out with a couple of lawyers and have a drink, but not very often. He's a loner and really doesn't care much for people. He likes being left alone and that's how it is most of the time. Even when it comes to me, he doesn't care if I continue to live in the same house with him, but he wants me to stay the hell away from him when we're both there. I might see him a few times a week, even though we live in the same house."

"I hate to say this because I don't want to disparage him, but you must take after your mother."

He laughed, as he said, "That's a compliment, believe me. She's the best. I can't wait to move—to live near her."

"He always been this way, or did something happen to change him into the man he is today?"

"As long as I've known him, he's the same as he is now."

"I wonder—you mentioned something about some trouble he was in during his younger years. Might that have affected him somehow?"

"I really don't know. I don't know much about that. I would on occasion, especially when I was younger, overhear my folks discuss and sometimes laugh about his earlier years, when he got in trouble. Mom would talk about how she turned him around. They separated for a period after I was born. That was when he got in trouble—while he was living away from her in Nashville."

"What year would that have been—I mean the year he was in all the trouble?"

"It would have been about twenty years ago."

She tried not to show any emotion—to remain uninterested in obtaining information and only interested in making conversation, but it was extremely difficult to do, after what he had just said. The judge had apparently been in trouble in Nashville the year her mother was murdered.

"Was he ever in trouble after that, or did your mother take care of business once she got him settled down?"

"He never had another problem with the law."

"How'd he get out of the trouble he had in Nashville?"

"My grandfather was a good man. He had a little pull in the city. The problems dad got into didn't amount to all that much, but it was enough he would have been left with a record. My grandfather made a few calls and got him out of it by having dad plead to a couple of simple misdemeanors, I guess. At least that's what I understood while overhearing the conversations between mom and dad."

"What happened once the problems in Nashville disappeared?"

"He finished law school, practiced law and eventually was appointed judge. He hasn't been a judge very long. He was involved in private practice and when a vacancy came up, he pulled a few strings and was appointed to fill it."

That was all she needed to know. She carried on what she hoped was an interesting conversation, but the purpose for meeting with him had been achieved. She left a few minutes later.

That night, once Jack arrived home, he apologized. They had supper and later went for a walk. He never asked, nor did she ever offer any information concerning her trip to Lebanon.

She had learned a good lesson today. Jack was tired of hearing about the trauma she endured years ago—he had finally reached the point where he wanted to hear no more. She would not bother him with it unless something tangible came about as a result of the fingerprint. If Matt was able to help, she would discuss it with Jack. Otherwise, her mother's murder would remain absent from any conversation between the two of them from now on.

Chapter 47

Ann was handling only those more important issues upon which she could maintain her concentration. All remaining, more trivial matters, would need to be handled another day. It was early morning. Matt was to arrive for his appointment in about an hour. Beth was already working. She had not been in to see Ann yet, but Ann heard her arrive and start her routine for the day.

It had once again been *one of those nights*. This time, her nightmare was one of the most intense she had ever endured. It didn't last all that long, but it *did* continue on through the murder of her mother. Normally, they were either shorter than that, or she woke up before it happened. But last night was different. Last night, he made her watch. And of course, the *he* was the same *he,* it had been since she met him. Judge Dunn was, once again, the center of attention.

She heard Beth walking down the hallway. Once she arrived at her doorway, she smiled and said, "Morning." As she continued to look at Ann, her smile quickly turned to a frown, as she said, "Oh, my gosh, you look tired. You didn't have another dream, did you?"

Ann leaned back, and said, "Oh yeah, sure did. Worst one ever. This one took me all the way through mom's murder. It was a doozy. Jack finally woke me up, but it was around two and I didn't get back to sleep until, I think, around four-thirty. Not one of my better nights for sure."

"I'm sorry, Ann. I wish that would end for you. By the way, I see you have Matt coming in today. Does this pertain to any particular case? I'll pull the file and get it back to you if it does."

"It does pertain to a case, but there is no file. It pertains to my case—my mother's murder. I want him to do a little investigating for me."

"Really? Are you on to something?"

"Most likely not, but Matt's good at what he does, and if anyone can help me, it's him. I'll let him take a look at what I have, and we'll go from there. He should be here in about an hour. I don't want anybody interfering with that appointment. Hold my calls while he's here."

"Sounds like this is pretty important—at least to you. I won't let anyone near your office or put anyone through on the phone. I just hope this works. I hope you can finally find some peace."

"Thanks. So do I."

Matt arrived on time, as usual, and Beth escorted him back to Ann's office.

Ann stood and smiled as she said, "Morning, Matt."

"Good morning. This must be pretty important. It sounded to my secretary like you were frantic to get in touch. Sounds like you want me to work on some personal business—something which you didn't care to discuss on the phone. What's going on?"

As Ann sat down, she said "I need you to do some work for me, and yes, it's personal, if you're available."

"I'm available and I certainly owe you after you sent both those clients to me. What is it you need?"

"My mother was murdered 20 years ago. The murderer was never identified. He was never caught."

Matt considered her comments for a moment, then said, "I'm sorry. I didn't know that."

"It's not really anything that I normally talk about, and it happened so long ago, most people have forgotten. Most of my friends, the children who were my age when it happened, were never told about it. The fact not many know about it now is fine with me. I'm not looking for sympathy in this life, so the fewer that know is a positive for me."

"I understand. Are you, at this late date, some 20 years later, wanting me to try to find out who did it? I can tell you right now, I probably won't have much success concerning something like that. It's been too long. Contacts having any information will be tough to find. I'll be glad to try I guess, but certainly no promises on this one."

"I understand. Matt, I think you're really good at what you do, but I would never go so far as to ask you to try to uncover who actually committed a crime now 20 years old. But let me ask you, do you have contacts at the police station here, like you did in Lebanon?"

"Contacts? Well, I have people in law enforcement that I can turn to when I need some help, yes, if that's what you mean. That's what happened in Lebanon—I had a contact there and it worked out well. I do have law enforcement officers in Nashville that will assist me if I need some assistance."

"Okay, let me explain where we're at. I have these nightmares, have for years. They are always about the murder. I witnessed it when I was five years old. I was in a back bedroom when this guy murdered my mom. I was watching through a space between the door and the doorframe. I saw him, only briefly, and I was just a child. So, as you can imagine, it's all pretty fuzzy this many years later. I've been to shrinks everywhere, and they've hypnotized me, drugged me and done everything they can think of to help me put a face on the killer. None of that ever worked."

"I understand. Well, obviously, something's changed or I wouldn't be here. What happened?"

"I met a judge in Wilson County, the one that was trying the Cline case. Ever since then, it's his face I see in my dreams. The nightmares have become much more violent. I had another one last night, the worst ever. Unfortunately, for some reason, it's his face on the face of the killer that I see in every dream I've had since I met him."

Matt sat up on the edge of his chair. "Now wait. You're not saying the judge killed your mother, are you? I hope you got something to go on beyond your dreams, because I know that guy. He's not going to take being called a murderer, lightly. I'll have to rethink working for you on this one if that's the path we're going down."

She laughed and said, "No, no just relax. I wouldn't have asked even you to solve this mystery based only upon that."

He settled back in his chair. "Thank God. What else do you have? Anything, anything at all?"

"His son is a deputy clerk in Wilson County. I had an opportunity to talk to him a number of times during the trial and again yesterday."

"Was that beneficial in some way?"

"Well, first of all, he says his father is a jerk. He abused his mother, and their own relationship—father and son—is really rocky. But the one thing he was able to tell me that might help, is that about 20 years ago, the judge lived in Nashville. During that time, he was, as I understand it, arrested multiple times for multiple offenses. He couldn't tell me exactly what the offenses were. He said the judge's father, his grandfather, was able to get him out of most of his problems, but the judge did plead guilty to a few misdemeanors in Davidson County. They started as felonies, but were reduced down to misdemeanors."

Matt had taken out a small notepad and started writing.

"His name was Dunn correct?"

"Yes, Rodney Dunn."

"Well, I can ask around and check the record, but I don't think that's going to help much." He stood. "I'll let you know what I find out."

"No, no, wait. Have a seat. There's more."

He sat down, as she continued.

"While I was in the middle of a nightmare a few weeks ago, I kept seeing this box. I had no idea what that meant. I did have a box of items I put away when I was five, after the murder, but I hadn't looked through it since."

"You mean like personal items—a five-year-old child's storage chest?"

"Exactly. So, the other day, I got that box out, and started looking through it. All of a sudden, I remembered I had watched as the murderer picked up a picture frame. I was watching him through a small opening from inside the closet in the bedroom and saw him pick it up and look at the picture of my mother and myself. He set it back down when he heard sirens outside the building."

Matt thought for a moment, then said, "And you still have the frame, correct?"

"I do."

"And the frame has his print on it, correct?"

She smiled. "It does."

"So, we have him in Nashville during that time period, we most likely have his prints downtown because of his illegal activities, and we have a print on the frame." He sat back.

"That's a pretty good piece of detective work, Ms. Connors, just a pretty nice piece of work."

"Everything is right there, it's just whether or not it all matches up. Can you have the print on the frame compared to his prints within the records of the police department? Can you get that done?"

"Absolutely."

"I have to tell you, there may be another print or two on there. I picked it up yesterday before putting two and two together, so I know mines on there. My mothers would be on there. I was the one that put it in the box after her death. I don't know if anyone touched the frame before mom had it, but I do know once she got it, the most recent prints were hers, the killer and mine."

"Do you have the frame here?"

"Yes." She turned around and picked up the brown envelope, handing it to Matt.

"This is going to take a day or two, but it shouldn't take long to match up one print. I'll let you know as soon as I know."

"Thanks, Matt. I'm not going to sleep very well until I know the results, but these nightmares keep me up anyway, so I guess the underlying reason for a sleepless night doesn't much matter. Just do the best you can."

He left shortly thereafter, promising to contact her as soon as he knew anything.

Later that afternoon, Beth messaged Ann that Sally was on line one.

"Hi, Sally. How're you?"

"Good. How are you coming along?"

"Tired."

"Nightmares still keeping you up?"

"Sure are. Nothing's changed in that area. Hopefully though, if things work out right, that could change."

"Why? What's happened? There you go again—not telling me until long after something's happened. What's going on, Ann?"

She started to tell her, then stopped. She thought for a moment, before she said, "Sally, I really can't say anything. I promise I'll let you know when and if something develops, but I can't say anything right now."

That seemed to satisfy her for the moment. Ann was done going through multiple explanations of her issues and her problems concerning her mother's death. She wasn't going to say a word to anyone until Matt let her know the results of his research. Jack had made it clear he had heard enough, and if he had heard enough, she figured everyone else had too.

Chapter 48

Ann waited for a call from Matt the remainder of the afternoon. Common sense told her it was too soon to expect a response, but that didn't stop her from hoping the call would come sometime before she left the office.

That night at home, Jack asked her if she was feeling alright a couple of times. She knew how quiet she must have seemed, but this was a life-altering event and as great of importance to her as anything she had ever been a part of. But his call didn't come before it was time to retire for the night.

Sleep didn't come easy. She tossed and turned, finally nodding off around 3:00 a.m. She knew Matt wouldn't call during the night, but that still didn't help her shut down—to shut off the thought process and fall asleep.

Thursday morning she was up, even as tired as she was, at the crack of dawn. She was in her office long before she figured Jack even woke up.

There were plenty of important issues, along with an expanding number of unimportant issues, that needed her attention. But after handling each matter, she would lean back and consider all the possibilities Matt's eventual phone call could hold.

If he found out nothing, obviously her investigation was over. There was nothing more she could do. It certainly didn't take a brain surgeon to reach that conclusion. The pressing issue was what if he *did* find out the print matched—whether it matched the judge's print or someone else's print now on record. That was the issue she continued to consider—exactly what she was going to do if there *was* a match. She contemplated a number of options, but she never did finally come to a conclusion concerning which option she would pursue.

Beth arrived on time. Shortly after she had pulled files for the day and reviewed the schedule, she walked into Ann's office.

As she sat down, she said, "Whoa, once again, we must have had another nightmare."

"Thanks a lot. It's always encouraging to know I'm starting my day looking my best."

"Sorry."

"Actually, I didn't have a nightmare last night. I've just got a lot on my mind. How's the day look?"

"Nothing's changed. The schedule's the same as what we discussed before I left last night. Nothing earth-shattering, but you do have quite a few appointments lined up."

"One thing about today—if Matt Armstrong calls and wants to talk, or if he wants an appointment sometime during the day, get him in. Move appointments around, or cancel one or two, I don't really care, but just make sure he gets in here."

"That sounds important."

"It is."

She had just finished her 10:00 a.m. appointment when Beth informed her Jack was on line one.

"Morning. What time did you get up? I got up at seven and your side of the bed was cold. What time did you go to work?"

"You know, I'm not really sure. Somewhere around six. Couldn't sleep so I just came to work."

"Another nightmare? I didn't hear you."

"No, I just couldn't sleep."

"I got some good news for you."

"What?"

"I just got a call. We're going to be able to settle on the house the middle of the month. We're not going to need to wait until the end of January. We can settle and move in about the 15th."

"Great! You're right, that is good news."

"Maybe we can go out for supper tonight—celebrate a little."

"Let's wait and see how we both feel, but that's a good idea. By the way, there's something I continue to forget to ask you."

"What's that?"

"What do you think about getting a dog?"

"When?"

"When we move into our new home. Obviously, we couldn't have one while living in the apartment, but now, with a home of our own, I'd like to get a dog."

He hesitated. "What do you have in mind?"

"Something small, like Rags—a house dog. Nothing that's going to take up much space or be much of a bother for either of us."

"Sure, that's not a problem for me. Maybe we can discuss it when we go out tonight."

The call ended as her appointment walked in the office door.

She heard nothing from Matt the rest of the day.

Once she arrived home, Jack wanted to go out to eat. Her heart wasn't in it, but it wasn't in anything right now, so to pass the time as much as anything, she said she would go.

During the meal she continued to check her phone, but heard nothing.

Sleep again proved nearly impossible. She finally sat up in bed a little after five and just decided to, once again, go to work. She had plenty to do and maybe it would help her think of something other than Matt.

The day remained unremarkable, until shortly after the noon hour, when Beth contacted Ann while Ann was discussing some estate planning ideas with one of Mr. Dale's old clients. She told her Matt would be in around three. Her heart skipped a beat, as she continued her conversation with the client, all the while thinking about Matt and what information he might or might not provide her.

At this point she simply wasn't sure what to hope for. If he had no information for her, it was over—for good. If he did, she would know who her mother's killer was, but that would certainly bring about a whole new set of issues as she made sure there was some form of justice rendered for the murder.

Matt arrived on time, as usual. Beth escorted him to Ann's office, and as he sat, Ann said, "Well, were you able to come to any conclusions?"

"Yes. I was able to get in to see the individual that takes care of this type of work with the department, yesterday morning. He called me this morning. I don't have anything in writing, but he's sending me the results which I should have in a couple of days."

Ann waited for him to continue, but when he didn't, even though her heart was in her throat, she said, "What conclusion did he come to?"

"Well, there were three sets of prints on there. Two he was unable to confirm and I'm assuming those prints belonged to you and your mother."

"What about the other set?"

He hesitated briefly before he said, "They were Judge Dunn's."

She said nothing. She couldn't. The news literally took her breath away.

Her hands were shaking so badly, she couldn't pick up her coffee cup. She looked away.

"You okay?"

She said nothing.

"Ann, look at me. Are you okay?"

She finally turned toward him, and whispered, "Yes, I'm fine, I'm fine, Matt."

"Now, I think we better talk about your next course of action here. I'll accompany you to the police station in Lebanon if you wish, whenever you want to go."

Again, Ann turned away. She knew figuring out her next step would take some time, and it would need to be done without input from anyone. She needed to figure this out herself. There were two or three options she had in mind. The decision to pursue the option she felt was most appropriate, would be *her* decision and her decision alone.

She turned toward Matt and said, "I need to think about this. You've been a huge help, Matt. I couldn't have finished off any of the last few matters I've handled without your help."

"Ann, let me help you with this. Let's figure this out together. Let's talk about the options and which direction you may want to move."

Ann stood. "Thanks Matt, but I'm going to do that on my own."

"So, I take it by your actions, that you're dismissing me."

Ann laughed. "Only until I need you again, which if the past is any indication of the future, will probably be very, very soon."

He stood and embraced her.

Once he reached her office door, he turned and said, "Ann, I know how important this is to you. I know you've been waiting over 20 years to figure out who did this, and that you probably never figured it would happen. But don't blow it now. You've got the guy right where you want him. Don't do something foolish based on emotion and only on emotion. Let law enforcement do their thing. Let them handle this. Just take a little more advice from me. Let them handle everything."

Ann smiled as she said, "Thanks, Matt. That's good advice, and I'll most likely follow it, but as you can imagine, I'm a little emotional right now. I need to let go of the emotion and do what you just told me to do. But for now, I want to think this all through. I'll be in touch soon."

Shortly after he left, Ann cancelled her appointments for the rest of the day. She needed to figure out her next move concerning the judge, and she couldn't do that while advising someone on how they should draw up a will—she needed peace and quiet.

Beth left the office at five. Ann went home shortly thereafter. The evening was spent with Jack asking her on more than one occasion why she was so quiet—whether she felt alright—what was on her mind.

Sleep for the third night in a row, was nearly impossible. She finally dozed off sometime after 1:00 a.m., but she awoke shortly before 5:00 a.m., and the first thing she thought about was the judge.

Finally, near 7:30, she came to a conclusion. Jack had left for a run, and she was alone.

She put her clothes on and worked with her hair, using a minimum of effort. Her physical appearance was the least of her concerns.

It was Saturday. She needed to know he was home, that he was physically located *in* his home in Lebanon before she did anything else.

She remembered a legal directory at the office Jack had picked up from the Wilson County Clerk's office while they were trying the Cline case. It contained the phone number, office and home, of each judge and attorney in Wilson County.

She drove to the office and found it lying on the desk which Jack would soon be using on a regular basis. She looked through the directory until she found his name, the name of Judge Rodney Dunn.

His court house chambers phone number was located just above his home phone number. It was too cold to play golf. At this time of day, she figured he would be home. She punched in his number.

After the fifth ring, Judge Dunn answered and said, "What the hell are you doing calling me at this hour, on a Saturday morning, at my home? How dare you!"

Chapter 49

"**G**ood Morning, Judge. You going to be home all morning, or you going out to play a little golf?"

"What's it matter to you? To goddamn cold to play golf, as you already know. But I can assure you if and when I do, you won't be part of the foursome. Is that *really* why you called? You want to play golf with me? Or did you have some other menial, idiotic reason for calling?"

"I sure do. I need to see you."

"You can see me when I'm in the courthouse. Now I've got a few more important matters to deal with this morning, like trimming my toenails. So, take care now, and don't get hit by a truck—then again, I don't give a shit whether you get hit by a truck or not. Good luck, and bye-bye."

"Sorry, we need to talk—today. I'll be there in about forty-five minutes."

"You're coming here? To see me? Oh, I think not."

"*Oh, I think so,* and if you know what's good for you, you'll be there and the door will be unlocked—unless you want me to go directly to the police with what I know about you."

He hesitated. She had no doubt that statement would at least get her in the front door.

"You know nothing about me. What kind of information do you think you have?"

"I'll be there in half-hour. I'll visit with you then. Bye-bye."

She terminated the call, got in her vehicle and started the drive to Lebanon.

She pulled up in front of his home forty-five minutes later. She pulled out her phone and called Jack.

He was still breathing heavily from his run, as he said, "Hi, hon. I just got home. Where are you? You working today?"

"No. Now Jack, you need to listen carefully. I never said anything to you about this, but I remembered one day while going through some of my old things, that whoever killed mom picked up a picture frame. I figured whoever killed her might have left a print on that frame."

"You're right, you never told me that."

"I forgot about the frame until just recently. You remember, I told you I kept seeing that box in my dreams? Well, I finally remembered what box I was dreaming about. It contained a number of my personal items I put in there after mom was murdered. The picture frame the killer picked up was in there."

"Just a minute. I'm sweating all over the floor. Let me towel off."

"Hurry, Jack. I don't have much time."

A few seconds later he said, "What do you mean you don't have much time. Where are you?"

"I called Matt Armstrong and asked him to do me a favor. I asked him to check the print on the frame against the prints of Judge Dunn, which I assumed were on file with the police department from the time he got in all that trouble in Nashville."

"You what? Ann, I told you this needed to end. I told you…"

"Jack, please let me finish. The print on the frame and the prints of Judge Dunn on file, were a match. Jack, he murdered my mom. Judge Dunn is a murderer."

He said nothing.

"Did you hear what I said?" She heard him stand. Finally, he said, "Are you sure? Is there any question about the match? I mean, if you tell law enforcement about that and you're wrong, he'll sue your ass for sure. You need to be sure that…"

"I am. There's no question about the match."

"Okay. You need to come home. Let's discuss what to do from here. I'll be waiting for you, and we can figure this out together…"

"Listen to me. I'm parked in front of the judge's house. I called and told him I was coming to see him. I'm going to tell the son-of-a-bitch what I think of him before he's arrested. *I need to tell him, Jack.* I'm not waiting to face him in the courtroom with a victim impact statement after he's been convicted. Those victim impact statements are a joke anyway. I need to tell him now, face to face, and that's exactly what I'm going to do. I need to tell him what kind of effect this has had on me, what he did to me, as well as tell him what I personally think of him murdering my mother in cold blood."

"No, no Ann, you can't do that. You can't go in there alone."

"I've already made up my mind. Now here's what I want you to do. Give me about 15 minutes, then call the police and tell them what's going on. Do you know anyone in the Wilson County sheriff's office—someone that knows you and will take notice if you explain what's going on?"

"Yes."

"Then call him in about 15 minutes and tell him to send the cops to Judge Dunn's house as quickly as they can get here. I need that time Jack—I need 15 minutes alone with the bastard. Do you understand what I'm telling you?"

"Would you wait until I get there? I'll go in with you."

"No. This is my problem. It's what I want to do, and I'm doing it by myself. I need to go. Do you understand what *you* need to do?"

She could hear him take a deep breath, after which he said, "Yes, I understand. Please, Ann, be careful. I love you."

"I love you, Jack. I'll see you soon."

She terminated the call, and stepped out of her vehicle. Ann walked up the sidewalk toward a large two-story home. White columns from the ground to the roof were located across the entryway. She assumed the house had to be worth hundreds of thousands of dollars. She concluded Judge Dunn would have lived in nothing less.

Ann tried the door. It was unlocked. She walked in to a large open space, with hallways to her right and left. Straight ahead was a large living area, with a massive fireplace located upon the far wall.

She had no idea which direction to proceed. It really didn't matter. She would search every hallway, every room, all day if necessary. She wasn't leaving until she said what she needed to say.

Suddenly a voice from her right echoed down the hallway. "I'm down here—in my office. Walk down the hallway and you'll find me."

She turned to her right and started walking down the hall, until she reached the only open door. She turned the corner, and walked in.

Judge Dunn was sitting behind a massive desk which faced the doorway.

"Come in, come in, you little bitch. Get on with what you need to tell me you know about me, so I can get on with my day. I have way more important things to do than screw around with an idiot like you."

She walked in, but stopped well short of his desk. She smiled and said, "We know each other."

He smiled. "That has to have been the dumbest thing ever to come from an individual's mouth in this room. What a brilliant statement. Anything else? You got anything else for me or are we done here?"

"No, I don't mean as a result of the trial, I mean before that. From another time. You and I, we've had some up close and personal contact before. I just never knew for sure you were the one until recently."

He leaned back in his chair, as he said, "Oh, really. I think not, but why don't you humor me. Where have we met before?"

"In Nashville—while you lived in Nashville about 20 years ago."

Again, that sickening smile. "Oh, I don't think so. And by the way, how do you know I lived in Nashville? You been checking up on me, have you?"

"Oh, I know all about you Judge—all about *your kind*, you sick bastard. Yes, I've been checking up on you."

"Those are pretty big words for a simple-minded dunce like you. By the way, you're a piss poor lawyer. I would suggest you find a new profession—one you can handle—like maybe washing dishes."

She smiled. "And you sir, can go fuck yourself. But I digress. Do you remember dating a woman by the name of Laura Johnson?"

He hesitated. The smile left his face. "Hell, no. Never heard of her."

"Well, she was my mother and you dated her, about 20 years ago."

"Don't remember, I guess. That all you got?"

"You murdered her."

He laughed. "Now this is just getting plain stupid. I've about had all I can take of you. Is that what you wanted to see me about?"

"I saw you do it."

"First of all, you're full of shit. Second of all, if you saw me do it, why haven't you done something about it before now?"

"I just wasn't sure. But now, when I have my triweekly nightmares, it's your face I see as the killer. You're the one, Judge. You murdered her. You're the piece of shit that took her from me. You're the asshole that almost ruined my life. You're the one, Judge. You'll rot in hell for what you did, but that's right after you rot in prison for the rest of your natural life. I've been waiting to say that to someone for a long, long time. Thanks for the opportunity."

"Is that all you got? Is that all you got to prove I murdered your mother? I told you you're a piss poor lawyer. I guess that just proves it. You got nothing."

"Well, I just happen to have a little more than that, Judge. You remember when you leaned over and picked up that picture frame in the bedroom? I saw you do that. It took a while to remember, but I saw you do that."

"I have no idea what you're talking about, but just for arguments sake, what the hell would that have to do with anything?"

"I just had the print on the frame compared to your prints when you got in all that trouble in Nashville—they were a match. *Now*, what do you think, Judge? Still not enough to convict you?"

The smile left his face. He leaned forward. "Who knows about this?"

"The cops will be here in about five minutes. Does that answer your question?"

He stood. It was clear to Ann this conversation for him, had just become serious. The smile left his face. He leaned on his desk. He stared directly at her, as he considered his next move.

Without ever looking down, he opened the top desk drawer and the next thing she knew, she was looking squarely into the business end of a pistol.

Her heart skipped a beat. She hadn't planned on this. She had no countermove. He had her right where he wanted her.

As they stood there, both silent, she heard footsteps coming down the hallway.

Mark Dunn entered the room as he said, "Hey, what's all the commotion?"

Mark's smile quickly left his face, as he too, eyed the pistol pointed directly at Ann.

Chapter 50

"**D**ad, what's going on?"

"Well, son, it seems we have an intruder."

He looked at Ann, and shrugged his shoulders. "What so you mean an intruder? You know who this is. Why are you pointing a gun at her? And where did it come from? I never knew you had a weapon in this house."

"Oh, I've had it a while. I purchased it for the very purpose for which I'll use it today—to kill an intruder,"

Mark, who continued to talk to the pistol, rather than his father, said, "Come on, Dad, you know she's not an intruder. You know her well. She would never break into someone's home. That doesn't even make sense."

The judge looked at her, then him. "No, you're probably right. It doesn't. I'll need to go to plan B."

Mark hesitated. Then clearly disgusted with the overall situation, said, "Okay, Dad, what's Plan B?"

"Let me think a minute. Actually, I don't have one."

Mark started to walk toward his father as he said, "Give me the damn gun. You aren't going to shoot anyone. Just give it to me."

"Stay back."

Mark stopped. He smiled. "Or what? You going to shoot me?"

Ann said, "Mark, do as he says. Your father's a murderer. That's why I came here—to confront him. He murdered my mother 20 years ago, in Nashville."

"What the hell are you talking about? He's no murderer, Ann. He may be a lot of things to a lot of people, but he's no murderer."

"I have proof. The cops are on their way here now."

"What kind of proof? *My Dad's no murderer*. There's just no way."

"I saw him do it, Mark. I was only five then, and the trauma was horrific. I couldn't remember whose face I saw until I met your father. Then it all came back to me. After he killed her, while he was looking around, he picked up a picture frame in my room. I had the print compared to the prints on file as a result of all that trouble he got into in Nashville the summer he killed my mother. The print was his, Mark—it was your father's print on my picture frame."

Mark turned to face his father

"Is that all true?"

"Now look what you've done. You've turned him against me too. What a little bitch you are—just like your mother was. She was a little bitch too, you know. If she hadn't held out on me, none of that would have happened."

"Held out on you—is that what happened? She wouldn't have sex with you so you killed her? You know, that would have been a little difficult since I was sleeping in the bed where she would have taken you. What a fool you were—what a fool you *are.*"

"You know, I've listened to about all I'm going to listen to. I've still got a little work to do before I make my exit. I think it's time the conversation ends and my work begins. By the way, I'm *never* going to jail. If all those people I've already sent there over the years find me in amongst them, I'll never make it out alive. I'm just not going to jail, especially for killing a whore like your mother."

Ann started walking toward him, as she said, "You know, you're the worst humanity has to offer. I could strangle you with my bare hands, you…"

She stopped as he redirected the pistol from his son, to her. Assuming he was about to pull the trigger, she flinched just slightly as the gun went off. The bullet struck her off center, in the right side of her midsection. She dropped to the floor, remained conscious, but never moved. She never knew anything could hurt that bad. She wasn't sure she could remain quiet and still, but she knew she needed to, or he would more than likely pump another round into her body.

Mark yelled, "Jesus, Dad what have you done? You shot her. What the hell are you thinking?"

"You know, son, I never did like you. You are way to much like that fucking mother of yours."

He fired twice this time, and Mark dropped first to his knees then to the floor. He fell facing her. There was no doubt he was gone. His eyes remained open. He never moved. He never blinked.

Ann heard the judge humming some song and then heard him apparently clearing a few items out of his desk. She needed to keep her eyes open, as if she too, had died where she had fallen.

She heard him coming around the side of his desk. She saw his feet stop, and watched as he kicked at his son.

"Too bad. Just too bad for both of you. Such a loss of two fine young people—the kind of people we need in this world."

As he walked out the door, she heard him say, "Oh, well. Life goes on." He laughed, then said, "At least for some of us."

Two days later

Vanderbilt Hospital
Nashville

She slowly opened her eyes. A stark white ceiling first caught her attention, along with the smell of some type of antiseptic. What had Jack done? Had he replaced the light bulbs and spilled something on the carpet in their bedroom all at the same time?

As she turned her head ever so slightly, she realized it wasn't her bedroom—in fact she literally had no idea where she was. As she continued to look around, she noticed Jack with Matt Armstrong huddled together near the windows along one wall.

"Jack what...what..."

They both turned toward her. Matt stayed near the window, while Jack smiled and approached her bedside.

He took her hand, and said, "Just relax. Everything's fine. You'll be like new before long."

She then felt the pain in her right side. She reached down to identify the source of the pain, but Jack grabbed her hand before it reached the area which seemed to be causing the problem.

"You remember anything?"

Ann remained silent as she looked around, but finally whispered, "Just start from the beginning and refresh my memory. I'll tell you when I remember."

"Do you remember going to Judge Dunn's house?"

She thought back...Judge Dunn, Judge Dunn...she did remember going to his home...and she did remember...

She turned away, as she tried to remember how it all ended.

As she turned toward Jack she said, "Yes, I remember most of what happened, but what about Mark? Is he..."

"He didn't make it."

She turned away and started to cry.

Matt, who had now joined Jack at her bedside, said, "He killed his own son, Ann. He was an animal. Now everyone is wondering what else he might have done without anyone knowing."

"But, if I hadn't gone there, if I would have just called the police, maybe..."

Jack said, "Hey, enough of that second guessing. You had a right to confront him. Who the hell knew he had that pistol...who could have anticipated Mark was home and would end up in his office...who knew he would pull a pistol, kill his own son, *and* try to kill you? You aren't responsible for his actions, Ann. Let's just concentrate on you at this point and get you up and going." He smiled. "And back to work."

"How long have I been here?"

"This is Monday. It happened Saturday morning, so it's just been a couple of days."

"What about my wound? Am I going to be okay?"

"Yes. The doctor will be here before long. He'll explain it all to you, but you were really lucky. You lost one hell of a lot of blood, but you're going to be fine. A couple of more days in here, and you'll be ready to roll." His eyes filled with tears. "I really thought I was going to lose you. I didn't know whether you were going to make it."

"I'm sorry for putting you through all this, I really am."

He wiped away a tear and said, "I love you so much I just don't know what I'd do without you. I was so worried."

"We need to quit this emotional stuff. I'm fine. Help me out here. I need to know what happened after I got shot and passed out."

"When the police arrived, he was gone. They found both you and Mark in his office, but apparently, he had anticipated, at some point in time, he would need to make a quick exit. The cops figure he had some of his clothing and personal items already packed, threw them in his car and got out before they ever arrived."

"They weren't able to stop him even after he left Lebanon, with some kind of roadblock or something?"

"No. He must have taken the backroads, because everyone involved in law enforcement in Wilson County was after him. But somehow he had just enough of a head start to evade them all."

She turned away, as she considered the fact he was still on the loose. When she reengaged in conversation she smiled and said, "You know, I guess I don't really care. At least I know who it was. At least I know even though he's not in jail, I might have helped make his life somewhat as miserable as he's made mine. He'll be on the run the rest of his life, if he's not captured. If he's captured, I'll testify against him. I'm just glad, after all these years, we know—I know. Maybe now, the nightmares will at least let up a little, and I can find some peace."

Matt said, "He'll turn up. They'll get him. He may have gotten away for now, but they'll eventually find him."

"I hope so, Matt. By the way, I want to thank you for what you did. Without the fingerprint matchup, none of this would have ever worked out." She reached out and took his hand as she started to cry. "I don't know what I would have done without you."

He smiled. "I would admit, your firm and our firm have been pretty successful since you've become an attorney, if I do say so myself."

Matt left a few minutes later, leaving only Ann and Jack. Shortly after he left, the doctor arrived, and explained to her that while she did lose a lot of blood, she was lucky. Her injury was not life threatening and she would be ready to go home in a few days.

Once he walked out the door, Jack said, "You know you and I have a lot to look forward to in the next few weeks. We need to purchase a little furniture, move into our new home, and I need to move into my new office. It's a start-over for us, and from now on we're going to think nothing but positive thoughts. This *cloud* we have both lived under since I've known you, has disappeared, and we're going to take advantage of it."

She smiled. "Thank God that part of my life is over. Maybe now mom can finally rest easy."

Jack smiled as he whispered, "Maybe now, *you* can rest easy."

Epilogue

Three weeks later
Offices of Connors and Connors, Attorneys at law

Life had returned to normal, or at least as close to normal as Ann's life had ever been.

She had appointments scheduled every half-hour for the rest of the day. Jack was still moving some of his items from his other office into his new office and would be in and out most of the day.

She had just finished one appointment. Her next had not yet arrived. Jack just left to go pick up one more load of additional items and his move would be mostly completed.

Beth appeared in her doorway and said, "We didn't get to have our usual visit this morning with that first appointment walking in about the same time you did. How you feeling? Any residual issues from that wound?"

"None. The doctor told me as long as I took it easy, I could work all I wanted. The stitches are out. I feel great. Ready to move on."

"Has anything else happened as concerns finding that asshole Judge? Have they been able to locate him yet?"

"I haven't talked to anyone with law enforcement in a few days, but the last I talked to them, all they had determined is that he apparently headed south out of Lebanon. I plan on contacting them weekly until they get him."

Beth hesitated, before she said, "What if they never get him? You okay with that—because they just may never find him."

"I've thought about that a lot. I'd rather they catch him, obviously not only because he should be made to pay for what he did, but I really don't care to have another run in with him, anywhere, anytime."

Ann thought for a minute, then said, "You know, even that non-life-threatening wound hurt like hell and I have a feeling the next time, I might not be as lucky as I was this time. He's a sadistic son-of-a-bitch. I'm afraid he'd have a very painful, carefully considered, life-ending plan for me if he ever gets another opportunity. I'm just glad I now know, and I'm *really* glad he's removed from the position he was in as a judge in Wilson County."

Ann heard someone walk through the front office door.

Beth looked toward the door and then turned toward Ann as she said, "It's just Jack carrying in another box. I'm not sure I'm going to know him without a box in his hands."

Beth stepped inside Ann's office as Jack squeezed by.

"Not much left, Ann. Most all my stuff is here now."

"When does the new girl start, Beth?"

"Tomorrow. I hope she works out. I don't know much about her, but she's got really good credentials, so we'll just have to see."

"You have Thursday and Friday of next week marked off for both of us, right?"

"Yes. You mean when you're moving to the house?"

"Yes. I just wanted to make sure you hadn't forgot. We're not seeing anyone during those two days. Hopefully that's all the time we'll need to get everything all set up."

"Neither of you have any appointments for those two days."

Ann heard Jack walking toward her office. As he did, he said, "Come on Beth, would you get back to work? You surely have things to do, people to call, you know, all that stuff. Move along."

Beth smiled. "You know, I'm still not sure I can handle both of you." She walked away from Ann's office door as Jack walked in.

"You have anything left to bring over here?"

"Just one small box. I'm going to get it now. Shouldn't take long."

"You remember we go pick up the dog tonight, don't you?"

"Yes, yes, I remember. You know, I didn't realize how small that little sucker actually is. Not much to him."

"It's a she, Jack, not a he. She's got a hell of a bark though. What she lacks in size she provides with noise. But you're right she's never going to amount to much of a watchdog. I think I told you, but I'm going to name her Rags too, as in Rags also. Not the number two, but…"

"I get it, I get it. We'll go pick her up after we leave here." He moved forward, and whispered, "By the way, are you planning on staying here through the noon hour—just getting a sandwich and eating at your desk, or are you going somewhere for lunch?"

She thought for a moment before she smiled and said, "Not going to happen today, Jack—at least not here. We'll do that when we get home tonight. I've got to much work to do to put it all aside and try to concentrate only on you over the noon hour."

"Okay, okay. But don't forget you just said that. I'll wait. I don't want to, but I will."

She smiled as she watched him walk out her door and heard him tell Beth he would be back shortly.

Her cell rang. She looked at the number, but didn't recognize it. She figured the call could go to voicemail. She could return it later.

Whoever it was, left no message, but five minutes later, it rang again. Once again, she let it go to voicemail.

The third time, she answered it.

"Good morning, Ann, how's your day going?"

She nearly dropped the phone. "How'd you get my number?"

Judge Dunn said, "I got the same legal directory you got. Again, how's your day going?"

"Where are you?"

"Oh, come on. You don't really think I'm going to tell you, do you? I'm close, Ann, I'm really close. Can't wait to see you again."

She took a deep breath. "You sick bastard, bring it. I'll be glad to meet up anytime, anywhere."

"Oh, you'll get the opportunity. Just a matter of time."

"You know, this time, you won't have the only gun. I'll have one too." Ann had never considered arming herself. She had just made that up, hoping it would somehow alter the flow of the conversation.

"I'll have a knife this time. And when I take you where I want to take you, I'll enjoy gutting you from between your legs all the way to your throat. I was surprised to read the online account of what happened. I just couldn't believe I was that bad a shot. This time you won't be so lucky."

"You murdered your *own son*. You are one depraved bastard. He was as nice a person as I've ever met. How could you do that? How could you murder your own son?"

"It was easy. He was an idiot. I hate idiots. But let's get back to us, to you and I. You better not let your guard down, Ann. I'll be right there. I'll be breathing down your neck every day of the week. You'll never know..."

She heard a loud commotion in the background—muffled voices.

"Gotta go, Ann. See you soon. Very, very, soon."

The call was terminated at his end. She put her phone down, and leaned back in her chair. Time to buy a gun. She wasn't going to meet him again and not be prepared. This time...

"Hey. This is it—the last of my files."

She said nothing.

"You okay."

She remained silent.

Jack walked in and set the box on the edge of her desk. "You look a little pale. You okay? You having a problem with your wound?"

"Better sit down."

He sat down, as he said, "Okay, what the hell's going on?"

"We're going to need a really... bigger...much bigger dog. In fact, were going to need a whole bunch of dogs—maybe pit bulls, or something that's mean."

"Why?"

"Because I just got a call from the judge. Apparently, he has a desire to cut me up into little pieces. In addition, he told me it wouldn't be long before that was exactly what he was going to do."

Jack leaned forward as he said, "Goddammit, where is he?"

"I don't know. He must have been using a burner phone, because no data came up on my phone as to who he was or where the call was emanating from."

"Did he really say he was coming to get you?"

"In no uncertain terms."

"Have you called the cops yet?"

"No. I will right now, but I need to quit shaking first. Jack, I told him to bring it on. Maybe I shouldn't have done that. Maybe I should have just hung up. Oh god, Jack, are we going to need to be looking over our shoulders for the rest of our lives?"

"Just call the police department in Lebanon and tell them what happened. Maybe we should have police protection for a while." He stood. "Call them. I'll take this box back to my office. I've got a guy in the department I can call and visit with him about what's going on."

Ann went to get a cup of coffee. She sat at her desk continuing to review the phone conversation she had just finished. Now, she wished she hadn't said what she had—would that provoke him even further? Would he make his move that much sooner? Would she and Jack continue to live their lives wondering where he was—if he were near—if he was watching?

She took care of her appointments the early part of the afternoon, and was still considering *the call* when her cell rang. It was from him! Should she answer or let it go? She immediately figured the more she knew, the better off she was. Perhaps he would make a mistake during the conversation. Maybe she might pick up a bit of information that would lead to his arrest. She had no choice. She had to answer.

"What do you want, you perverted bastard?"

No one answered.

"Speak. I don't have all day. What do you want this time?"

"Ma'am, whom am I talking to?"

It wasn't his voice. Good god did he have a partner?

"Who am I speaking with?"

"I'm an officer with the Atlanta police department. Who is this?"

She was now completely confused, but just in case he was who he said he was, she said, "I'm Ann Connors. What are you doing with this phone?"

"Did you just receive a call from this phone?"

"Yes."

"Was the call from a Judge Rodney Dunn, a Judge from Lebanon Tennessee?"

"Yes. What's going on officer?"

"Why was he calling you? How do you know him?"

"He called to threaten me—again. I was shot by him. My mother was murdered by him 20 years ago. He called me to tell me how he was going to kill me. Now, what's going on."

"Let me call you right back."

She terminated the call. Ann sat quietly waiting for her cell to ring. About 15 minutes later, it did.

"Is this Ann Connors?"

"Yes."

"Sorry for putting you off the first time. I just needed to verify who you were. We found out the judge was staying in a hotel here in Atlanta. We broke into his room. He reached for his weapon. He was shot and killed."

Ann gasped. "He's dead?"

"Yes. You won't have to worry about him anymore, ma'am."

The call lasted but a few more minutes. She put her phone down, thought about what she had just heard, and started to smile as she stood. She walked out to Beth's desk, and said, "Cancel all our appointments for the next seven business days."

Beth said, "What?"

She was starting to walk away, as she said, "You heard me. And call those people that sold us the dog. Tell them we'll pick her up later next week."

She walked into Jack's office and said, "Stand up."

"Why?"

"Just do it."

He stood and she put her arms around him.

"Do you remember what you and I said we were going to do as soon as a very special, life-altering event occurred—an event that demanded a celebration?"

"Not really. What'd we say?"

"Oh, come on Jack. It wasn't that long ago. *Think.*"

"You know, a hell of a lot has gone on with us lately. You were shot, I thought I was going to lose you, you were in the hospital, you lost all that blood, we found out who shot your mother. No, I don't remember. Now, what's going on?"

"Come with me. I'll tell you on the way."

She took him by the hand and walked to Beth's desk.

"We'll see you near the end of next week, Beth."

Jack said, "Wait. What the hell's going on?"

"You'll soon find out, buddy."

As they both walked out the front door, Beth yelled "Where you going?"

Ann, without ever turning her head, yelled, *"We're going back to Gatlinburg!"*

About the Author

JB Millhollin resides near Nashville, Tennessee. He has published a number of novels and continues to write, using the city and surrounding area as a backdrop for his stories. If you enjoy his style of writing, stay in touch through his Facebook author page, on twitter (@jbmillhollin), and through his website at www.jbmillhollin.com.